don't forget me

VICTORIA STEVENS

FARRAR STRAUS GIROUX • NEW YORK

Farrar Straus Giroux Books for Young Readers
An imprint of Macmillan Publishing Group, LLC
175 Fifth Avenue, New York, NY 10010

fiercereads.com

Library of Congress Cataloging-in-Publication Data

Names: Stevens, Victoria, author.
Title: Don't forget me / Victoria Stevens.
Other titles: Do not forget me
Description: First edition. | New York : Farrar Straus Giroux, 2018 | Summary:
    Forced to leave her mother, who has early-onset Alzheimer's, in a nursing
    home in England and move to Australia to live with the father she has never
    met, seventeen-year-old Hazel Clarke struggles to build a new life for herself
    until she is befriended by Red and his quiet, grieving twin brother, Luca, who
    help her learn to love her new home and realize the importance of honesty
    and family.
Identifiers: LCCN 2017011002 (print) | LCCN 2017033507 (ebook) |
    ISBN 9780374305628 (ebook) | ISBN 9780374305604 (hardcover)
Subjects: | CYAC: Grief—Fiction. | Families—Fiction. | Friendship—Fiction. |
    Alzheimer's disease—Fiction. | Australia—Fiction.
Classification: LCC PZ7.1.S7447 (ebook) | LCC PZ7.1.S7447 Do 2018 (print)
    | DDC [Fic]—dc23
LC record available at https://lccn.loc.gov/2017011002

Our books may be purchased in bulk for promotional, educational, or business
use. Please contact your local bookseller or the Macmillan Corporate and
Premium Sales Department at (800) 221-7945 ext. 5442 or by e-mail at
MacmillanSpecialMarkets@macmillan.com.

For my Nana,
who always believed I could
And for Lilly
(no more excuses)

"Don't forget me," you said,
and I laughed softly—
because that
(more than anything in this entire, endless universe)
would be impossible.

—J. E. STARLING, "REMEMBERING YOU"

PROLOGUE

AT NIGHT, THE SCREAMS WERE WORSE.

Maybe it was the way they echoed around the apartment, bouncing off the walls; maybe it was because they startled Hazel awake and she was still bleary with sleep as she made her way down the hall to her mother's bedside.

She knew her way through the darkness, one hand trailing along the faded walls to guide her. Past the kitchenette, past the living room. Past the bathroom. Her mother's door was always propped open, just in case she needed Hazel. The nightmares often left her mother's forehead damp with sweat, hair sticking to her skin in dark strands. Hazel knew how to calm her, how to place her hands gently on her mother's cheeks until she stopped writhing, until she stilled.

"It's okay," Hazel would promise, voice even and calm, a lie that came too easily. "It's all right. You're going to be all right."

Her mother would turn to her with wild eyes, gripping Hazel's arms with cold fingers as if her daughter were the only solid thing left she could still hold on to. "Don't go," she would beg. "Please don't leave me."

Her mother never seemed to realize that it wasn't her being left behind.

At some point in the last few hours that Hazel and Graham had been driving, the sky outside the window had faded from dusky blue to starry black, sinking them into complete darkness. Only the faint moonlight allowed Hazel glimpses of her surroundings, submerged almost entirely in shadows.

Her legs were stiff from so many hours of traveling, the side of her face cool from being pressed against the window. The soft music from the radio and the gentle hum of the car were making it hard to keep her eyes open. The dashboard read 12:06.

She stole a glance at the man in the driver's seat, who she'd first met just forty-eight hours ago in the lawyer's office back in London. *Graham Anthony Bell.*

Her father. The man who'd waited seventeen years before making contact with his only daughter. The man whose name she'd had to find out from Social Services when he was already on the plane over.

His focus was on the road, eyebrows knitted together as his fingers tapped out a soundless rhythm on the steering wheel. He had two days' worth of stubble dusting his jawline, and even in the half-light of the car he looked weary. His dark hair was flecked with gray, and he had fine lines around his green eyes—Hazel hoped they were from laughter and not just from time in the Australian sun.

"We're almost there," he said without taking his eyes off the road. It was the first time he'd spoken since they left the airport and started driving toward Port Sheridan.

Hazel nodded, fixing her attention back out the window, and a few minutes later Graham pulled into the driveway of a huge white country farmhouse with a wide wraparound porch.

He killed the engine, and they sat there for a moment, the quiet stretching out between them.

"Well," he said eventually, "this is it. This is home."

Your home. Not mine. Hazel looked up at the house with a tightness in her chest that wouldn't shift and said nothing. Graham ran a hand through his hair as if this was as difficult for him as it was for her.

"Shall we go in?" he said, and she nodded like she had a choice.

Hazel wondered as she stood in the oversize entrance hall if the house always felt this empty. This unwelcoming. Graham led her wordlessly up the stairs to a room at the far end of the hallway, placing each of her suitcases beside the bed.

He cleared his throat. "You must be exhausted, so I'll let you get some rest. I can give you the tour in the morning."

Hazel turned to look at him. He was watching her with the pity she'd grown used to.

"Thank you," she managed to say.

"It's no problem, Hazel," he said softly, and shut the door behind him.

Hazel dropped her purse on the floor by the desk and sat on the end of the double bed. She drew her phone from her pocket, dialing the usual number.

You've reached Isabella Clarke. I can't take your call right now, but leave a message after the tone and I'll get back to you as soon as I can.

Hazel waited until she heard the beep, and then she hung up. She curled up on top of the bed and redialed, lying perfectly still as she listened to the sound of her mother's voice.

You've reached Isabella Clarke. I can't take your call right now, but leave a message after the tone and I'll get back to you as soon as I can.

This time when the beep sounded, Hazel didn't hang up right away. Instead, she curled into herself even tighter and listened to the silence as it stretched out endlessly.

part one

HAZEL WOKE AT NOON TO THE SUN streaming through cotton curtains, flooding the room with bright light. She stared at the unfamiliar ceiling as memory settled heavily in. She wasn't in her apartment anymore; she was in Australia, more than sixteen thousand kilometers from London.

From home.

She buried her head in the pillow. *You have ten seconds to wallow in your self-pity,* she told herself firmly, *and then you're going to act like everything is totally fine. One. Two. Three. Four. Five. Six. Seven. Eight. Nine. Nine and a half. Nine and three-quarters . . .*

She took a deep, steadying breath and kicked back the covers.

. . . Ten.

Hazel climbed out of bed and surveyed her surroundings. The room was tastefully—albeit minimally—decorated, and everything from ceiling to carpet was a crisp, spotless white. The walls were bare, with no photos or anything else to show they were part of someone's home and not a hotel.

She crossed the room to draw back the curtains. Behind them was a sliding glass door that opened onto a balcony, and down below was a well-kept garden ending in a row of palm trees. Beyond that, on the horizon, lay the vast open sea; it was close enough that she could count the waves as they crawled up the empty stretch of sand. A rush of longing for the busy, familiar streets of London hit her and she yanked the curtains shut again.

Hazel showered and changed quickly and let herself out of the bedroom and into the hallway. She could hear music from a radio downstairs. She followed the sound and found Graham sitting at the kitchen table, surrounded by piles of paperwork, a mug of coffee in his hand.

At the sound of her footsteps, he looked up and said, "Good morning! Did you sleep well? Are you hungry? If you'd like to go out for brunch, I own this place in town . . ."

"You own a restaurant?"

"Yep, the Anchor—they're not expecting me back until Monday, but I can call and get us a table. If you want."

Graham seemed so much more relaxed and comfortable

here in his own domain, yesterday's guarded awkwardness all but gone. She envied him.

"That sounds great."

"How are you holding up?" he asked then, studying her closely.

I'm surviving. That was the only word for what she was doing, wasn't it? Getting up each day, putting one foot in front of the other? But she said nothing, not trusting herself not to cry.

"Well," Graham said, clearing his throat, "I'm ready to leave when you are."

"I'll get my things," Hazel said, turning on her heels and leaving the room.

Graham hardly paused for breath the entire ten-minute journey into town, his low voice filling the silences with trivial chatter. As Hazel listened to him talk, she took in her surroundings through the open window. The sky was a bright, clear blue and the sides of the road were lined with the occasional yellow-leafed poplar or wisp of shrubbery. On her left, running alongside the highway, was the glittering sea. Port Sheridan was so different from what she was used to and she knew it was going to take some time to adjust to everything—like this balmy weather, which was typical here despite the fact that it was the middle of August and Australia's winter.

When they arrived at the Anchor, they were greeted enthusiastically by the staff and led to a table with an amazing view of the sea. When a waitress came over, Hazel ordered grilled barramundi and Graham ordered a steak. While they waited for their food she listened to him talk about the area and the local hangouts and her new school; she was to start at Finchwood High on Monday, where Graham had been a student himself some thirty years ago.

After brunch, they left the Anchor and walked along the beach toward a bustling promenade of shops. Graham pointed out each one as they passed, telling Hazel all about who worked there and what they sold and if it was overpriced. She tried to keep up, but he spoke so fast that most of it went completely over her head—not that he seemed to mind. They stopped to pick up her uniform and some other bits and pieces for school, and then for a midafternoon snack of ice cream and coffee, after which Graham finally suggested they go home so she could settle in and unpack. It wasn't until they were in the car that he quieted. Hazel, completely exhausted, was grateful for the silence.

Back at the house, Graham left her to organize the contents of her oversize suitcases, which was easier said than done—hanging her clothes in the closet and arranging her things on the desk felt far too real and not nearly temporary enough. In the end, she just collapsed onto the bed, falling immediately into a deep, dreamless sleep.

2

IT WAS CLOSE TO MIDNIGHT WHEN HAZEL
woke, and moonlight was streaming into the room through
the glass doors; she'd been asleep for hours.

Wondering if Graham had been in to check on her, she
eased open the bedroom door to see if he was still awake. The
hallway was dark, but on the carpet in front of her was a tray
with a chocolate muffin and some orange juice. Taped to the
glass was a handwritten note, which Hazel crouched down to
read:

*Thought the jet lag might have caught up
with you. Didn't want to wake you.*

Sleep well, Hazel.

Hazel read the note twice and then folded it in quarters and tucked it into her pocket, ignoring the sudden lump in her throat. She carried the tray into the room and shut the door quietly behind her, setting the food down on her desk.

She thought about going back to bed, but she felt too awake, too wired. The room was stuffy, as if someone had sucked out all the air. She went over to the balcony door, and though the cold glass felt good beneath her palms, it wasn't enough. She needed to be outside where it was cool.

She let herself out the back door in the kitchen and into the garden, edging her way through a gap in the undergrowth at the end and onto the beach beyond.

Oh my God. The moonlight, the sea, the endless curve of the beach—it was so beautiful. Hazel walked right up to the water's edge, where the waves moved smoothly toward the shore and then crept back again in an even, calming rhythm.

It was a few minutes before she realized that she wasn't alone. There was a figure standing a little way down the beach, half-hidden in the shadows and facing her direction. As she watched, it began to make its way across the sand toward her. Hazel froze.

"Hello?" the person called when he was close enough. It was a boy, with a deep, lilting voice.

Hazel licked her lips nervously before answering. "Hello?"

He came to a stop in front of her. He was tall, a good foot

taller than her, and around her age. He had dark hair and dark eyes, and pale skin. A camera hung from a strap around his neck. "Who are you, then?"

"Who's asking?" she said, and the boy let out a bark of surprised laughter.

"You're a Pom, huh?"

"Pom?"

He smiled. "English."

"Oh. Half."

"Sweet," he said. "I'm Red. Red Cawley."

"Like the color?"

"Yep. Short for Redleigh. Yourself, Pom?"

"Hazel."

"No kidding," he said. "Like a color too—guess we match!"

"Guess we do."

"We should sit," he decided suddenly, dropping down to the ground and stretching his legs out across the sand. He patted the spot next to him. "Come on. I don't bite."

Hazel sank down beside him, crickets chirping in the undergrowth behind them. She fixed her eyes on the horizon, at the faint line where the black of the sky met the indigo of the sea. Above them, the sky was full of stars. There were no clouds or any of London's orange nighttime glow obscuring them, so she could make out entire constellations.

"It's pretty, huh?" Red said.

She murmured her agreement.

"Okay, Hazel-from-England," he said then. "I have to ask because it's driving me crazy—what are you doing out here in the middle of the night?"

"I couldn't sleep," Hazel admitted.

"Jet lag?"

"How did you know?"

"You've got that look about you," he said. "When did you land?"

"Last night."

"Nice! Welcome to Australia! How do you like it so far?"

"Well, it's—"

"Amazing?" he offered. "Beautiful?"

"Different," she said.

"I'll bet! Don't worry; you'll fall in love with it soon enough. Everyone does."

Hazel nodded—because that was easier than explaining how much she'd lost by coming to Australia, or how she'd only come because she'd lost so much. This stranger didn't need to know that.

"It was nice to meet you," she said instead. "But I should be getting back . . ."

"Sure, yeah!" Red jumped to his feet, offering her a hand. She grabbed it and straightened up, meeting his eyes. He was smiling warmly at her. "I guess I'll see you around then, huh?"

"Maybe," she said.

"Hopefully," he corrected. "Good night, Hazel-from-England."

She stood on the sand and watched him walk away, keeping her eyes on him until the shadows swallowed him whole and she was alone again.

When Hazel got back to her room, she found a sheet of paper and a pen, and sat down at her desk to write.

Dear Mum,

I remember the time we went to the zoo for my birthday. We saw every animal there, and then when my feet started to hurt, you put me on your shoulders so we could walk around again. I got my picture taken with a parrot, and you bought a copy for my bedroom wall. I wonder where that photo is now.

I miss you, Mum, but I remember.

Love,
Hazel

She read the letter over twice and then sealed it in an envelope and put it away in her desk drawer.

3

IN THE CAR ON THE WAY TO SCHOOL MONDAY
morning, Hazel couldn't decide whether she was more scared
or nervous. At least nobody here knew what she'd gone
through; she was so tired of people looking at her differently
because of what had happened with her mum.

Graham parked the car and turned in his seat to face her.
"You sure you want to do this so soon?"

She glanced out the window. The school was a collection
of modern, single-story buildings surrounded by palm trees and
open space. Students were arriving, milling around the parking lot, sitting on walls and benches, grouped in small huddles.
Was one of them Red? She hoped so.

"Yes," she said, tugging at the hem of her uniform.

Graham studied her face for a moment and then reached

across the car to give her shoulder a squeeze. "All right," he said cheerfully, opening his door. "Let's get you enrolled, then."

Finchwood High was a coed school for students between the ages of eleven and eighteen. It was home to over seven hundred pupils and had a staff dedicated to providing an enriching and unique experience for each student—or at least that's what the principal, a balding man named Mr. Lynch, told them proudly as he ushered them into his office.

He was completely different from the sharp, suited principal at her school back in London; Mr. Lynch wore tan trousers and a polo shirt, and his eyes were kind as he chatted to Hazel.

"So, welcome to Finchwood!" he said.

"It's just temporary," Hazel said immediately, and looked over at Graham, who had his lips pressed tightly together. She swallowed and turned to Mr. Lynch. "I'm hoping to be back in England by Christmas."

"Well," Mr. Lynch said with a broad smile, "rest assured we'll do everything we can to make this transition smooth for you, even though the school year is well under way. Shall we get you to your homeroom, then?"

Hazel looked at Graham again, and he raised an eyebrow as if to say, *It's not too late to change your mind.* She just nodded.

Mr. Lynch led them out of his office and into a crowded hallway filled with students hanging around in groups or getting their things out of their lockers. Once they reached the end of the hallway, Graham said a brief goodbye and Mr. Lynch took Hazel to her classroom. Outside, he introduced her to a redhead named Ashley who was to show her around for the rest of the week and make sure she settled in okay. He handed Hazel a map of the school printed in bright colors, and then wished her good luck before returning to his office.

Ashley took one look at Hazel, eyes dragging up and down her body in a way that made Hazel feel incredibly self-conscious, and sighed.

"So he asked me to do this because we have the same schedule," she said, arms folded across her chest.

"Thank you," said Hazel. "I appreciate it."

Ashley let out a laugh. "Oh, don't thank me! There's no way I'm going to spend the week babysitting you. It's not a big place; you'll find your way. Right?"

Hazel blinked at her. "Well, I—"

"Right?" Ashley pressed again, and Hazel nodded hastily. Ashley broke into a dazzling smile, flipped her hair over her shoulder, and stalked into the classroom, leaving Hazel alone in the busy hallway.

Most of the desks in the room were already occupied, so Hazel made her way to a seat somewhere between the middle and the back, where she figured she could avoid any unwanted attention.

She settled into her chair, slumping down to make herself as small as possible.

The teacher arrived a few minutes later, and the loud chatter in the classroom died down to a murmur. Hazel got up to hand the teacher the enrollment slip Mr. Lynch had given her, desperately praying that she wouldn't make her introduce herself to the rest of the class. But the teacher just welcomed Hazel, said her name was Mrs. Baxter, and sent her back to her desk. Even so, Hazel could feel the students watching her as she took her seat again. She thought how unusual it must be for a student to join Finchwood halfway through the year—the school year in Australia began in January and ran through to December.

Hazel spent the rest of the morning trailing after Ashley from one class to the next with just enough distance between them that she was sure the other girl wouldn't notice she was being followed. She thought she'd done a good job of it until the lunch bell rang and Ashley disappeared from the classroom before Hazel had a chance to gather her things. She packed her bag hastily, throwing it over her shoulder as she rushed from the room to catch up, and ran straight into someone.

"Oh God, I'm so sorry, I didn't . . ."

Hazel trailed off, raising her eyes to meet Ashley's. Ashley was standing with two friends, one hand on her hip as she glowered at Hazel.

"You," Ashley said accusingly, stepping toward her, and

Hazel took a step back, wishing the ground would swallow her up.

"Me?"

"Yes, you. New girl. Whatever your name is. Would you quit *following* me?"

"Sorry?"

"You've spent the morning trailing after me like a lost puppy."

"Because Mr. Lynch told me that—"

"I don't care what Lynch said, having a constant shadow is getting on my nerves!"

"I don't want any trouble," Hazel said, hands held up in surrender, and *oh God*, this was not the first day she'd had planned. She was supposed to lay low, blend in. "I just need to know where the cafeteria is."

"Use the freaking map, then," Ashley hissed. "I saw Lynch give you one. Or do they not teach you how to use those in England?"

"They . . . um. They do."

"God, I know, it was rhetorical. What's wrong with you?"

"Just leave it, Ash," one of her friends said. "I'm starving."

Ashley held Hazel's gaze for a few seconds before finally saying, "You're right. Let's go."

The three of them headed off down the hallway, in what Hazel assumed was the direction of the cafeteria. She took a moment to collect herself, taking a deep breath and letting it out slowly before heading in the same direction. When she found the cafeteria, she bought a sandwich with the money Graham had given her and sat at an empty table in the far corner.

The tables around her started to fill up with loud, chattering students until every table was full except for hers. A wave of loneliness washed over her, and Hazel fought back tears. She willed the moment to pass—which, as always, it eventually did.

It's okay, she told herself, like if she thought it enough times, it might make it true. *You're going to be okay.*

Graham was waiting for her outside the school entrance at three o'clock as promised. Hazel climbed into the passenger seat beside him, overwhelmed by how relieved she was to see a familiar face.

"Hey!" he said. "How was it? Did you have a good day?"

Hazel nodded as she buckled her seat belt, fixing her eyes on the dashboard because she wasn't sure she'd be able to meet his eyes without welling up again. It had been a long day. The afternoon hadn't been any better than the morning, and she'd turned up ten minutes late to the first class after lunch— Psychology—because she couldn't find her way to the right room and she was too afraid of Ashley even to attempt to follow her. She hadn't seen Red around, and she was starting to think Graham was right—maybe it *was* too soon for her to start at a new school. She knew she could explain it to him, but she didn't want to burden him with anything else. Not when her entire existence was a burden already.

He was quiet for a moment. "I know moving is hard," he said finally. "Fitting in is hard. Especially in the middle of the school year."

She waited for the *but*, for him to elaborate or offer advice, but he didn't; he just started the car and drove them out of the parking lot.

Moving is hard, fitting in is hard. You just have to deal with it.

After Graham and Hazel ate a dinner of Indian takeout together in the living room in front of the television, Graham excused himself to finish some paperwork in his office, and Hazel headed upstairs to her bedroom to start her homework. She got most of it done, but when her vision began to blur from staring at math equations, she gave up for the night. She pulled her desk chair across the room and out onto the balcony so she could watch the waves. The moonlight was casting long shadows across the sand and painting silver lines across the water.

Hazel wondered if Red would turn up again; theirs was the first conversation she'd had since she arrived in Australia that hadn't made her feel uneasy. From where she sat, she should be able to see anyone walking along the beach. What would she do if she *did* see him? Would she go down to meet him on the beach again? Was she already that lonely?

Yes.

She kept her eyes on the shoreline and focused on the quiet

sound of the waves, refusing to let her mind turn to England or her mother or the big white house that was a poor substitute for a home or the stranger she was now living in it with. She waited to see if Red would show, with his easy smile and bright eyes.

At midnight she finally gave up, dragging the chair back inside and closing the door behind her.

HAZEL CAUGHT THE SCHOOL BUS THE NEXT
morning instead of getting a ride because Graham had to go
to work early. She didn't mind; she'd known she'd have to make
the journey alone eventually.

Tuesday mornings she had Modern History, followed by a
free period, which she spent in the library finishing her Math
homework, followed by Spanish. Still wary of the wrath of Ashley, Hazel struggled to find her classrooms, and when she did
finally arrive, it was usually a few minutes after the final bell—
which gave the students already there another reason to stare
at her as she settled into a chair.

Rather than sit on her own in the cafeteria again at lunch,
she bought a sandwich and found a bench in a quiet corner

outside where she could watch people go by. Tuesday afternoon included a double session of Health/PE, which meant Hazel changed into the gym clothes Graham had bought her and took part in a game of cricket—a match that mainly involved her classmates goofing off and having fun around her.

Graham arrived back at the house that afternoon just after she did. For dinner, he ordered in Thai food and they ate in the living room again with the sound of the television drowning out the silence that settled over them once Graham realized she wasn't going to engage in his cheerful attempts at a conversation. When they said good night and headed their separate ways, Hazel went straight out to her balcony and waited for Red to appear.

Once again, no matter how hard she willed otherwise, he didn't show.

The rest of the week, Hazel rode the bus to and from school alone, sat in her classes alone, and ate her lunch on her bench alone. Evenings were a little better, because even though she and Graham didn't have much to say to each other, he was at least there in the room with her, which she appreciated more than she knew how to vocalize. She continued to spend her nights out on her balcony looking for Red, putting off the inevitable moment she had to go to sleep.

By Friday, people had stopped staring at her so openly. She was still a mystery to them, if the occasional sideways glances were anything to go by, but she'd almost returned to her usual invisible self.

On Monday, the girl sitting at the desk in front of hers in homeroom struck up a conversation while they waited for the teacher to arrive.

"Hey!" she said as soon as Hazel sat down. "You transferred recently, right? What's your name?"

"Hazel."

"All the way from England!" the girl said. "Awesome accent! I'm Madison, but everyone except my mum calls me Maddie. Maddie Wynter. Like the season but with a *y*. How are you finding it?"

"It is a lot," Hazel admitted.

"Didn't Lynch assign you a settling-in buddy? He usually does that."

"He did. Ashley. But she wasn't . . . interested."

Maddie glanced in Ashley's direction before looking back at Hazel. "I'm not surprised. She doesn't really care about anyone but herself."

Hazel shrugged. "It's okay."

"No, it's not. If I hadn't been out sick, he might've assigned you to me—but you should definitely stick with me from now on. I won't abandon you."

"Are you sure?"

"Of course I'm sure!" Maddie said. "School sucks at the best of times, let alone when you're on your own. You can meet Hunter, too, when he turns up."

Just then a tall, curly-haired boy slid into the seat beside Maddie. "Who's this, then?"

"This is Hazel," Maddie said. "She's from England, and she's *nice*, Hunter, so don't even try it."

"Try what?" he said innocently.

"He flirts with everything that moves," she explained to Hazel.

"I do not!" he said. "I don't, Hazel, I promise. She's just jealous I never try it with her."

"Right." Maddie snorted. "That's exactly it. I'm so, so in love with you, Hunter Emery. You are the light of my life, my sun, my moon, etcetera."

Hunter reached over to pat her sympathetically on the arm. "I know I am, babe. I'm the light of everyone's life."

Hazel hid her smile behind her bag. They seemed so nice— maybe being invisible wasn't what she needed after all.

After homeroom, the three of them went their separate ways for class, but they arranged to meet for lunch behind the main building at Hunter and Maddie's usual shady spot on the lawn beneath a blue gum tree. Then, at the end of the day, they both got on Hazel's bus home, even though it meant a longer walk to their houses. They didn't seem to mind that Hazel didn't say much, content to bicker back and forth between themselves.

Hazel thought there must've been people like Maddie and Hunter back in England, relaxed and easygoing, but if there were she'd never met them.

Then again, there hadn't been time to make friends.

When Hazel got home Graham was still at work, so the house was empty. She let herself in with the spare key from under the doormat, which felt weird—almost *wrong*, like she was breaking into someone else's home. She supposed she was, in a way. How long would it take for her to feel as if she wasn't trespassing on Graham's life? To adjust to their awkward, one-sided conversations. She stood in the middle of the kitchen, overwhelmed by homesickness.

Temporary, she reminded herself. *This is only temporary.*

When Graham called to check in, Hazel was on the sofa reading the book her English teacher had assigned.

"Hazel, it's me," he said. "I'm sorry I didn't call sooner; work's been a nightmare. Two of our waitresses called in sick. Is everything okay?"

"Everything's fine."

"Are you hungry? I'm going to be here for a while, but I think there's a pizza in the freezer. Or the numbers for takeout are on the fridge if you prefer; just give them my name and I'll sort the money out later." He paused. "Is that okay?"

"It's fine," she assured him.

"I'll be home as soon as I can."

Hazel wanted to tell him not to rush back on her account, that she was used to being alone and was more than capable of looking after herself, but instead she hung up the phone and went searching for the pizza. Graham's fridge was surprisingly empty for someone who was a chef. There were just some cans of beer and a bottle of barbecue sauce—and a lone pizza in the bottom drawer of the freezer. Hazel shook her head in amusement, unwrapped it, and threw it in the oven.

It was past nine by the time Graham got home. He came upstairs and knocked on her door. "Hey," he said. "Good day at school?"

She thought he looked tired, even more so than usual. "Yes, thanks."

"The television's on downstairs if you want to join me."

"I think I'll have an early night, if that's okay."

"Sure."

He hovered in the doorway, half-in and half-out. "You're doing really well, Hazel. She would be so proud."

Hazel said nothing, her throat suddenly tight. She wished he would leave without saying another word.

"I just . . . It will get *easier*, you know?" he continued. "It really will. One morning you'll wake up and it won't be the first thing you think about."

Graham left the room, shutting the door behind him. *One morning you'll wake up and it won't be the first thing you think about.* Hazel didn't know whether that thought was comforting or terrifying.

5

IT HAD BEEN A LONG TIME SINCE MEALTIMES in Red Cawley's household had resembled something conventional. It was hard to maintain the façade of normalcy when it was just Red and his mum, Claire, sitting around the kitchen table, the empty chairs a reminder of the family they'd once been—four down to two.

Conversations with his mum were always nice enough, but Red knew both of them were secretly relieved when the dishes were loaded into the dishwasher, and Claire could disappear into her office and Red into his bedroom for the rest of the evening. Sometimes, though, shutting himself away wasn't enough and he had to get out of the house; on those evenings, he climbed out his bedroom window and went down to the garden, ducked through a hole in the hedge at the bottom and out onto the beach beyond. On nights like tonight, when the tide was low enough, he could walk along the entire stretch of beach without ever getting his feet wet, using a flashlight to guide the way.

At just after ten, Red grabbed his drawstring bag and made his way barefoot across the sand, his camera around his neck. The sky was clear and full of bright stars. It was the first thing he had noticed the first night they spent in their new house back in February, that the stars were so much brighter here than in Sydney, and it wasn't a consolation, exactly, for being uprooted from his old life, but he definitely clung to it when the nights were long and the house was lonely.

It had been over a week since he'd ventured this far up the shore. He'd meant to come sooner, hoping to see Hazel again, but he'd been busy with schoolwork. Red arrived at the stretch of beach where he'd met her the last time, and crouched down to clear a space just at the edge of the undergrowth. He settled cross-legged on the sand, and emptied his drawstring bag out onto the ground, using his flashlight to illuminate the contents: colored and graphite pencils, his trusty sketch pad, and a banana for emergency sustenance.

He buried the flashlight in the sand so its beam lit up his page, and then chewed absentmindedly on the end of one of the pencils as he studied his most recent drawing. It was only half-finished, a sketch of the beach at sunset. He hunched over the paper, shading in the skyline and adding texture to the rolling waves.

Red was almost done when the soft thud of footsteps on the sand made him look up, his eyes settling on Hazel making her way toward him. He put his sketch pad back in his bag and said, "Hey, stranger!"

"Don't you have a house of your own to sit outside of?" she said when she got close.

"The view of the sea isn't as good from the other end of the beach."

"Doesn't it look the same wherever you stand?"

"Spoken like a true amateur! What are *you* doing out here, anyway? It's late."

Hazel lowered herself to the ground beside him. "Couldn't sleep."

"Well, it can't be jet lag this time. What is it? Insomnia?"

She shrugged and dug her hands into the sand in front of her. "What about you?" she asked without looking up.

"Me? I'm just enjoying the night air. How have you been, Hazel-from-England?"

"Homework is keeping me busy."

"Lucky you. Which school are you going to?"

"Finchwood?"

"Awesome!" he said. "It's a good place; I know a bunch of people who go there."

"Really?"

"Yeah." Red was about to explain why but thought better of it. "Are you enjoying it?"

"Well, it's *school*, so . . ."

Red let out a burst of laughter, and she ducked her head. He could just about see the pleased pink flush on her cheeks through the near-darkness.

"What about you?" she asked then. "Where do you go to school? I was . . . hoping we'd end up at the same place."

"I go to West," Red said. "It's an art school for the gifted and talented."

"Gifted and talented?"

"Yeah," he said, grinning. "God knows how I got a place."

"You're an artist then?"

"Trying to be."

"Is that why you carry that camera everywhere?"

Red glanced down at it. It was nothing special or high-tech, but he loved it. "Yep. You never know when you might need to capture a moment. Hey, maybe I'll show you some of my stuff one day."

"I'd like that."

"I know how hard it can be, moving to a new place and leaving everything you know behind," he said then. "Back in February, I was the new kid in town too."

"You were?"

"Yep. We moved here from Sydney." Red paused and studied her face. "It can be tough, going to a new school, meeting new people. Starting over again. But you'll get there. You'll settle in."

"I don't need to settle in," Hazel said, brow furrowed. "I won't be here long. This is temporary."

"Really? Where are you staying?"

"With my dad. His name's Graham Bell?" She gestured toward the houses behind the undergrowth. "His house is the one with the porch."

"Yeah, I know it!" Red said. "And I know him too, kind of—my mum works in his restaurant. Have you been there yet? The Anchor?"

"We went on my first day."

"Mum says it's the best place she's ever worked. Hey, you should come over for dinner tomorrow and meet her!"

"Really?"

"Definitely. She'll love it—I know she's secretly disappointed that I'll never bring a girl home for real."

Hazel raised an eyebrow in question, and Red winced slightly. He hadn't meant to say that, not really. There was just something about her that made him feel comfortable. Too comfortable.

"It's because I'm not into girls," he explained carefully, watching her expression to see how she'd react. "Not in that way. Not romantically, I mean. Or sexually. Shit. It isn't . . . It's not a big deal."

"No," Hazel agreed quickly. "It's not a big deal."

Red had seldom met anyone who hadn't completely accepted his sexuality—his family and friends in particular had always been one hundred percent supportive—but he still felt a wave of relief.

"My mum'll love you. And not just because you're cool; she

pretty much loves anyone. She's a lot like me in that respect. Superchill about everything. We're both *people* people, you know? And she's the best chef. Everything she cooks is amazing." He paused, stealing a sideward glance at her. "What's your mum like?"

Hazel said nothing.

"Is she like you? Or are you more like your dad?"

"I . . . don't know," she said. "I hardly know him. I only found out that he existed a couple of weeks ago."

Red nodded slowly. He thought briefly about his own dad; he knew a thing or two about absent fathers himself.

"I used to have a mum, though," Hazel added.

"Used to?"

"It's a long story."

"I've got time."

"I don't really like to talk about it. Too many people felt sorry for me in London. I don't want it to be like that here."

"I won't tell anyone," he promised.

Hazel wasn't sure why she believed him, but she did. She took a deep breath, and let it out. "Well, I wasn't very old when she first got sick . . ."

Red listened closely as she told him everything that had happened back in England, about everything she'd lost. He didn't interrupt, didn't say anything at all until Hazel had finished talking—and then he just scooted closer to her and placed an arm around her as she cried into his shoulder.

Dear Mum,

I remember the time we went to the fair. We had chocolate, and popcorn, and lemonade, and fries. You warned me that I shouldn't eat anything else, but I made such a fuss about having cotton candy that you bought me some—then later, on the bumper cars, I got sick. But you weren't angry. You just gave me a hug and won me a stuffed animal from one of the stalls to cheer me up. It was a blue rabbit, with soft fur and floppy ears. I called him Justin.

He was my favorite toy ever.

I miss you, Mum, but I remember.

Love,
Hazel

6

THE FOLLOWING MORNING BEFORE SCHOOL,
when Hazel told Graham about meeting Red (she didn't say
when or where and, surprisingly, he didn't ask) and being invited for dinner, he agreed readily.

"Of course you can go!" he said. "It'll be good for you to
make some friends, especially ones like Red. The Cawleys are
a lovely family. I went to school with his parents, did he mention that?"

"He didn't," Hazel said, slightly dazed. Port Sheridan was
a small town, but it wasn't small enough for that to not be a
pretty huge coincidence.

"Well, he's a good kid," Graham said. "Go, and have fun.
You deserve it."

Hazel wasn't going to disagree with that.

*　*　*

During her free period, Hazel called Red on her cell phone to arrange to meet him at Graham's house after school, and he was there just after four, as promised, grinning. She wondered if he was always so happy, whether he went to bed smiling and woke up smiling like there was nothing in the world that could hurt him.

Because their houses were only linked by the beach at low tide, they spent twenty minutes walking to his house, a journey that would've been much quicker had Red not stopped so often to take photographs.

"Well," he said brightly when they arrived, unlatching the front gate. "Welcome to my humble abode."

Red's house was as big and white as Graham's, and also had spacious rooms and big glass windows that flooded them with light. Apart from that, though, it was the complete opposite. Red's was *lived* in, and Hazel felt oddly safe and calm among the clutter of such a homey, domestic place. It reminded her of her own home in England.

As Red got them something to drink, Hazel looked around the kitchen and then outside the back door to the garden. Like Graham's, it was fairly large, with a wooden table-and-chairs set under a dark green umbrella just past the veranda, a few chaise longues farther out on the lawn, and a shed at the bottom. Beyond the grass was a row of hedges and the beach and sea.

Hazel scanned the horizon. "The beach really *does* look different from here."

"Told you!" Red said, handing her a drink. "Less sand and more sea, right? Wait until you see the sunset later, the colors are completely . . ."

He trailed off, frowning. Hazel turned toward the kitchen doorway to see what he was looking at.

Oh.

She couldn't help but stare. The boy's skin was considerably more tanned and his hair lighter, but his eyes were just like Red's. Brown and dark and intense.

"Hazel, this is my brother, Luca," Red said tightly. Luca's expression was even, but there was something unsettling there too, a barrier.

"Wait," she said slowly. "Are you two . . . ?"

"Twins," Red finished with a curt nod, at the same time that Luca muttered, "*Un*-identical."

"You look so alike," she said—although, on closer inspection, not as much as she'd first thought. Red was taller and leaner, made of more angles.

"What have you been up to?" Red said to Luca. "Feels like I haven't seen you in days."

Luca just glared. His and Red's eyes locked across the room until Red finally tore his away and muttered, "Jesus, Luc."

Luca turned and left. Hazel stood frozen, waiting until Red started to move a little too briskly around the kitchen again before she spoke. "Did I . . . do something wrong?"

"No, Hazel. You didn't."

"Then what was that?"

"We don't get along," he answered flatly, and didn't offer any more on the subject.

Red's mum breezed into the kitchen a little after five, laden with groceries. She looked a lot like the twins, with Red's bone structure and Luca's coloring, and long blond hair pulled back in a ponytail.

"You must be Hazel!" she said warmly as Red began unpacking the bags. "I'm Claire. It's so lovely to meet you!"

Hazel found herself smiling at her. Red hadn't been exaggerating when he said the two of them were similar. "You too."

"It's nice to be able to put a face to the name!" Claire said. "When Red said his new friend Hazel was coming over, I had no idea it was going to be you until Graham mentioned it too. He's been talking about you at work for days, saying we should all get together. Coincidences, huh?"

"Coincidences," Hazel echoed.

"He was almost as excited as Red was about you coming over for dinner tonight."

"And *neither* of us," Red said, "was anywhere near as excited as you. Don't deny it."

Claire just laughed. "What can I say? It's nice to have a girl around for once. It's tiring being surrounded by you boys all day. Speaking of which—have you seen your brother today?"

"Briefly, yeah."

"How was he?"

Red looked up from the groceries, and there was a split second of shared, secret pain between them, so brief it was almost imperceptible. "The usual."

"He's not taking his meds, you know," Claire said. "He just keeps throwing them in the garbage like I won't notice. And I had to call him in sick again today. The school's being patient and talking about *extenuating circumstances*, but if his attendance gets any worse, they won't let him graduate next year."

"Shall we talk about it later?" Red said, looking pointedly at Hazel. Claire glanced over in her direction as if she'd forgotten she was there.

"Of course. Sorry. I take it he won't be joining us for dinner?"

"Does he ever?"

Another pause. Hazel watched Red's expression carefully, sure she'd been privy to something extremely personal and private. Claire shook her head and said, "Why don't you show Hazel the fish tank while I rustle up something for dinner?"

Red gestured for Hazel to follow him out of the kitchen. "It's just through here . . ."

Hazel's mind was still on Luca when Red dropped her off at Graham's porch later that night. The rest of her evening at the Cawleys' had been normal enough, but Hazel had been left curious; there was something off about Luca, something neither Red nor his mother were willing to talk freely about.

"How did it go?" Graham asked as soon as she came through the front door. "Did you have a good time? How was everyone?"

"It was nice, Red was great—Claire was lovely, and Luca . . ."

She trailed off. Luca was *what*? Cold? Rude?

Graham nodded; he obviously knew enough about the family not to need further explanation. "Was Marc there?"

"Marc?"

"The boys' father," he said. "Which I guess means he's still away for work. I'm glad you had a good time, anyway."

"Me too," she said, and hesitated. "Did . . . Did anyone call today?"

Graham didn't answer. When Hazel raised her eyes to his, he was studying her closely. She wondered if you could see the cracks in humans the same way you could see them in crockery, the fissures and the fractures, waiting for the one knock that would break the thing apart.

"I'm sorry," he said finally. "No one called."

Later that night, once the tide had crept out far enough that Red could walk across the sand, Hazel met him on the beach as they'd arranged earlier. It was pleasant out, cool but not cold, and the air was still and peaceful.

"It's nearly midnight," Red said. "Aren't you tired?"

"Not really."

"Insomnia again?"

"It's not that I *can't* sleep," Hazel said. "I can sleep if I want to."

He turned his head to her, brow furrowed. "Why don't you, then?"

"My dreams."

"Nightmares?"

She nodded. "About her. About Mum."

He was quiet for a moment. "When I was seven I watched a movie about alien abductions," he said. "Kept me up every night for months. I was so scared of sleeping alone that we had to put my bed in Luca's room. Of course, that's not the same."

"Monsters are monsters," Hazel said. "It doesn't make a difference if they're from space or your mind."

Red murmured his agreement, turning his gaze up to the sky. She thought she could probably watch him for hours; he was so relaxed, so at home in his own skin. The opposite of her.

"Luca has trouble sleeping too," Red said. "Sometimes I'll get up for water in the middle of the night and see him sitting on the garage roof."

"I'm sorry," she said, without knowing quite what for.

"Monsters are monsters," he murmured. "We all have them, huh?"

Hazel found Red's hand on the sand, squeezed tight, and said nothing.

7

WHEN THEY'D MOVED TO PORT SHERIDAN, the first and only alteration Luca made to his new bedroom was to push the bed away from the center of the room and back against the far wall. From there, he had a perfect view out the large bay window without even having to raise his head from his pillow.

He couldn't remember the last time he'd drawn his curtains—he found comfort in always being able to see the world outside. When he couldn't sleep, Luca would gaze at the constellations as they edged their way across the sky to prove to himself that the world hadn't stopped turning. At dawn, he liked to watch the sun rising, chasing away the remnants of darkness as it crept up from the sea. He focused his attention on the vivid colors instead of on the ache that had long settled inside him.

That morning, the sky was a startling shade of bright blue. Luca fixed his eyes on a solitary cloud in the middle and began counting backward from a thousand. When he finished, he sat up in bed and pulled out the worn calendar from the bottom drawer of his bedside table, using a red pen to draw an X through the box bearing the day's date. Wednesday the 31st of August. *Two hundred and seventy-nine days.* Time was a funny thing, wasn't it? Fitting itself into seconds and minutes and months; one week running seamlessly into the next; days melting into one another. The *really* funny thing about time, Luca thought, was how people always thought it was endless. They never seemed to have enough of it, yet they always thought they'd have more.

He put the calendar back in the drawer and padded out of his room toward the bathroom. The house was so quiet that he could hear the clock in the kitchen ticking; his mum always drove Redleigh to school in the morning and then went straight on to work at the Anchor, so Luca never had to interact with anyone first thing. He needed that, needed the space and the silence to gather himself together for the day ahead.

He turned the water on in the shower and stood back to wait for it to heat up. When the steam had fogged the bathroom mirror enough for him to pretend his reflection didn't exist, he shrugged off his T-shirt and boxers and stepped under the spray, wincing as it scalded his shoulders. His skin was pink and blotchy when he finally emerged, the temperature of the water just shy of dangerous, the sting just shy of comforting. He toweled off, went back to his room, and pulled on his uniform. He'd never bothered to customize it the way his classmates had—standing out only meant drawing attention to yourself, and he'd perfected the art of blending in.

Downstairs on the kitchen table, his mother had laid out his breakfast for him like she did every morning. One piece of toast, lightly buttered and cut into four triangles as if he were a child, a glass of orange juice, and a bowl of cornflakes with the milk on the side so the cereal didn't get soggy. Beside the cereal, lined up next to the spoon, were two small pills—each inscribed with a little *M*.

Luca didn't bother sitting down. He ate two triangles of toast and drank a little of the juice and poured the rest down the sink with the milk, tipping the dry cereal back into the box in the cupboard. Finally, he picked up each of the pills from the table and weighed them in his palm. They felt like air. Felt like air and tasted like nothing, but changed everything. Made him numb. For a second he considered actually putting them in his mouth today, then tossed them in the trash can along with the rest of his toast.

The walk to school was long, but it was less claustrophobic than taking the bus. Luca took the scenic route through the backstreets, arriving just before the final bell rang. When he reached homeroom, he paused outside in the empty hallway to take a deep, steadying breath. He braced himself and pushed the door open.

The room was full and *loud*, students making the most of their final few minutes of freedom before the school day started. He spotted Hunter and Maddie in their usual places, and . . . *what*? That English girl Red had brought over last night was next to them. What was her name? A color. What was she doing with his friends?

She was the first to notice him approaching, and her eyes widened. Shit. He lowered his gaze to the floor as he waded through the desks.

"Morning!" Hunter said as Luca slid into the empty seat beside him. "How are you doing?"

"Fine," Luca answered, the lie bitter on his tongue as he turned his attention to the front of the classroom.

8

HAZEL COULDN'T STOP STEALING GLANCES AT
Luca. Red's brother went *here*, to Finchwood? How had she
not noticed him in class before? Granted, she hadn't known he
existed until last night, and he hadn't stuck around then, but
still. He didn't look Hazel's way once. She wondered if he even
recognized her.

"I didn't know Luca went to school here," she muttered to
Maddie as they packed up for their first class.

Maddie's eyebrows shot upward. "You know him?"

"I know his brother," she said—and come to think of it,
why hadn't Red mentioned anything before about his twin
going to the same school she did? Was he hoping their paths
would never cross?

"You know *Red*?" Maddie said.

"*You* know him?"

"Everyone knows Red! You should see him on a night out—people just flock to him. How did you two meet?"

"He was loitering on the beach outside my house."

"Sounds like him," Maddie said, laughing. "They're heaps different considering they're twins, right?"

Hazel couldn't imagine them being any more opposite.

Luca joined them at lunch, the four of them sitting in their usual shady spot on the lawn. He slotted in seamlessly the same way Hazel had, as if he'd been there all along and they just hadn't noticed. Hazel kept an eye on him as she listened to Hunter and Maddie talking about what people did for fun around Port Sheridan.

Both of them had part-time jobs. Hunter worked at a tourist hot spot just outside of town, giving guided tours of a waterfall, and Maddie helped teach dance to a class of twenty or so four-year-olds. That aside, it seemed their weekends were left to chance; depending on their work schedules, they went to the beach or hung out at the pier or relaxed at someone's house. The way they talked made it seem so carefree and spontaneous, two things Hazel was completely unaccustomed to; she'd always been too preoccupied with her mum to socialize.

"Are *you* going to get a job?" Maddie asked Hazel.

Hazel hadn't even thought about it. Part of her wanted to say no immediately because it didn't make sense when she was only here temporarily—but then the other part thought that maybe she *should* get a job. It would be another distraction.

"Maybe," she said. "Graham owns a restaurant in the town center. Maybe I could waitress."

"Oh yeah?" Hunter said. "Which restaurant?"

"The Anchor?"

"No way! We love that place, don't we, Mads? And isn't that where your mum works, Luca?"

Luca nodded, and Hunter turned back to Hazel. "And you know the guy who owns it? Graham? And he's your, what, uncle?"

"He's . . . my dad," she said, and wondered if she'd ever get used to saying that.

"That's *so* cool! I'd love to work there. They make the best burgers in town."

"Not that you're eating burgers for a while," Maddie reminded him. "No junk food until you find a sport, remember? Or have you already backed out of that?"

"Excuse you," he said indignantly. "I never back out of anything. Although at this rate, I'll never get to eat a burger again."

Hazel had spent enough time with the two of them over the last few days to know how set they were on helping Hunter find a sports team to join. From what Hazel understood, he had decided to work methodically through each of the sports that Finchwood offered, attending open practices to see which one he might want to try out for next year.

"Why is getting onto a team so important to you, Hunter?" Hazel asked.

"Well, it's Callum's fault, really," he said.

"Callum?"

"My older brother. He was captain of the rugby team for four years in a row, played soccer in the offseason, and entered the state championships for fun. It's like he's made it his life's mission to make me feel completely inferior."

"He's a dick," Maddie supplied helpfully.

"Right, a total dick," Hunter agreed. "I figured that if I was part of a sports team like he was, he might stop teasing me about it."

"So you only want to get on a team to prove to your brother that you can?"

"Basically, yeah."

"And we'll get there," Maddie said firmly. "I'm not giving up until we find you a sport that you don't suck at."

"Ever the optimist." He grinned.

Maddie shook her head. "You wait. I'm going to be there when you tell Callum all about it. I want to see the look on his face."

"When do you *not* want to see his face, though?" Hunter said. "Everyone knows you've been crushing on him since you were five years old."

"I have not!"

"You have so, Mads."

"Hunter!"

"Maddie!" he said, laughing. "You said you thought he was cute that one time, remember?"

"That was truth or dare; it doesn't count!"

"So you don't think he's cute?"

"Of course he is—he's an Emery, isn't he? Your whole family's unnaturally good-looking."

"What, even me?" he said, eyebrow raised.

Maddie just shook her head again, glowering at him. Hazel smiled and glanced over at Luca. Their eyes met, and he looked away.

"Anyway," Hunter said, "volleyball practice is Friday, and I've got a really good feeling about it. I think it could be the right one."

"He also said that about baseball and soccer," Maddie said drily.

He narrowed his eyes at her. "Ye of little faith."

The bell rang, signaling the end of lunch. They each gathered their things, and when they went their separate ways outside the main building, all Luca said was, "Later."

Hazel realized as he walked away that it was the only word he'd said the entire time.

Red was waiting for her on the beach that night, sitting cross-legged on the sand.

"Evening, sunshine," he chirped as she approached. He was always so upbeat, and just like with Maddie and Hunter, it helped take her mind off England and her mum and reminded her to smile. "How are you today?"

Hazel collapsed on the sand beside him. "I'm okay, thank you."

"That's what I like to hear." He slung an arm around her shoulder. "You know, I was thinking that we should go for a swim."

"What, *now*?"

"While it's not busy!"

"I don't think there's much chance of this beach getting crowded, seeing as you're the only person I've ever seen here."

"That might be the case, Hazel-from-England, but skinny-dipping is much easier under the cover of darkness."

"Hey!" Hazel said, pushing him away. "We are *not* skinny-dipping!"

"Not tonight, maybe," he said. "But tomorrow's the first day of spring, which means summer's just around the corner."

"So?"

He winked. "So, never say never."

She shook her head, amused, and focused her attention on the gentle rush of the waves moving up the shore. It was one of the few constant, familiar things about this entire weird, alien place.

"I have a bone to pick with you," she said then.

"Yeah? What did I do?"

"You failed to mention that your brother goes to Finchwood."

Red shifted on the sand to face her. "You saw him, then?"

"Hard not to. He's in my homeroom."

"Christ."

"Why didn't you say anything?"

"Because I was hoping you wouldn't realize?" he said. "I don't know. Things with Luca are . . . tricky. I didn't want to complicate things."

Hazel squeezed his arm. "Families *are* complicated, Red. You don't have to be embarrassed. Besides, it's not like I don't have baggage of my own, is it? I understand tricky."

"I know," Red said, and he was half-smiling now, which was good. "Does this mean you've been hanging out with Hunter and Maddie too?"

"Yep. They're lovely."

"They are," he agreed.

They were quiet for a moment, but the silence that settled over them wasn't awkward. It was nice. It was peaceful.

"I'm not embarrassed about him," Red said then, his voice low. "Luca, I mean. I'm . . . worried."

Hazel just nodded and rested her head on his shoulder.

Dear Mum,

I remember the time we went to the Natural History Museum in London. It was so fun looking at all the different animals, but the dinosaur exhibition was my favorite. You didn't mind that I dragged you back there to see it three times, and you didn't mind that all I wanted to do was stand and stare. You bought me a book about dinosaurs from the gift shop so I could take them home with me. You read it to me each night for a long, long time.

It was my favorite book ever.

I miss you, Mum, but I remember.

Love,
Hazel

9

ON MONDAY MORNING, INSTEAD OF GOING TO homeroom with the others, Hazel went to a meeting with Miss Allen, the school guidance counselor. Apparently, it was just to check in with how she was adjusting to life at Finchwood now that she'd been there two full weeks, but Hazel was worried that Miss Allen was going to ask probing questions about England and her mum that she wasn't ready to answer.

Hazel signed in with the lady at the desk in the administrative office and took a seat on one of the green chairs lining the wall of the waiting room. She hadn't been sitting long when a student and a parent filed out of Mr. Lynch's office. Hazel realized that it was Luca and Claire Cawley.

"Hey!" Hazel said, jumping to her feet as they approached. "You're here early, why—"

"None of your business," Luca cut her off.

Hazel blinked at him, taken aback by his vehemence, the sharp edges of his voice. "I was just—"

"Well, just *don't*," he said, glaring at her over his shoulder as he walked away, leaving Claire and Hazel staring after him.

"It was a meeting about attendance and his plans for the future," Claire said, eyes still fixed on her son's back as he disappeared into the crowd outside in the hallway. "Mr. Lynch called it. He's getting concerned. We all are."

"Oh," Hazel said softly, not knowing what else to say.

Claire exhaled and forced a smile. "We'll get through it. It's good to see you, Hazel. Come over again soon?"

"Sure," she said as Claire waved goodbye and headed out of the office, no doubt on her way to join Graham at the Anchor to start prepping for lunch. Hazel watched her go with a pang of sympathy. It must be so hard for her and Red to live with Luca when he was like this.

"Hazel?" the receptionist said from the desk. "Miss Allen is ready for you."

Hazel nodded and made her way through the waiting area and into the guidance counselor's office.

The session was longer than Hazel had expected, but relatively painless, with Miss Allen giving England a wide berth. They spoke about her classes and teachers instead, and about how she was getting on. When the bell rang, signaling the end of first period, Hazel thanked her and headed toward the arts building for her next class.

At lunch, Hazel joined Hunter, Maddie, and Luca at their usual spot.

"How was Miss Allen?" Maddie asked.

Hazel looked over at Luca, their encounter in the waiting room still in the back of her mind. He was staring at her, lips pressed into a thin line.

"She was fine," she said eventually, tearing her eyes away to look at Maddie. "She's very friendly."

"She didn't try and psychoanalyze you, did she?" Hunter asked. "I got sent to see a guidance counselor by my dad when he and Mum got divorced. She kept going on about stability and forgiveness. You remember, Mads?"

"I remember. She was probably right, though, looking back. You were pretty fragile."

He pulled a face. "She thought I was certifiable because I told her I was glad my parents were separating."

"Glad?" Hazel said.

"They used to fight all the time," Hunter said. "Like, *all the time*. Now that they're not constantly under each other's feet, they can be civil."

"I guess that's an improvement," Hazel said, and Maddie changed the subject. Hazel glanced over at Luca again to see if he was still staring at her, but his gaze was fixed firmly on the grass.

* * *

Hunter's volleyball practice on Friday had gone poorly, but he remained upbeat and enthusiastic about his next endeavor: cricket. He was staying after school to work on his batting technique with one of the guys from his Health/PE class, so Maddie and Hazel caught the bus home together. Hazel waited until they were sitting tucked away at the back of the bus before bringing up Luca.

"Maddie, can I ask you something?" she said.

"Of course! What's up?"

Hazel hesitated. "It's . . . about Luca."

Maddie shifted in her seat to face Hazel. "What about him?"

"It's just that Red's so friendly and confident and cheerful and Luca's . . ."

". . . not?" Maddie finished for her, and Hazel nodded.

"What happened to him?" she said.

"God knows," Maddie said. "He never talks about his past, but it's clear something's troubling him. Hunter tried to ask him about it once, and Luca shut him down. But look, he's not . . . He's not *mean*. I don't want you to think he's a bad person or anything."

"It's not just me he hates then?"

"He doesn't hate you, Hazel."

"Well, he definitely doesn't *like* me."

"He's just . . . adjusting to you. He'll warm up eventually."

"Is that the reason he barely talks at lunch? Because I'm there?"

"I doubt it. He's always pretty quiet. But once you get to know him, he can be sweet, and he's got a killer sense of humor, and sometimes he'll forget to be shy for a moment. *Then* you can tell that he and Red are twins."

Hazel wondered if she'd ever get to see that side of him. "How did you guys become friends, anyway?"

"Hunter was assigned to show him around when he moved here," she said. "Like you and Ashley. It was only supposed to be for a week, but he stuck around. He's a good guy, and we're glad we have him—just like we're glad to have you."

"I'm glad I have you too." Hazel smiled.

"It's nice to have a female friend for once, actually," Maddie said then. "I've got a bit of a history of scaring people off. I'm sort of . . . intense."

"About what?"

"Everything?" she said, laughing. "I don't know. I get obsessed easily, like with helping Hunter find a sport he's good at. It also probably doesn't help that I've been dux for three years straight."

"Dux?"

Maddie flushed pink. "It means I got the highest marks in our grade."

"That's amazing!" Hazel enthused.

"Yeah, well. Not everyone thinks so." Maddie shook her head, glancing out the bus window and then down into her lap.

"When I was younger, some kids bullied me about it, so I stopped trying to be the best at everything for a while."

Hazel couldn't imagine why anyone in the world would want to be mean to the bright, bubbly girl sitting beside her. "What made you want to get good grades again?"

"I realized that people are assholes, and they'll always find something about you to criticize. I figured I'd rather they picked on me because I tried hard and did well and made myself proud than because I let them make me feel small."

"When I was growing up," Hazel said, "my mum always used to tell me never to compromise myself for anyone else."

"Your mum sounds very wise."

"She was," Hazel said, ignoring the pang in her chest. "She . . . used to be a nurse. She made people feel better for a living."

Maddie looked at her carefully. "Past tense?"

"She . . . got sick when I was younger. Very sick."

"You want to talk about it?"

"Not yet."

Maddie nodded once and pulled her in for a hug. "I'll be here when you're ready, all right? I'm really, really happy that I met you, you know that? I'm so glad you're here."

Hazel hugged her back tightly.

10

THERE WERE SEVERAL THINGS ABOUT PORT
Sheridan that Red had grown to love in the past seven months,
but the West School of Art and Design was pretty much at the
top of the list. When he'd found out that they were moving
away from Sydney and heading two thousand kilometers up the
coast, it was the first thing he did: google art schools in the area.

Well, that wasn't *entirely* true—the first thing he did was
sulk bitterly.

If Red had to move away from his home city for a quiet,
suburban town so that Luca could have a fresh start, then Red
deserved a fresh start too. And Red's fresh start came in the
form of a school that not only tolerated but actively *encouraged*
his penchant for drawing and daydreaming when he should've
been listening in class.

West was more than just a school; it was Red's sanctuary. Even on days like today, when he was standing waiting for his teacher's verdict on his work and feeling like he might throw up from nerves.

Monday afternoons used to be Red's favorite of the week; lunch was followed by an hour of free time, which he usually spent sketching in one of the studios, followed by two blissful hours of Photography with Mr. Hodgkins. Not anymore, though. Not since Hodgkins had started them on their final big project of the year, a portfolio of carefully collated photographs that encapsulated the theme of family.

Family. Yeah, fucking right.

Red usually found that sticking to a theme gave his work focus—last term's exploration of dark versus light had generated some of his favorite pictures—but not this one. This one was a major pain in his ass, which explained why Hodgkins had kept him after class to check in on his photographs. Red knew he needed some help, but his teacher's scrutiny was making him sweat.

"Well," Hodgkins said finally, looking up from the photographs and taking off his glasses to study him closely. "I don't know what to say. Your work is usually much better than this, Redleigh."

Red sighed. *Tell me about it.* "I know, sir. I'm sorry. I think it's the subject matter. My heart isn't in it."

"Why? Do you not think it's a good theme?"

"No," he said. "It's not that. I'm just struggling to find a way to shoot my family that doesn't feel . . . forced."

"Forced?"

"It's like every time I try and take a photo it ends up looking like something out of a catalog, you know? Like a stock photo of a stock family."

Hodgkins gestured at his portfolio with a wry smile. "Yeah, I can see that. They're not bad photographs, Redleigh, all right? The composition is sound, the quality's impressive. It's what they're *showing us* that isn't working. Like you said, they're not real. What is it that's holding you back from losing yourself in the moment and letting the photos happen spontaneously? What are you afraid you might capture on film?"

Everything, Red thought.

He was afraid that the photographs would show Hodgkins and his class just how fractured and useless his family had become—that they'd convey his mother's pain, and how broken Luca was. And his father? *He* wasn't even around for Red to photograph.

"Don't overthink it," Hodgkins said when Red didn't answer. "And remember that our families aren't limited to the people who raised us—sometimes they're just the people that we care about the most."

Red hadn't looked at it that way—had only considered including photographs of his parents and his brother—but he doubted that would help. Who did he really, truly care about other than them?

Hodgkins handed his portfolio back. "Stop trying to get the perfect shot and concentrate on getting some authentic ones, okay? Families are complicated and ugly and messy sometimes, Redleigh, and if that's how you see yours then that's what I need you to show us. If you can capture that honesty, you'll be fine."

If only it were that easy, Red thought as he shoved his portfolio in his satchel beside his camera and let himself out of the studio.

When Red finally got home from school, his mum was waiting for him in the kitchen with a tray of gingerbread cookies. She looked a little flustered, a smudge of flour on her cheek, her hair spilling out of its usual neat ponytail. Red knew she only baked when she was stressed.

He cocked an eyebrow and helped himself to a cookie. "Rough day?"

"You could say that. Luc and I had that meeting with his principal after I dropped you off this morning."

"How'd it go?"

"Not great," she said with a frown. "Mr. Lynch seems to think your brother would be an excellent candidate for university."

"That's . . ." Red trailed off, confused. "That's *good*, isn't it?"

"It was, until he handed Luca a list of schools that offered track scholarships."

Holy shit. "He did *what?*"

She sighed. "Exactly. Apparently, he's been reading Luca's file. He seems to think Luc should start training again and try for another one."

"How did Luc react?"

"He didn't, really. But I could tell it upset him." She shook her head and took a big bite out of her cookie. "I keep waiting for the day when he gets better, you know? When things are different."

"They will be, Mum. You know it takes time."

"I know," she said. "I just . . . I wish there was something I could *do*. I might talk to the doctor about trying a new medication, maybe one he'll actually take."

"Again?" Red said doubtfully.

A few months back, the doctors had changed Luca's medication from Zoloft to mirtazapine. At first, Red had barely noticed the difference in him, but then one evening out of nowhere Luca fell asleep on a chaise longue on the veranda outside. He slept there all night underneath a blanket Claire tucked around him and stayed that way until morning.

After that, Luca went from barely sleeping to sleeping all the time, and his mood swings disappeared completely. He became steadily more withdrawn and shut off, but it was more than that. It was as if someone had taken the energy and life and

Luca out of him and left him empty. On the mirtazapine he was nothing. Red was secretly glad he had stopped taking the pills; he liked having his brother back, no matter how hard it was to watch him suffering.

"It's for his own good," Claire said. She looked completely crushed, like this was her fault. Red wanted to tell her she was wrong, that none of this was *anyone's* fault. Sometimes life just fucks you over and leaves you to pick up the pieces.

He thought back to his conversation with Hodgkins. Maybe this was what he meant about honesty—because this scene right here, seeing his mother surrounded by baked goods with flour on her apron and worry in her eyes, made his fingers itch to reach for his camera and steal a snapshot. Not one of her smiling, or posing, or pretending. One of her being upset, and worried, and raw. Real.

He reached across the counter instead and covered her hand with his own. "I love you, Mum."

"When Luca got home from school, I told him we'd take out another mortgage to pay for college if we had to," she said quietly. "That he didn't need to worry about scholarships."

"What did he say?"

"That he'd think about it," she said, sighing. "I think he just forgets sometimes, you know?"

"Forgets what?"

She raised her head to meet his eye. "That *he* still has a future."

FRIDAY NIGHT. *TWO HUNDRED AND EIGHTY-eight days.* It had been a long, long week and Luca needed to do something to release the anger and frustration that had been building up slowly inside him ever since Monday morning and that ridiculous meeting with his mum and Lynch and all his talk about track scholarships. Like it was that easy for Luca just to pick up where he'd left off last year with his running. Like Luca hadn't already spent countless nights out on the track by his house trying to force himself to get back into the one thing that used to come as easily to him as breathing. But being on a track made so many memories come flooding back, memories that he still couldn't deal with. So running wasn't just hard; it was impossible.

The urge to beat the crap out of something or someone

spread over him like a rash, putting him on edge, making his skin crawl. He had to get out of the house; he had to get away, or he'd explode.

Luca got onto the first bus that arrived, not caring where it was headed, and rode on it until the light outside the windows had faded to black and they'd pulled up to the final stop in town.

People stared as he walked past, their eyes following him, halting their conversations midsentence, and he knew exactly what they saw—a young, healthy, wholesome teenage boy. That was why they looked, but it wasn't why they *stared*. They stared because they couldn't figure out exactly what was going on beneath his boy-next-door exterior, but they knew something wasn't right.

Eight o'clock. Nine. Ten. He was in a dimly lit bar full of middle-aged men drinking pints of ale and bickering over who got to play darts next. It was shabby, and it was grimy as hell, but it was also perfect. He was invisible. And the bartender hadn't asked for ID, not caring that Luca was still half a year away from being eighteen.

Luca couldn't even stand being in his own house. Redleigh and their mum were constantly on his back, breathing down his neck, suffocating him, and they couldn't seem to understand why he didn't like to be around them, not even for dinner. It was their stupid questions. So many stupid questions it drove him insane: *Are you okay? Do you want to talk about it? Is there anything I can do to help?* On and fucking on.

That was the one good thing about his dad not being around—his radio silence. Not that his dad would bother asking how he was even if he *were* home.

Luca ordered another beer. There was someone watching him as the bartender handed him his change and pushed the bottle across the bar. Luca could feel his eyes on him but didn't look up, taking a long swig of beer instead. He was about halfway through the bottle when the man from across the bar jumped off his stool and walked by him toward the bathroom, shoving into Luca with his shoulder as he passed.

"Hey," Luca said, turning around to face him. "Apologize."

The man was huge, with a thick neck and small red-rimmed eyes. "Piss off, you rat," he said. "Are you even old enough to be in here?"

Luca glanced down at the bottle in his hand and then back up at the man, his jaw set. "I can handle myself."

"Yeah, right. *That* I'd like to see."

"Don't push me," Luca said, standing from his own stool. He could feel the anger welling up inside him, white-hot and burning. "You don't know shit."

The man stepped toward Luca. He towered over him like an ugly, meaty giant, but Luca refused to be intimidated, not by this clown. Not by anyone.

"Language, kid. Mummy wouldn't approve."

Luca clenched and unclenched his jaw, his hands balling up unconsciously into fists by his side. The bartender was watching them closely. "I told you not to push me," Luca said.

The man burst out laughing, a low, growling sound that shook his whole body. He laughed and laughed, and it made Luca's skin crawl, the anger building until he snapped and threw the hardest punch he could muster right at the left side of the guy's jaw.

The laughter stopped abruptly, replaced by a sudden, hushed silence. The guy staggered backward, his hand gripping the side of his face tightly. Pain shot through Luca's arm, but he stifled a grimace—because whatever happened next, he wouldn't show any weakness.

"You little shit!" the guy barked, lunging toward him. Luca ducked, narrowly avoiding a flying fist, and straightened up just in time to lay another punch, this time on the guy's left eye. The man lunged again and his fist collided with Luca's stomach, winding him, and Luca stumbled backward, his face colliding with the hard surface of the bar. He gasped for breath, unable to stand up. Someone grabbed hold of his collar and yanked him away, dragging him across the room and throwing him out the door. Sprawled on the pavement, Luca looked up and came face-to-face with the bartender.

"You're an idiot," he said. "You could've gotten yourself killed."

"Sorry," Luca muttered.

"Yeah, well. Don't bother coming back."

He slammed the door shut. Luca propped himself up on his elbows and took a deep breath, testing his stinging lungs. He could feel the pain starting to creep in. He got clumsily to his feet, the beer kicking in all at once and fogging up his mind, and followed the wall of the bar into an alleyway. Suddenly, the bar door flew open, throwing bright light across the dark pavement. Luca could hear voices, one of which he recognized—the guy he had punched.

"I'm gonna find him," the man promised. "I'm gonna find that little shit, and I'm gonna kill him."

Luca froze, inching backward across the wall until he was hidden behind a Dumpster, swallowed by the shadows. Now that the adrenaline had subsided, he felt an unmistakable stab of fear in his stomach.

"Leave him alone, Phil," another voice said.

"Yeah," someone else agreed. "He's not worth it. He's just a kid. He was probably drunk."

"What a pussy," he growled in answer. "I'm bleeding. He made me *bleed*."

"Let's go back inside and get it cleaned up, then. No point getting angry out here, he'll be miles away by now. You scared the shit out of him."

The man, Phil, hacked up a mouthful of phlegm and spat loudly into the gutter. "True. What a pussy," he said again, and the door banged shut behind them as they went inside.

The breath Luca didn't even know he was holding came out in a rush. He realized he was shaking. A siren wailed in the distance, and Luca had never felt so out of place. Missing home was like that—it came and went in waves and then hit you hard when you least expected it. Shit, he missed Sydney.

He still woke up every day wishing he could go back there. That he could reverse time to *before*.

He leaned against the wall, resting his head against the rough brickwork, nursing his hand. It was throbbing now, as was the right side of his face from where it had connected with the bar. The minutes ticked by and little by little his breathing and heartbeat slowed down to a steady rhythm, and his mind began to clear. He felt weary and nauseated. Hollow.

Every time Luca got in a fight, there were a couple of minutes afterward where he felt good, filled with an odd sense of complete calm. It never lasted long, but it was worth it. That's why he kept coming back for more. The aching, the stinging, the fear, it was all a distraction from the real world and himself.

The pain was worse now that the adrenaline was gone. Luca inspected the damage. Several knuckles were grazed, blood oozing sluggishly through his skin, and his entire hand was swollen—by morning, it would no doubt be mottled with dark bruises. His face, too. God, Redleigh was going to be so pissed. Luca still remembered how he'd reacted the last time he caught him with bruised fists, so disappointed, so betrayed, so let down. *You promised you weren't going to fight anymore,* he'd said. *You promised, Luc.*

Luca was so tired of breaking promises. He couldn't keep on living like this. He didn't *want* to keep on living like this.

He just didn't know how to stop.

12

WHEN LUCA WALKED INTO THE CAWLEYS'
kitchen on Saturday afternoon, his hair was mussed up from
sleep, dark circles were under his eyes, and there was a purple
bruise blooming across the right side of his face. He was still
wearing his pajamas, despite the fact that it was the middle of
the day; he'd obviously had a late night.

Hazel's eyes widened at the sight of him. Luca glanced over
and caught her staring, and pulled the fridge door open force-
fully. Hazel could see that his hand was battered—there were
bruises and cuts all along his knuckles, scarlet and swollen
and raw.

"Jesus, Luc," Red said as he noticed too. "Were you—"

"Redleigh," Luca said sharply, a warning. "Don't."

"Are you serious? Has Mum seen you? She's going to *kill* you!"

Luca kicked the fridge shut and stalked out of the room. For a moment, neither Hazel nor Red spoke. Red seemed frozen, staring out the doorway after his brother.

"Do you think he was in a fight?" she asked eventually, and Red nodded.

"He's in trouble," he said, voice heavy.

"He'll be okay," she assured him, even though she wasn't convinced that was true. "It was only one fight, Red."

He just shook his head. "I wish."

It took Red a while to perk up after the Luca incident, but Hazel managed to bring him around eventually. The two of them spent the rest of the afternoon out in the garden, playing cards and drinking lemonade. Hazel was the most relaxed she'd felt in a long time, and the realization made her feel sick—that she could sit there and enjoy herself so easily like everything back in England had never happened.

When Claire found out that Graham would be at the restaurant until closing, she refused to let Hazel go home without having dinner with them. It was the kind of motherly concern Hazel hadn't had in years, and she found herself fighting back tears as she agreed to stay.

Red had been right that night on the beach: Claire really

was a phenomenal cook. Tonight, the three of them sat around the kitchen table and ate prosciutto-wrapped salmon on a bed of lemongrass-and-chili rice. Like the last time she'd eaten at Red's, Hazel was reminded how sick she was of takeout.

After dinner, Hazel said her goodbyes to Red and Claire and headed down the road toward Graham's house. The sun was just beginning to set, bathing the streets in the soft orange glow of dusk. It was a pretty neighborhood, Hazel thought as she walked. Quiet and peaceful. The houses were all the same: big and angular with slanting roofs and meticulous front gardens. She crossed the street, took another right, and noticed that there was a bright light shining through the trees up ahead. Hazel remembered passing a community sports field with Red on the way to his house that first day—it must be the floodlights from that.

Curious, she walked in the direction of the lights until she arrived at the open gates of the stadium. She went through and came to a stop at the edge of the illuminated field. It was empty. Except no, wait, there was someone there, tucked away in the farthest corner. Hazel knew it was Luca the second she laid eyes on him; she recognized him by his sandy-blond hair. He was sitting on the grass in the middle of the running track, his legs stretched out, scowling down at the ground.

Hazel felt a pang of sympathy for him. Red had told her that they'd moved to Port Sheridan because of something that happened to Luca in Sydney, but she didn't know what. She did know that it had hit Luca really hard—not because of his anger, or the way he pushed everyone away—she knew because sometimes, when he thought no one was looking, his eyes went dark and it was clear that he was remembering. It was the same helpless, hollow look that filled her own eyes when her thoughts turned to home.

It was *that* that made her step forward out of the shadows and walk over to him—knowing that deep down, underneath it all, Luca felt the same sort of pain she did.

"Luca?" she said when she was close enough.

He started at the sound of her voice but didn't respond.

"Luca," she repeated, this time less tentatively, and he looked up. He didn't say anything right away, and Hazel didn't push him. She just waited.

"I used to be able to do ten laps around a track this size in twelve minutes."

"So why can't you now?"

"I'm not a runner. Not anymore."

"Then what are you doing here?"

"It doesn't matter!" he snapped. His eyes flashed with familiar anger and irritation. "You wouldn't understand."

Hazel exhaled, trying not to lose her temper at his defensiveness. How *could* she understand, when everything about him was shrouded in mystery?

"Look," she said. "If it's *that* important to you, just ask someone for help. That's how it works, isn't it? A problem shared is a problem halved?"

Luca glared up at her. "Who am I supposed to ask?"

"Anyone! Your brother? Hunter? Maddie? Even *I* could help, probably."

He shook his head and turned away from her. "I'm fine," he muttered. "I don't need anyone's help."

"Great. I'll leave you to it, then."

If he responded as she walked away, Hazel didn't hear him. She was too wound up, too irritated and confused. What was *wrong* with him? What had she—or anyone for that matter—done to deserve his animosity? She'd tried to give him the benefit of the doubt, but perhaps the truth was that he was just a jerk.

She didn't understand why the others put up with him; if he wasn't Red's brother, she would've given up on him the moment they met.

Red. Red, who had to live with him every day, who had a brother who refused to talk to him or let him in but was still trying to make the best of a bad situation.

She stopped walking to catch her breath. Despite everything Red had to deal with, he still loved his brother unconditionally. What was worse for him? Having Luca shutting him out at every given opportunity, or not having Luca there at all? The second. Of *course* it was the second. Red was losing his twin the same way she'd lost her mum, and she knew exactly how much it hurt to have someone slip away from you, for them to always be just out of reach.

Hazel turned on her heels, hurrying back toward the track.

She didn't know what she was going to do when she got there but maybe, *just maybe*, being there would be enough. Maybe if someone had been there for her when she needed them, things wouldn't have been quite so hard. She didn't stop until she was back on the grass, but she was too late.

Luca was already gone.

Dear Mum,

I remember the time we went to the seaside. It didn't stop raining all day, but we still had fun. We stopped in a little café on the beach for a hot chocolate with extra whipped cream and a slice of sponge cake, and we sat and watched all the people swimming in the sea despite the rain and the cold. We were both so happy, and I never stopped laughing, not even for a second.

That was the best day ever.

I miss you, Mum, but I remember.

Love,
Hazel

13

LUCA WASN'T IN SCHOOL FOR MOST OF THE next week. Hunter and Maddie seemed unperturbed by his absence, like it happened regularly, and on Wednesday night on the beach, when Hazel asked Red about his brother's whereabouts, he just shrugged.

"How should I know? I'm not his keeper."

"But you do *live* with him."

He pulled a face. "In the same house, yeah, but it's not like he ever leaves his room."

Hazel knew that was true, but it didn't help ease her worry. She couldn't get the image of how he'd looked on Saturday night out of her mind. "What about your mum? Did she see the bruises from his fight?"

Red didn't answer for a moment, and when he did his voice was hollow. "Yeah. She did."

"What happened?"

"She cried and begged," he said. "Then she threatened to call Dad and came downstairs and cried some more."

Hazel's stomach twisted. "Red . . ."

"I'm sure he'll be back in school by the end of the week," he said, forcing a smile, and changed the subject.

Sure enough, Luca was back on Friday morning, showing up in homeroom and sliding into his usual seat with no explanation for his absence. At lunch, Hazel met Maddie and Hunter on the lawn, but Luca didn't join them. When Hazel asked about it, Maddie just said, "He's probably in the library catching up on schoolwork or something."

Hazel was on her way to her last class of the week when she saw Luca again. He was heading her way down the hallway, but instead of passing her by, he stopped in front of her.

"Hazel."

The word sounded strange coming out of his mouth, foreign. Perhaps it was because it was the first time she'd ever heard him say her name.

"Yes?"

"I . . . I just wanted to apologize for Saturday night?" he

said, running a hand nervously through his hair. Up that close, Hazel could see the faint yellow smudges where the bruises had been on the weekend. "I shouldn't have talked to you the way I did. You were only trying to help."

Hazel managed a bewildered nod, and Luca took a deep breath and said, "The thing is, I don't even know if you were offering, but if you *were*, then I'd really appreciate it if . . . Will you help me with the running thing?"

"You want *me* to help you?"

"I've tried everything else," he said.

Hazel thought again about Red, and about Claire—about how worried they were about him—and surprised herself by nodding. "Okay."

"Really?"

"I can't promise anything," she warned. "I've never done any running myself, but I'll try my best. When would you like to start?"

"As soon as we can," he said.

"Tonight? Eight thirty, on that field?"

"Okay," he said. "But this is . . . This is private, all right? You can't tell Red or the others about it. Not yet."

"But why? I—"

"Promise me you'll keep it between us."

"I don't understand *why*," she said. "But okay."

Luca nodded curtly, turned on his heels, and walked away down the hallway and out of sight.

* * *

As Hazel made her way to the track that evening, she wondered what it was exactly that she was supposed to be helping Luca with. She didn't know anything about running, especially not *competitive* running, so it wasn't like she could give him any advice—and if he used to be a runner, then he probably didn't need it anyway. He'd said he'd tried everything, but what did that mean? Was she just there for moral support? To cheer him on from the sidelines? Wave some pom-poms around and be his personal cheerleader?

Because she would, if she had to. She wanted to help—wanted to try, at least—but she wasn't doing it for Luca. She was doing it for Red.

The lights were on at the field when she arrived, but the track was empty. She'd half-expected Luca to be there already, warming up or stretching. She took a seat on a bench by the starting line to wait for him.

She waited. And waited. By nine o'clock, when there was still no sign of him, Hazel stood—disappointed but not entirely surprised—and headed back to Graham's.

14

HAZEL STAYED AWAY FROM THE CAWLEYS' house on Saturday so that she wouldn't risk seeing Luca—the more she thought about him not showing up at the field, the more upset she got. On Sunday, Red came over to Graham's. They spent the day out in the garden sprawled on the grass talking, and when Graham returned that evening from his shift at the Anchor with pizza, the three of them ate outside at a table underneath the stars. It was a good distraction from the twisting feeling of humiliation in the pit of her stomach.

At school the next week, Luca repaid the favor and spent Monday and Tuesday avoiding Hazel. He sat across the room in homeroom, and at lunchtimes, he didn't join them on the lawn to eat. By the third day, Hazel began to get a little irritated by his refusal even to make eye contact with her—what reason did he have to ignore her? It was *him* who'd asked for help and then stood her up with no explanation or apology.

Hazel caught sight of him heading down the hallway at the start of lunch on Wednesday, and although she was still angry, she couldn't stand the tension between them. It didn't just affect her; she could tell that it was also upsetting Maddie and Hunter—they didn't understand why he was ignoring them too.

When Hazel marched up to him, though, ready to call him out, he just pushed past her in the direction of the library.

"Really?" she called after him. "How long are we going to do this for?"

He turned back around to face her, expression stormy. "What do you want?"

"Just to give you a tip for next time someone tries to be nice to you—don't make plans and then stand them up. I don't know if you thought it would be funny, some sort of hilarious prank—"

"No," Luca cut her off, cheeks flushed pink. "It wasn't a prank."

"Then what was it?"

"I . . . panicked."

"About meeting me?"

He shook his head, jaw set. "It's got nothing to do with you. And I know that's not an excuse and I shouldn't have bailed, but it's not . . . I keep trying, and I just. I can't do it."

"What can't you do? Run?"

"You wouldn't understand. It's complicated."

"Fine!" she said. "Whatever. But we all have our issues, Luca, all right?"

He opened his mouth to argue and then clamped it shut again, settling for glaring at her instead. Hazel wondered what it was about her that seemed to infuriate him so much.

"Let's just . . . Let's forget it, shall we?" she said, taking a deep breath. "But you have to stop avoiding Maddie and Hunter because of me. They're your friends and they care about you, so it's not fair for you to take this out on them too. Please come to lunch. They miss you."

Luca hesitated for a brief moment and then nodded and followed her to the lawn to join the others.

Luca stopped avoiding her after that, but it took him another few days before he plucked up the courage to ask about the running again. It was Saturday, and Hazel was at the Cawleys' house for lunch. Red had just left the kitchen to grab something from upstairs when Luca appeared in the doorway.

"I want to try again," he said. "With the training, I mean. Can we try again? Please?"

"Are you going to stand me up this time?"

Luca shook his head, looking a mixture of sheepish and mortified. "No. I swear."

Hazel thought about it for a moment. "Fine. Tonight, eight thirty. But this is your last chance."

Luca nodded once and turned and disappeared from the room. Hazel stared after him, trying to wrap her head around what had just happened. If he wasn't a runner anymore, then why was this so important to him? Because it *must* be, if he was willing to swallow his pride and come back to ask for her help again.

Red walked in a moment later and caught her frowning. "Everything okay?"

"Everything's fine," she said, forcing a smile and hoping that was the truth.

Luca was waiting for her when Hazel arrived at the track that evening, much to her relief. He nodded at her once in greeting, and Hazel took a seat on the ground to watch him warm up. There was a sense of determination about him as he stretched that had his forehead creased in concentration and his jaw set.

"All right," she said when he finished. "What's the plan here, then?"

"I . . . don't have one."

Hazel resisted the urge to roll her eyes. "Okay. Why don't you start by telling me what kind of running you do, then? Sprints? Relays?"

Luca kept his gaze on the ground. "Long-distance."

She didn't know why, but that surprised her. Long-distance running took a lot of dedication and patience, and she just couldn't picture him running endlessly around a track. Couldn't imagine him doing much, really, except scowling and sulking in the corner.

"What distance did you do?"

"Three thousand meters was my specialty," he said. "But I did five thousand meters too."

"You said you used to do ten laps of a track this size—how far was that?"

"Four thousand meters."

"And you used to be able to do it in twelve minutes?"

"Yep."

"What happened?"

He raised his eyes to hers, looking annoyed. "It doesn't matter."

"Luca. I'm trying to help."

"I just *stopped*, all right? I stopped running. That's it."

Hazel knew that wasn't it from the defensiveness in his voice, but she let it go. "How long has it been since you ran?"

"Nearly a year. But running isn't the main problem— starting is."

"Starting?"

"I can't even finish a lap."

"Why not?"

He didn't answer. Hazel waited, but he still said nothing.

Just stood there with his hands balled into fists and his jaw clenched.

"Why not?" she pressed. "Is it because it's too hard? Because you're out of shape?"

"No."

"What, then?"

"I'm afraid I won't be able to do it again."

"That's it?"

Luca nodded reluctantly. "I figured that if someone else was here it would help."

"What, by them forcing you to carry on if you try and stop?"

"Something like that."

"That's the plan?" Hazel said. "I stand here and yell at you?"

"You got a better one?"

"I . . . No."

"Like I said"—he shrugged—"I've tried everything else. If you don't want to help . . ."

"I'll help," she said firmly. "Shall we get started?"

Luca nodded again and arranged himself behind the start line on the track, crouched down to the ground. He looked over at her when he was in position, waiting, and Hazel began to count him in.

"Three. Two. One. *Go.*"

Luca took off down the track, feet flying across the grass. He got about a quarter of the way around before he came to a halt, sinking to the ground. Hazel got to her feet and jogged over to meet him.

"See?" he said. "It's like I'm hitting a fucking *wall* or something."

"Get up," Hazel told him. "Try again."

"It's pointless," he muttered, but he did as he was told. She followed him back to the start line, and this time when he got into position, she followed suit beside him, copying his stance.

Luca looked across at her weirdly. "What are you doing?"

"Running with you."

"But you—"

"I'm running with you, all right? Are you ready?"

"Yes?"

"Good. Three. Two. One. *Go.*"

This time, they both started running. Hazel had never been very good at sports, but she tried her hardest to match his pace and find some sort of rhythm as her feet thudded against the track in time with his. It felt clumsy and awkward, but it didn't matter; she wasn't doing this for herself.

She kept her focus on Luca as they ran. When they approached the point where he'd stopped before, his face got all pinched like he was preparing himself to hit his imaginary wall.

"Luca," she ordered. "Don't stop."

He said nothing, but they kept running, and he didn't falter. She kept saying things like *You can do this, You've got this, You're doing great.* He didn't respond but he definitely heard.

They passed the start line and began their second lap, and still Luca didn't fumble. By lap three, Hazel was hopelessly out of breath. She slowed to a halt halfway around and continued shouting her encouragement from the side of the track: "Keep going, Luca! Just seven laps left!"

Running on his own, Luca fell into a steadier, easier rhythm. Hazel found herself a little in awe watching him, taking in how he landed on his feet with each step, the bend of his knees, the swing of his arms. Around and around the track he ran, and then he was finally finishing his tenth lap and walking back over to Hazel. He looked worn out and breathless, but also calmer than she'd ever seen him.

"You did it," she said when he reached her.

He collapsed on the ground to catch his breath. "That was way, way longer than twelve minutes."

"Yes," Hazel said. "But you did it, Luca. You started and you got past the wall."

He didn't respond right away—but, then, "I did."

"And now that you know you can, you'll be able to do it by yourself."

"Actually—" he started. "I was thinking . . . Could you help me with my time, maybe? Getting it back?"

She considered it for a moment. "Okay. But we should have a routine—how are Mondays and Thursdays for you?"

Luca sat up to unlace his shoes. "Mondays and Thursdays are good."

Hazel waited to see if he would thank her, or at least

acknowledge her, but when he didn't, she said, "All right. See you at school, then."

"See you," he echoed, without any real feeling, and Hazel turned on her heels and left him to it. She didn't understand why he'd given up the running if it was so important to him or why it seemed so difficult for him now, but one thing was clear: he looked good at it. Really, really good.

That night on the beach, Hazel had to fight the urge to tell Red about her and Luca's session. She might not have understood why it was so important to Luca that she keep it a secret, but she had to respect it anyway.

Red, fortunately, had other things to talk about—namely Hazel's dad.

"Hey, so how are things with you and Graham?" he asked as soon as they were settled on the sand. "Mum said today that he basically never stops telling people at work how happy he is that you're here."

Hazel felt her cheeks heat up without really knowing why. Graham had never shown any real indication that he was pleased to be sharing his house with her or, in fact, that he was pleased to have a daughter at all. It wasn't like Hazel would hold it against him if he wasn't. Finding out that your seventeen-year-old child that you'd never met was coming to live with you was a lot for *anyone* to adapt to.

"They're . . . okay."

Red looked thoughtful. "It must be so weird for both of you, right? One minute you don't know each other and the next you're stuck together."

Weird was one way to describe it—hard was another. Though she and Graham had begun to adjust to life with each other, the situation was still awkward and difficult to navigate. The worst moments, though, Hazel had found, weren't the silences when she and Graham couldn't find anything to talk about. It was when they *could*. It was the moments when Hazel recognized herself in his laugh or his sense of humor and started thinking about how different her life could have been if he'd chosen to be a part of it before he absolutely had to be.

When Hazel didn't answer, Red looked sideways at her. "Sorry. That was . . . insensitive. It'll get easier, you know that, right? You'll get used to each other."

She had her doubts about that.

THE FOLLOWING WEEK, HAZEL MET LUCA ON Monday and Thursday at the stadium, and each evening he ran his ten laps of the track. It was clear that Hazel's presence wasn't necessary—the only thing she did was call out his times from a stopwatch—but she didn't mind just being there for moral support if that's what Luca needed. They quickly figured that the average time it took him to complete the laps now was roughly sixteen and a half minutes. Hazel didn't know whether to be daunted by the number or encouraged, but at least he was running, and it seemed to make him feel better. When he was on the track his anger was in check and he seemed less . . . agitated.

* * *

Friday was the night of what Hunter had spent the entire week referring to excitedly as "the biggest party of the year," which Kayla, from their grade at Finchwood, was throwing to celebrate the beginning of the half-term break. For some reason, Hazel had been invited too, and Maddie was determined that she should experience her first Australian party. Hazel didn't have the heart to tell her it was her first party *ever*.

It was tradition, apparently, for them to eat out at a restaurant in town before a party—even Luca came for the dinner part and then afterward usually went home or went out somewhere by himself because he, unsurprisingly, abhorred parties as much as he abhorred any event that required social interaction. Tonight was no exception.

They had decided to go to the Anchor. Hazel hadn't been since her first day in Australia. The hostess showed them to a round table in the corner with a decent view of the sea, and Hazel sat down opposite the window, safely nestled between Red and Maddie. When their waitress came to take their order, Hazel chose the grilled barramundi again, hoping she would be able to appreciate it more now that she wasn't feeling sick with nerves. The conversation around the table was light and easy. It was nice, everyone being together.

After they'd eaten and paid the check—complete with a huge discount courtesy of Graham—they split up. The boys took a taxi back to Red's house, and the girls caught a bus to Maddie's. She had insisted on lending Hazel a dress and doing her hair and makeup. By the time they were ready to leave for the party, Hazel looked like an entirely different person. Her hair was out of its usual braid and hung loose around her shoulders, and Maddie had painted Hazel's lips a soft coral to match her heels. Her outfit was nothing like what she was used to wearing, but Hazel liked it.

Kayla's house was already crowded by the time they got there just after eight o'clock. The pathway to her front door was lit with fairy lights that twinkled in the darkness and there were people spilling out the door and into the front garden. Hazel followed Maddie wordlessly through the crowd and into the entranceway, her heart thudding in time with the heavy bass blaring out of the speakers somewhere farther inside the house.

They made their way to the kitchen to get something to drink and found Hunter and Red sitting around the table playing a game of Arrogance.

"Hazel-from-England!" Hunter cried at the same time that Red said, "There you are!"

"Here I am," Hazel said with a laugh, sliding into the seat beside Red. He was wearing a burgundy top that made his skin look even paler than usual, his eyes even darker. "Have you guys been drinking?"

"That was my fault," Red said. "I found Mum's sherry and we had a few shots."

"Sounds . . . dangerous."

He nodded gravely. "Totally dangerous and totally manly. You look nice, by the way."

"Thanks. You too."

He sipped his drink. "I brought Luca."

"You did? How'd you get him to come?"

"Well," Red said, "let's just say I'm not above blackmail if it gets him to act like a normal teenager."

"Where is he?"

"Who knows. We lost him pretty quickly."

Red's gaze slid over to a boy in the corner of the kitchen with bright blond hair, and then back to Hazel. She raised an eyebrow, and when he realized he'd been caught out, Red's face flooded with color.

"Friend of yours?" she asked under her breath.

"Not yet. But I think we had a moment on the stairs earlier."

"Well, he keeps looking over this way."

"Really?" he said.

"Really. You should go talk to him."

Red just shrugged. "Maybe later."

Hazel bumped his shoulder with hers and turned her attention back to the others. As Hunter shuffled the cards, Maddie explained the rules of Arrogance. It was the first time Hazel had played a drinking game, but she picked it up easily enough. They played until everyone had finished their drinks, Hazel sipping carefully on the drink Red had poured her as she got used to the slightly bitter aftertaste. Then they refilled them from the bottles on the counter and moved into the front room where the music was loudest. The room was packed full of people dancing, and the four of them worked their way through the crowd to an empty sofa in the corner.

Hazel stayed glued to Red's side for the next hour or so until Maddie pulled him away to dance with her. Then she and Hunter chatted happily for a while, about school and his latest failed attempt at cricket.

"Hey, I'm going to find the bathroom," he said eventually, voice raised over the music. "Are you okay here?"

"I think I'll go get another drink," Hazel said. "Do you want anything?"

Hunter shook his head, squeezing her arm. "I'm good, thanks. Catch you in a bit!"

Hazel followed him out of the room and headed toward the kitchen. It was almost as busy as the living room, and she had to weave through the crowd to get to the counter filled with drinks. She settled on a bottle of something pink. When she arrived back in the living room, Hunter hadn't returned to the sofa, and Red and Maddie were no longer dancing.

Hazel looked for them in another room and then in the kitchen. Nothing. Her head began to swim and she couldn't tell if it was panic or the drinks. She yanked the back door open to get some air and stepped out onto the patio. She shut the door behind her, shut out the people and the *noise*, and took a few big breaths, in and out, until she felt a little calmer.

"Hazel," someone said from behind her. She whirled around. Luca was sitting on a low wall off to the side, hands wrapped tight around the neck of a beer bottle.

"Oh, hi," she said hastily. "I didn't mean to—"

"No, no. Don't go." He patted the wall beside him. "Stay. Please stay."

Hazel hesitated but made her way over anyway. She glanced sideways at him. He was looking at her, mouth curving upward into a sleepy, hazy smile. Hazel couldn't remember ever seeing him smile before. She wondered how long he'd been out here on his own.

"Thanks for staying," he murmured, eyes falling shut.

"Are you okay?"

"M'great. Can't you tell?"

He was slurring his words, stumbling over them until they began to blend into something almost incomprehensible.

"Hey, Luca?" she tried again.

His eyes flew open, focusing on her blearily. "Hmm?"

"Are you sure you're all right? Do you want me to get Red?"

"Red?"

"Your brother?"

"Ha!" He snorted. "Fuck off."

She stood abruptly from the wall. "Fine, I will."

"Wait!" He grabbed hold of her arm, pulled her back down onto the wall beside him. "Wait. I'm sorry. Didn't mean it."

Hazel's mouth was set in a tight line. "Sure about that?"

He looked up at her with woeful brown eyes. "You don't like me, do you?"

"Look," she started, "I hardly *know* you—"

"No one knows me." He cut her off. "But *you're* still trying to help."

An awkward silence settled over them. He was still looking at her, too closely, too intensely, his eyes glazed.

"Don't know why Red cares so much about me being here," he said then. "When he disappears on me."

Her forehead creased. "He just wants you to be happy."

"No, he wants me where he can keep an eye on me," Luca argued.

Hazel thought that was probably true. She should go and find him and let him know that she'd located his brother. "Well, I really need to—"

"What are you drinking?" Luca asked, leaning forward to study the bottle she had balanced on her knee.

She looked down at the bottle, momentarily distracted. It was pink and tasted sweet, but beyond that, she didn't have a clue because she'd never drunk alcohol before tonight. She held it up to him so he could examine the label. "No idea. You tell me."

Luca squinted at it, brow furrowed. "Smirnoff Ice," he decided finally.

"What's that?"

He looked at her as if he was trying to figure out if she was being serious. "Well, it's a vodka mix, I guess." He shrugged. "Raspberry flavor."

Hazel made a face. "You're joking. It's supposed to taste like *raspberries?*"

"That's why you stick with beer," he said, grinning. "Beer

is reliable. Drinking Smirnoff's like drinking liquid candy, you know?"

She *didn't* know, but she nodded anyway to placate him. He swayed again, this time dangerously close to falling off the wall. Instinctively, Hazel's arm shot out to steady him. It was weird, seeing him so relaxed and chatty when she was used to him being so withdrawn.

Once Luca regained his balance, he smiled up at her. "Ryan says alcopops are for wimps," he told her then.

"Ryan?"

"My best friend."

"Oh." She frowned down at her drink. "I don't think I've met him yet."

"Course you haven't. Never will."

"Why not?"

"Because he's dead, isn't he?"

"He's *what*?"

"He's dead. Ryan's dead. He died last year. Back in Sydney."

"I'm sorry," she whispered. This was it, this was why Luca was the way he was. "I didn't know that."

"No one does. No one knows."

"I really am sorry, Luca."

"No one knows," he said again, slowly. "No one except my family. No one *can* know. Don't want them to feel sorry for me. Don't wanna be the boy with the dead best friend."

"Okay," she agreed. "I understand. I won't tell."

"Thank you," he mumbled, and rested his head on her shoulder. Through the kitchen door, she spotted Red.

"Are you sure you don't want me to get someone?" she asked again, tearing her eyes away from Red just in time to see Luca slump forward and tumble off the wall, landing passed out on the patio beneath them.

Dear Mum,

I remember the time we went to the theater in London. We went to see <u>The Lion King</u>, and I got scared by the costumes. You let me sit on your lap for the rest of the show, and you wrapped your arms around me tight so that I wouldn't be frightened anymore, and every time Scar came onstage you held my hand because I didn't like him. By the second act, I was having the time of my life.

Thank you for helping me face up to my fears, Mum, and making me stick it out. It was so worth it.

I miss you, Mum, but I remember.

Love,
Hazel

THE NEXT MORNING, RED MADE HIS WAY OVER to Hazel's. When she opened Graham's front door, she looked like she'd barely slept. Her hair was a mess, and there were smudges of leftover makeup underneath her eyes.

"Morning!" Red said cheerfully, and she broke into a smile.

"Morning. How are you feeling?"

He'd been a tad worse for wear at the end of the evening when the two of them had put Luca into a taxi and taken him home, but it was nothing that a good night's sleep and a bacon sandwich couldn't fix.

"Not too bad," he said. "Not as bad as Luca, anyway. He spent the entire night with his head down the toilet."

"Is he all right now?"

"He's sleeping it off." Red shook his head. "He's an idiot,

though. He knows he can't handle that much beer in one go and he drinks it anyway. When I saw him this morning, he said he didn't remember much past the walk from our house to the party."

Hazel opened her mouth like she was going to say something, and then shut it again. "That . . . sucks," she said instead.

Red waved his hand dismissively, following her into the house. "He'll be fine. I left him some Tylenol."

"You take good care of him, considering the two of you don't get on that well."

"Why do you think I blackmail him into coming to parties sometimes?" he said, hating how bitter he sounded. "It's the only time we ever talk, when he's so drunk that he barely knows who I am and can't remember that we even had a conversation."

Her face fell. "Red, that's . . ."

She didn't finish her sentence, and he didn't prompt her—because what could she possibly say? *Red, that's pathetic? Red, that's terrible?* He already *knew* that.

"It's okay," he said with a smile that felt like a grimace. "I mean, it's *not*, but . . . it will be. Hopefully."

Hazel just nodded in response.

By the time they were out in Graham's back garden, Red's moment of melancholy was forgotten. The sun was already high in the sky above them; it was a perfect day for being outside.

Hazel sat down on the grass, and Red stretched out beside her, resting his head in the crook of his arm.

He let his eyes wander over Hazel's profile, studying her the way they studied the bowls of fruit in Still-Life Drawing class. Red knew that she was objectively beautiful—but only in the way that he knew flowers were beautiful. Not in any other way. Despite how much he liked everything about her— which was a *lot*—he wanted to kiss her roughly the same amount that he wanted to kiss one of Graham's frangipanis.

"Man, I love this style of house," he said after a while. "Do you think Graham would let me paint it?"

"*Paint* it? Like a different color?"

"No." He grinned. "Like on an easel."

"Hey!" she said. "You still need to show me your work, you know. Don't think I've forgotten."

He shifted onto his elbows. "You really want to see?"

"Of course I do."

"Well. If we go back to my house, I could show you some stuff . . ."

Hazel nodded enthusiastically, climbing to her feet. "Let's do it!"

"What, *now*?"

She laughed and held out her hand. "Yes, now! Let's go!"

When they got to Red's house, his mum—who had the day off from the Anchor—greeted them in the kitchen with homemade lemonade. There was no sign of Luca, but when Red asked his mum if she'd seen him, she said that he'd gone down to the beach for a swim, so he must have been feeling a little better.

"Where are these paintings then?" Hazel asked when they'd finished their lemonade. "I know you're stalling."

"Maybe I'm shy."

"Shy?" She laughed.

Red didn't mind; he knew that *Red* and *shy* weren't exactly words that belonged together.

"Come on," she pressed. "I promise not to make fun of them."

He looked at her sideways. "Even if they're bad?"

"Even if they're completely awful. Which I know they won't be."

He sighed dramatically. "Fine. They're out in the shed. I'll show you."

The shed at the bottom of the Cawleys' garden was a carefully curated shrine to all things art. Red had spent weeks covering every inch of the inside with his work; there were watercolor paintings and pencil sketches, charcoal drawings and chalk pictures. The shelves that ran along the top of each of the walls were filled with art supplies and stacked canvases. It was art heaven.

"Oh my God," Hazel breathed beside him, turning in circles to take it all in. "This is so cool."

Red grinned at her, watching while she moved to look more closely at some of the pictures tacked to the nearest wall. Most of them were of colorful, intricate landscapes of beaches at sunset and dawn, but there was other stuff too: architecture, wildlife, food.

"Red," she said softly. "These are amazing. You're really talented."

Red felt his cheeks heat up. "You think?"

"These paintings look like *photos*! The amount of detail is incredible. Every one of these is so beautiful—I can't believe you kept all this to yourself!"

He ducked his head. "Thanks."

"Do you ever draw people?"

"Not usually. I hate drawing hair."

"But sometimes?"

He shrugged. "Sometimes."

"Have you ever drawn me?"

Red bit his lip. "Well . . ."

Hazel broke into a smile. "Can I see? Please?"

He rolled his eyes at her, but reached up onto one of the shelves and pulled down a thick, leather-bound sketchbook. The one he kept his very favorite drawings in. He flicked through the pages until he found the sketch he was looking for, and even then he scrutinized it for a long moment before finally handing it over to her.

Hazel studied the picture carefully, her forehead creased

slightly in a frown as her eyes tracked back and forth across the page. Red was pretty proud of this sketch; he knew he'd captured her delicateness almost perfectly, her curving smile, her glittering eyes framed by sweeping lashes.

Except Hazel didn't look particularly impressed.

"You don't like it," Red said eventually. *Oh God, I should've picked a different one. What was I thinking? This one's utter crap.*

"No," she said. "No, I do."

"But?"

"I mean, it's *good*," she said, showing him the page. "It's a great drawing, Red, but it doesn't look like me. This girl is more . . . well. She's just *more*."

Oh. That makes sense.

"Hazel," he said. "I drew you exactly how I see you. Just because this isn't how you see yourself doesn't mean it's not how you are."

She half-smiled. "Thanks, I think."

"You can keep it if you want," he offered.

"No, it's okay. I want you to have it. To remember me by."

He frowned at her for a moment, clamping his lips together. "Right," he said finally. "Temporary. Almost forgot."

"You should definitely show more people your art, though," Hazel said, hastily changing the subject. "These paintings should be in a gallery or something. I mean, not the one of me, but . . ."

Red shook his head. "Nah, I don't think so."

She placed the book carefully back on the shelf and squeezed his hand. "They're good. I promise."

"It's not that," he said. "What if I put my art out there and people don't *care*?"

"Don't you think that's how every artist feels? Every writer? Every musician? You can't just sit on all this, hoping that one day you'll be good enough—you have to trust that today you already are."

Red threw his arms around her and pulled her in for a tight hug. "How come you always know the right thing to say?" he said, voice muffled in her shoulder.

"Years and years of practice," she said, laughing. "So come on, tell me more. What kind of art is your favorite? Painting? Sketching?"

"I like all of them the same except sculpting," he said. "But I've been doing photography the longest."

"Hence the camera?"

"Hence the camera. Wanna see?"

She nodded earnestly, and Red pulled down another book from the shelf, this one filled with glossy prints. He handed it to her, and Hazel flicked through the pages in awe. Most of them were of city lights, lively urban landscapes made of vibrant colors.

"Is this Port Sheridan?" she said.

Red shook his head. "Sydney."

"It looks like a great place."

He was quiet for a moment, keeping his expression carefully blank. "It is."

"Do you miss it?"

Yes. So much that sometimes I feel sick with it.

"Occasionally."

"I'm sorry," she said.

"Hey, 'In three words I can sum up everything I've learned about life,'" he said. "'It goes on.'"

"Robert Frost?"

Red shrugged and flashed her a half smile. "What can I say? I'm a closet poet."

Hazel shook her head and turned to the next page, and her breath caught in her throat. Red knew what spread she was looking at; it was the one with a shot of the Sydney skyline on the left-hand page, and a picture of Luca on the right.

It was one of Red's favorite photographs that he'd ever taken, and if it wouldn't feel completely dishonest, he'd submit it as part of his portfolio for Hodgkins's assignment. He didn't remember exactly when it was from—he just knew that it was sometime before Ryan died. It had to be, because Luc was grinning, real laughter lines creasing the edges of his eyes, his shoulders back. He looked relaxed, comfortable, but it was more than that.

"He looks so *happy*," Hazel murmured, finishing his train of thought, and the confusion in her voice—that Luca had once existed as someone carefree and unbroken—made his chest ache.

Red snapped the sketchbook shut and took it from her, replacing it swiftly on the shelf.

" 'It goes on,' " he repeated softly.

17

GRAHAM ARRIVED AT THE CAWLEYS' HOUSE TO pick Hazel up just before five, intending to drop her off at home and then continue on to work. Claire was making small talk with him while Hazel went to find her things, and by the time she got back, Claire was trying to convince him to stay for dinner.

"Can't have you living off of takeout, Hazel," she said briskly. "You're a growing girl! And Graham, you can't work on an empty stomach—it's not like anyone can fire you for being late. You're both eating here, and I'm not taking no for an answer."

Graham looked from Claire to Hazel and then back again. "Fine," he said finally. "If you're sure you don't mind."

"Nonsense. We'll enjoy the company, won't we, Red?" she said, and Red just beamed in response.

Dinner was spareribs in a sticky barbecue sauce, with home-made sautéed potatoes and a fresh garden side salad, and the four of them sat around the table in the dining room—Graham and Claire on one side, Red and Hazel on the other. Hazel wondered briefly if Luca was somewhere in the house, perhaps shut away in his room, and then pushed the thought to the back of her mind.

"The house looks good," Graham said after a while of quiet eating, pausing momentarily to survey the room. "It looks *really* good. You've done a great job."

"It was mostly Marc," Claire said. *Marc*. Red and Luca's father—not that Hazel had ever heard him mentioned before in the Cawley house. "He always did have a good eye when it came to decorating."

"I remember your place in Brisbane, the one with the nautical theme. I loved it."

"Brisbane?" Red said. "As in the house where I was born?"

"Graham came to visit when you and Luca were four months old. He was a great help, actually. Your dad and I had our hands full—everything was double. Double stroller, double crib, double bottles, double dirty diapers . . ."

"Nice," Red said, grimacing.

"Then you moved all the way to Adelaide!" Graham said. "I wish I hadn't been too busy to visit. I bet it was just as nice."

Claire smiled fondly at the memory. "Oh, it was. My favorite house was in Canberra, though. Shame Marc couldn't handle the cold nights—it's a great city."

"Then after Canberra, we moved to Sydney, right?" Red asked. "That's the only house I really remember."

"Then we moved to Sydney, yes, when you boys were five."

"And you actually managed to stay there for longer than a year," Graham teased.

"Eleven, actually," Claire said with a laugh. "Which is a family record. And *now* we've come full circle. Back to Port Sheridan."

"Back to the beginning," Graham agreed. "It only seems like yesterday that we were bartending at Lee's."

"You and Dad and Graham were in the same year at Finchwood, right, Mum?" Red asked.

"That's right."

"I also showed her how to make her first cocktail," Graham said. "A mango-and-passion-fruit frozen daiquiri if I remember correctly."

"Really?" Red said. "Mum tried to teach me how to make a few cocktails a couple of months back, but I never quite got the hang of it, did I?"

"It wasn't exactly your thing," Claire said, ever diplomatic. "But only because you refused to follow the recipes and kept trying to add in extra ingredients."

"I was being *creative!*"

"You never were the practical one," she said fondly. "That was always Luc's job."

"Is he good at making cocktails, then?" Hazel asked, and Red and Claire shared a look across the table.

"We don't know," Claire said. "He's never tried to make one."

"Why not?"

"Because Luca doesn't do *anything*," Red said flatly. A heavy silence settled over the table, and the four of them ate quietly for a while.

"Have you heard any more about when Marc will be back in town?" Graham asked.

"He's had some problems with a client," Claire said. "He should be back in a few weeks."

"And he's still in Cairns?"

"Yep. So not too far."

"No, that's not too far," Graham agreed. "You and the boys must miss him, though."

Hazel had wondered why Marc Cawley wasn't here with his wife and sons, why he hadn't been here since Hazel had arrived in Australia. It had been almost two months, and that was a long time to spend away from home.

"We do," Claire admitted. "We could really use his help around the house too."

"Well, if you ever need a hand . . ."

"Thank you," she said gratefully. "It's just strange, that's all. Being back here and not having him around much lately. It's just . . . It's a reminder of how everything has changed. Everything always changes."

Hazel found Red's hand under the table and squeezed it tight.

part two

18

LUCA FOUND THAT TRAINING WITH HAZEL
was . . . a process. A very long and difficult one, at times.

During half-term week, they met every day on the track,
and then when school started again they went back to meeting
twice a week. Hazel never asked questions, just called out his
time for each lap as he passed her.

With each training session, he managed to shave a few seconds off his time. Some days were better than others—one
Thursday night they brought his time down by nearly ten
seconds, which Hazel had been particularly thrilled about.
She'd literally jumped to her feet in happiness when Luca finished his final lap, flushed with excitement. He hadn't known
what to do; it had been a long time since anyone had reacted

to anything he'd done with something other than concern or mild annoyance.

When they got under fifteen minutes, Luca offered to walk Hazel home after the session but she shrugged him off, telling him that it wasn't far and she could walk herself, which . . . wasn't exactly the point. Luca had thought it might be nice to spend even a couple of minutes with each other off the track.

Tonight, their final Monday training session in October, Luca was determined to do his laps in fourteen minutes. He made his way over to the stadium early, so that he could be ready to start as soon as Hazel got there, and was just finishing his warm-up when she arrived. He gave her an awkward half wave. She'd changed out of her school uniform into a pair of shorts and a T-shirt, and her dark hair was loose around her shoulders.

"So under fourteen minutes then?" she said when he approached the start line after finishing his stretches.

Luca nodded and crouched down in position, poised and waiting. "Ready."

She held the stopwatch up, about to press the Start button. "Hey, Luca?"

He twisted his head to look at her. "Yeah?"

"You can do this."

He held her gaze for a moment. *You can do this. I believe in you.* "Thanks, Coach."

Hazel rolled her eyes at the nickname, but she was smiling as she counted him in. "Three. Two. One. *Go.*"

* * *

He made it. Thirteen minutes and fifty-two seconds. When Hazel read him his time, he let out a brief whoop of happiness and collapsed on the grass in front of her.

"Pleased?" she asked.

Luca nodded, stretching. "Jesus. Under fourteen minutes. That's . . . That's good."

"That's more than good, Luca. It's amazing."

"Not amazing." He frowned. "Under *twelve* minutes would be amazing, but we're getting there."

"Yeah," Hazel said, smiling. "We are."

Luca lay still for a moment, taking in deep, measured breaths and then letting them out, slowing his heart rate back down. After a minute or two, he sat upright and shifted on the ground to face her. "Walk you home?"

Hazel hesitated, looking like she was ready to shoot his offer down again, and then shrugged. "Sure. Why not."

They walked in silence for a while before Luca spoke up. "So. Got any plans for the weekend?"

Luca knew that Hazel liked to keep herself busy while her dad worked—often she was round their house seeing Redleigh, or the two of them were off sharing long, relaxed lunches in town or having lazy days at the beach. His brother had, apparently, taken it upon himself to show Hazel as much of the area as he could. He was determined for her to fall in love with Port Sheridan before she left.

"Well, there's a party Friday night, and I think Hunter mentioned something about taking us to the waterfall?"

Luca laughed. Hunter had been trying to get him to visit him at work for months, but Luca had always made excuses. It wasn't that Luca didn't like Hunter—he *did*—but the thought of the two of them spending all day together was a little . . . daunting. Even back in Sydney, he'd never really gotten the hang of having lots of friends. It had always just been him and Ryan.

"Why don't you come to the waterfall with us?" Hazel said when he didn't answer.

"Oh, I . . . don't know."

"It'll be fun!"

"It'll be a lot of socializing," he corrected.

"What's wrong with socializing?"

"I wouldn't know what to say to anyone," he said. "I'm no good at talking."

"You're talking all right now, aren't you?"

"Yeah, but you're . . ."

Hazel looked indignant. "I'm *what*?"

"You're you."

"Thanks, Luca," she said wryly. "So charming."

Luca just sighed. "Forget it. You should go, though."

"I think we should *all* go," she said. "The five of us."

Luca didn't know if she was just being nice—being *Hazel*—or if she really meant it, so he said nothing, and they walked the rest of the way in silence. When they arrived outside the gate to Graham's house, they came to a standstill on the sidewalk and turned to face each other.

"Well," he said, "here you are."

"Here I am."

"Thanks for your help."

She just smiled at him. "Thanks for walking me back. It was a good session."

"See you in homeroom," he said, and headed back the way they'd come.

19

ON WEDNESDAY, HAZEL WENT TO THE CAWLEYS'
house for dinner—baked potatoes with chili and salad. Claire
kept telling her it was nothing special, but Hazel thought it
was categorically the best meal she'd had since last time she
came for dinner.

Claire burst into laughter when Hazel told her. "Oh, honey.
That's sweet."

"It's true," Hazel insisted. "I know Graham owns an
amazing restaurant and he's probably an amazing chef, but
at home he really does specialize in microwave meals and
takeout."

"Have you ever *asked* him to cook?" Red said.

Hazel pulled a face. "You know I couldn't do that. I'm
already forever indebted to him for his hospitality. I can't go

around demanding he cook on top of everything else he already does for me."

"You're not indebted," Claire assured her. "You're his *daughter*, Hazel, and he loves having you around. Trust me, he enjoys the company. He's lived alone in that house for far too long."

"Hey," Red said. "Maybe you and Graham could even cook together. That'd be nice, right?"

"Maybe. This really is lovely, Claire," she said, changing the subject as expertly as always.

"Thank you, it's my new . . ."

She trailed off. Hazel followed her gaze to the doorway.

". . . Luca?" Claire said, her voice laced with surprise. Hazel knew why—she hardly ever saw Luca out of his room when he was home, let alone near the kitchen at dinnertime.

He hovered where he stood, clearly uncomfortable with having so many pairs of eyes fixed on him. "Is there space for me?"

"Of course!" Claire jumped to her feet, rushing around and grabbing cutlery and a plate of food and setting them in front of the empty chair opposite Red.

"There's always space for you," she added softly, once he sat down.

For a moment, no one moved. Red had told her that Luca hadn't eaten with them in months, but here he was. Sitting at the table, about to have dinner with his family.

Wordlessly he picked up his fork and began to eat his baked

potato, breaking the spell. As the kitchen table burst into life again, Hazel thought that the expression on Red's face looked a little like relief and a little like happiness—but as he broke into a smile, she realized it was neither.

It was *hope*.

The four of them stayed at the table together long after they'd finished eating, making conversation. Luca didn't say much, like always, but having him there seemed to be enough. Hazel didn't know what had brought about his sudden change of heart, but she was grateful for it. She knew it would make Red and Claire immeasurably happy.

After an hour or so Claire made her excuses and slipped away, leaving the three of them on their own. Red brought up the birthday party they'd been invited to on Friday. It was for a girl named Sienna in Hazel and Luca's homeroom.

"Hunter said it's a costume party," Red said, leaving the table to refill the water pitcher. "Is that true or was he screwing with me?"

Hazel grinned. "No, it's true. We have to come as something that begins with the first letter of our name."

"*R?*" He frowned. "That's shit."

"No, it's not!" she said. "Loads of things begin with *R*."

"Yeah? Like what?"

"Robot? Rabbit? Raccoon? Robin Hood?"

"Runt?" Luca offered.

Red narrowed his eyes at him. "Laugh all you want, Luc. At least I'm making the effort to go."

"Who said I wasn't going?"

Red blinked at his brother. "I . . . *Are* you?"

"Maybe. I was invited—it would be rude not to, right?"

There was a moment of silence. Red opened his mouth and shut it again, speechless. Hazel was as surprised as he was; just over a month ago Luca had to be blackmailed into going to a party, and now he was going to go willingly? What had changed? Hazel wondered if Luca's decision had been prompted by their talk the other night about the waterfall.

"I thought you'd be pleased," Luca said when nobody spoke. "Isn't this what you wanted? Me to socialize? To make friends?"

"Of course," Red said quickly. He cleared his throat. "I just . . . I'm a bit concerned what you're going to dress up as, that's all. Little Bo Peep? Little Red Riding Hood?"

"Lifeguard, actually," Luca said smoothly.

"Hey. That's a pretty good idea."

Luca cocked an eyebrow, amused, and Hazel bit back her smile, glad that the awkwardness had passed. "Maddie's making mine," she said. "Apparently it's going to blow your minds."

"What is it?" Luca asked.

"No idea. She won't tell me until Friday."

"You know what?" Red said. "Maybe rabbit isn't such a bad idea. I can do the whole sexy-bunny thing."

"Now *that* I'd love to see." Luca smirked.

"I'll need to borrow your fishnets, then," he hit back. Hazel burst out laughing, and Luca just glowered at him across the room. Hazel could tell Red didn't mind, though. He was probably glad they weren't arguing.

It was a really weird experience, actually, seeing Luca and Red talking so amicably. And *that* was weird in itself, Hazel thought, because they were twins, so acting like they were friends should be second nature to them, and it *wasn't*. Or, at least, it hadn't been. It was weird too that this was the first time Hazel had seen Luca start to let his guard down the same way he did with her on the track. Surely he should be more comfortable around his own brother than around her?

When it got to half past nine, Hazel decided to head back to Graham's—she had homework to finish, and she knew if she stayed Red would talk her into watching a movie, and then she'd never get it done. She said goodbye to the twins and thank you to Claire, and let herself out the door.

She was halfway down the path when she heard footsteps following behind her. "Miss me already?" she teased.

"It's . . . It's not him. It's me."

Hazel spun around, coming face-to-face with Luca. "Hey!" she said. "What are you doing out here?"

"I just . . . I heard you saying to Hunter and Maddie that you were having some trouble in Math?" he said, hesitant.

"It's nothing," she said, although she was—she'd flunked the last test, and now her teacher was talking about moving her into the class in the grade below unless she showed improvement.

"Well, I was just going to say that I could talk you through a few topics, but if you're not worried about failing, then obviously—"

"*You'd* tutor me?" she said, dazed. Because this was Luca, the same boy who could barely even look her in the eyes a couple of months ago, and now here he was, offering his assistance.

He looked embarrassed. "Well, yeah. If you needed help."

"Seriously?"

He looked at her like she was the one acting strangely. "I mean, I'm no genius like Maddie or anything, but I understand it well enough."

She still couldn't quite get her head around it. "But why would you want to help?"

"Because you're helping me?" he said. "Is it really so unbelievable?"

"Just surprising, that's all."

"So what do you say?"

She considered it for all of two seconds and then broke into a smile. "Okay. That would be great. If you really don't mind."

"I don't mind," he assured her. "We can go over it after we train tomorrow and see what you need help with."

"Awesome. I'll see you at school then?"

"Yeah. Sure."

When he made no move to go back into the house, Hazel said, "Did you want something else?"

"No," he said, flushing pink. "Well, not exactly. I just wanted to . . . I want you to know that I've figured it out."

She frowned. "Figured what out?"

"The truth. About your mum."

"My mum?" Hazel echoed.

"She's dead, right?" he said.

What? The words barely registered; they didn't make sense.

"We don't have to talk about it," Luca said hastily. "I just wanted you to know that I know."

Nobody had mentioned her mum since that bus journey when Maddie had asked about her, and Hazel had been happy to let everyone draw their own conclusions about what had happened in England so she didn't have to think about it—but *this*? This hadn't been her intention.

"But Luca, what made you—"

"I asked Redleigh about it, and he said that she wasn't around anymore."

"He said that?"

"That's all he'd tell me—that, and that I should talk to you about it and not him because you'd asked him not to tell anyone. But that's the reason you're staying here with your dad for a while, right? Because she died? You never talk about her. Ever. Which means it hurts to talk about her, which is . . . I *get* that. Look, I'm not . . . I'm not trying to push you or anything. I just wanted you to know that I know, and I'm . . . well. I'm here if you need me. To talk to, or whatever. Because I . . ."

"Because you what?" she said, throat tight.

He didn't say anything for a long time, the silence stretching out between them. Hazel's mind kept replaying his words over and over again, a constant loop of *She's dead she's dead she's dead.*

"I . . . I just know what you're going through," he said eventually.

No mention of Ryan. Nothing. He really didn't remember telling her about him, did he? Luca clamped his mouth shut as if he knew he'd already said too much.

They fell back into silence. Then he raised a hand in farewell and made his way up the path toward his house. Hazel stood for a moment, frozen in the darkness. How was she going to fix this? How could she tell him the truth now without destroying their tentative friendship? Without destroying *everything?*

She felt completely numb inside. It was crazy, wasn't it? How the second you felt things might actually be starting to come together, you realized that they were still falling apart.

Relief flooded through Hazel when she heard the sound of Graham's car pulling into the driveway just before ten o'clock. There was something comforting about knowing she wasn't alone in the house anymore. On the walk home, she kept thinking about talking to Red, but she hadn't called him. She knew he'd be angry that she hadn't set Luca straight and wouldn't understand that she didn't know how, that she was too afraid of Luca's reaction.

A few minutes later, Graham knocked on her door.

"Come in," she called.

"Hey," he said. "Just wanted to let you know I'm back."

"How was work?"

He gave her a weary smile and ran a hand through his hair. "Long. Tiring . . . But it was good, I suppose. We didn't get any complaints, which is always a bonus."

"You should take a vacation sometime," she suggested. "You look exhausted."

"Trust me, vacations create more problems than they solve. The restaurant turns into chaos when I'm not there. How was your night, anyway? Did you go over to the Cawleys'?"

"I did. The four of us ate dinner together."

"The *four* of you?" he echoed in surprise.

"That's pretty much how we reacted too."

"Interesting," he murmured. "But you had a good time?"

"The best."

"Well, I'm glad. I'll let you get to sleep then. Night, Hazel."

"Good night."

He gave her a little wave and then closed the door. She was burrowing down underneath her sheets ready to close her eyes and forget about her day when the door swung open again.

"I almost forgot," Graham said. "I picked these up at the store earlier. I meant to do this sooner, but it just slipped my mind."

He handed her a wad of glossy brochures, which she took warily.

"I don't know how you want to do it. You could have a feature wall, or two walls one color and the other two another, or you can have all one color, or we can find some stencils and use those . . ." He trailed off, surveying the room. "Once you've chosen the color we can get new curtains and bedding and everything else. How does that sound?"

Hazel looked at him, and then back down at the brochures. He wanted her to decorate the room, wanted her to choose a color and make it her own.

"Thanks, but I don't think I'll be here long enough to make this worthwhile."

She held the brochures back out to him, and his face fell. "Oh. Well, I just thought it would be a bit of fun, but if you don't want to, then it's fine."

"It's not that I don't want to," she started, but realized that was a lie. It *was* because she didn't want to—but not because she didn't want to spend time with Graham, which she was sure was what he suspected. It was because if she painted the room, then it would start to feel more like a home than it was already starting to, and she couldn't have that. And even if she came back for visits after she left, this still wouldn't be her home. *England* and her mum were home. Graham might be her dad, but that didn't make him family.

"It's just—" she tried again.

"Just what?"

137

"I thought they'd have called by now."

"Oh, Hazel," he said. "I don't know if you should count on that."

Hazel didn't answer. She had to count on it. It wasn't a choice—she had to believe that this was temporary and that one day she'd be back where she belonged.

Graham didn't take the brochures from her. "You keep them, okay? Have a look if you want. If you change your mind, just let me know."

Hazel nodded and lowered her arm. She could do that much. He paused in the doorway to look back at her. His expression was impassive, but she could read the sadness in his green eyes. Was he sad for her, or sad for himself?

"It's never too late, you know," he told her.

"Never too late for what?"

"To start over," Graham said gently, and shut the door behind him.

Dear Mum,

I remember the time we went to the park to build a snowman. You spent forever showing me how to make it, and when we were done, we had the biggest and best snowman in the whole place. Everyone envied us, and I felt so proud of what we'd created together. We didn't have any coal, so you gave him coins for eyes.
I loved that winter.

I miss you, Mum, but I remember.

Love,
Hazel

20

ON FRIDAY NIGHT, EVERYONE WENT TO THE Anchor again to eat before Sienna's party. Hazel couldn't help but think, as they sat around the same table overlooking the sea, that it was the kind of tradition she could get used to. This time the boys went to Hunter's house after dinner, while Hazel and Maddie went to change into their costumes at Maddie's again. They would all meet at the end of Sienna's driveway at eight o'clock.

Maddie had Hazel sit at her dressing table so that she could curl her hair. As she did, she commented on what a good mood Luca had seemed to be in at dinner.

"I hadn't really noticed," Hazel admitted, because he'd just seemed normal—albeit a little more talkative than the last time they went out.

"Well, I can't believe he's voluntarily coming to a party," Maddie said. "We've been trying to get him to come out with us since, like, *February*. I wonder what changed?"

Hazel didn't say anything. She knew that Luca was becoming a little more relaxed and open with every training session that they spent on the track together, but she was glad that she wasn't the only one who could see the difference in him. That meant that he was doing better *off* the track too.

"The two of you seem to be getting along better now, anyway," Maddie went on, moving to the next section of Hazel's hair. "Hunter said that Luca's been helping you with some Math topics?"

"He has," Hazel said. "He's a surprisingly good tutor."

Maddie laughed. "Really?"

"Really. Very patient."

"Huh," she said. "Guess there's a lot we don't know about him yet."

Hazel knew that was true, just like she knew that she was looking forward to getting to know him better. Every time she learned something new about him, it felt like she was one step closer to understanding the kind of person he'd been back in Sydney. Before Ryan.

By some miracle, despite how long it took them to get ready, they managed to arrive at Sienna's on time. Hazel was dressed in a white knee-length tunic trimmed with gold, and she had gold bangles up both arms. Maddie had pinned Hazel's hair up at the back, leaving only a few tendrils hanging down beside her face, and the whole look was finished off with a wreath of gold leaves on her head. Maddie was dressed as Marilyn Monroe and looked stunning in her white dress and bright red lipstick.

"Wow, girls." Hunter whistled as they climbed out of their taxi. "You look *amazing*."

Hazel took in his round glasses, jagged lightning scar, and striped tie, and let out a laugh. "So do you, Harry Potter!"

"Let me see," Red said, stepping forward to look her up and down. "Helen of Troy?"

"How'd you guess?"

"What can I say? You look like a goddess."

She giggled and pushed him away. "What are *you* supposed to be, anyway?"

He spun around, showing off the blow-up guitar strapped to his back, and then tossed his head around so that his blond wig flew everywhere. "I'm a rock star! Can't you tell?"

"I see it now." She grinned. "What's with all the hair, though?"

"That's exactly what I said." Luca snorted.

Hazel looked past Red to get a glimpse of his brother. He was dressed in a yellow tank top, red swim shorts, and his usual flip-flops. He'd clearly gone with his original lifeguard idea; he was pulling it off too, his top showcasing his arms. His very tanned, very toned, very *nice* arms.

His eyes met hers, and Hazel resisted the urge to look away. Ever since their conversation the other night, she'd felt guilty. She knew he'd found solace in what he thought was their common ground, and she was still struggling to find a way to let him know that he didn't have the entire truth. She knew the longer she left it, the harder it would be to backtrack. She should speak to Red too, but she was still afraid of what he'd say.

"All you're missing is a whistle," she said to him finally, pushing everything to the back of her mind. Maybe she wouldn't have to say anything at all if she left in a few weeks.

Luca shoved his hand into his pocket and pulled out a silver whistle on a length of red string. "One step ahead," he said as he hung it around his neck with a half smile.

Sienna's house looked like something out of a movie. The bulk of the party was gathered outside in the back garden under a huge tent, which was filled with tables laden with snacks and mixers. At the bottom of the garden, there was a DJ and a dance floor, and there were fairy lights hung everywhere, so the entire garden was alight.

"Oh my *God*," Maddie breathed as they stepped from the house, and the others murmured in agreement, taking it all in. Hazel had never seen anything like it.

"Take note, Hazel," Red said. "This is what happens to girls whose parents have far too much money."

"Yeah, but it's pretty awesome, though, huh?" Hunter said, handing Red a beer from the six-pack they'd brought with them from his dad's house.

"I guess." Red frowned, opening the can and taking a long sip before passing it to Maddie. "I've always shared my birthday parties."

They all turned to look at Luca, who shrugged. "Sorry."

Red threw an arm around his brother's shoulder and pulled him in tight. "Wouldn't have it any other way," he told him, and although he kept his voice light, none of them missed the sincerity behind his words. They stayed like that for a moment, together, and it was the first gesture of affection Hazel had seen shared between the two of them. It was strange to see—not just for Hazel, either, if Maddie's and Hunter's surprised expressions were anything to go by.

For a while, the five of them sat in Sienna's garden talking, then the boys went off to find more drinks, and Hazel and Maddie waited for them on the bench, content to sit and watch the rest of the party unfold. It was a lovely night out, the temperature just right, the stars bright in the clear sky above them.

"Wow." Hazel whistled suddenly. "That girl looks *really* into Hunter."

Maddie followed her gaze to where the boys were standing at the edge of the tent; there was a tall, willowy brunette with her hand on Hunter's arm, her head thrown back in laughter.

Maddie didn't say anything, focusing instead on the label on her can.

"You think he likes her?" Hazel said.

"No idea."

"Aren't you curious?"

Maddie raised her head. "It doesn't really have anything to do with me, does it? He's a big boy."

Hazel frowned. She wondered if Maddie was just tired of people making assumptions about the nature of her and Hunter's friendship, or whether there was something else about it that bothered her.

"Hey," she said eventually, "you and Hunter, you never . . . You haven't . . . Have you?"

"No!" Maddie said. "God. No."

"No?"

"Hazel, he's my best friend," she said. "Gross. It'd be like you and Red. If he was straight, obviously."

Hazel said nothing, because in a way Maddie was right. Even if Red wasn't gay, he wouldn't be her type. They were just too similar; he felt more like a sibling than a friend. She didn't see that in Maddie and Hunter, though. Anyone with eyes could see how much they cared about each other.

Maddie finally cracked a smile, shaking her head. "Look, I don't know what I'd do without him, so I can't . . . I couldn't *risk* it, you know? I can't even think about it because there's no point. I wouldn't give up what we already have for the world."

"So you've never wanted to try anything?"

"No!" she said again, a little too quickly. "Never. I mean, it's *Hunter*. I don't even know if he's boyfriend material. It would probably be super weird, like kissing a cousin or something."

"Gross!" Red said, appearing beside them. Hazel and Maddie turned in unison to see him and Hunter standing there with an armful of beers.

"How much did you hear?" Maddie asked.

Hunter's expression was uncharacteristically blank. "Enough."

"Wait, *who's* been kissing their cousin?" Red said.

"No one!" Maddie said, flushing pink. "God. Where's Luca? We should go dance. I want to dance."

"Here," Luca said brightly, appearing between the two boys. He glanced between Hunter and Maddie. "Wait, what did I miss?"

"Nothing," Maddie said tightly, grabbing hold of Hazel's hand and dragging her toward the dance floor. Red let out a snort of laughter and followed them.

"Why wouldn't I be good boyfriend material?" Hunter wondered out loud.

Luca reached for a can of beer. "What?"

"Boyfriend material," he said. "Maddie said she didn't know if I would even be boyfriend material. What's *that* supposed to mean?"

"Who knows," Luca said, opening the can of beer and sitting

down on the bench. "Why do you care what Maddie thinks, anyway?"

"Well, I *don't*," Hunter said, collapsing beside him. "But still."

Luca just smiled knowingly into his can.

It took Hazel and Red nearly twenty minutes to convince Maddie it was okay for them to go and rejoin the others. She finally agreed, begrudgingly, and the three of them made their way back to the bench at the end of the garden.

"These beers are warm," Hunter was complaining as they walked up. "It's like drinking piss."

"Sorry, Princess," Luca said. "There were none left in the cooler."

"How do you know what piss tastes like, anyway?" Maddie said, taking a seat without looking at Hunter.

"Oh, hey," he said. "Still thinking about making out with your cousin?"

"Get lost, Hunter."

He just grinned at her, handing her a beer. She cracked it open and took a sip, before pulling a face and handing it straight back.

"That bad, huh?" Red said.

Luca stood up from the bench. "I'll go see if I can find some ice."

"I'll come with," Hazel said. "I need to use the bathroom."

Luca nodded, and the two of them made their way into the tent, through the crowd, and out the other side into the house. It wasn't as busy inside, and while Luca headed for the kitchen, Hazel went upstairs to find the bathroom.

When she came out a few minutes later, the hallway light had been turned off. She started feeling her way along the wall, searching for the switch, when suddenly someone appeared right in front of her. Or, rather, a shadow did.

"Hello?" she called out nervously, stepping away from the wall.

The overhead light flickered on, and she blinked in the sudden brightness. Her eyes adjusted and then focused on the figure at the top of the stairs. It was a boy, and he was staring at her in a way that made her skin crawl.

"Well, look who it is," he drawled then, stepping forward and coming to rest against the wall beside her. "Everyone's favorite Pommy."

Red and Hunter had often called her that before to tease her about being English, but now the word sounded tainted, cruel. Hazel vaguely recognized the boy in front of her from one of her classes.

"Um," she said, trying to inch her way along the wall to put some distance between the two of them. "I'm sorry, but someone's waiting for me. I should go."

"Whoa. Not so fast." His clammy hand grabbed hold of her and pulled her toward him, his fingers wrapped tightly around her wrist. "I'm not done with you yet."

"I need to *go*," Hazel repeated firmly, yanking her hand out of his grip, desperate to get back to Red and the others. "Now, if you'll excuse me . . ."

"Wait." He was in front of her again, blocking her path. His hands were on her shoulders, pushing her backward and pinning her against the wall. He wasn't incredibly tall, not like Red, but he still towered over her. His warm breath tickled her cheek, and he smelled of beer and something sweet, something exotic. *Coconut*, she thought vaguely. "Don't be such a tease," he murmured. "Let's just have one little kiss."

"No thank you," she said, and tried to shrug him off, but he was too strong, and his grip on her only tightened, his fingers digging painfully into her skin. Would anyone even hear her over the music if she screamed?

"Just one kiss," he slurred. He cupped her face roughly, while the other hand still pinned her against the wall as he leaned forward and covered her mouth with his own. One moment he was kissing her sloppily, trying to force his tongue past her lips as she fought against him, and the next someone was dragging him off her and she could finally breathe again.

"What the hell—" he started to say, but a fist collided with his face before he had the chance to finish his sentence. He dropped to the floor, blood gushing out of his nose, and stared up at Hazel in horror—except he wasn't looking at her, he was looking behind her at the person who had hit him. Hazel spun around and came face-to-face with her rescuer.

Thank God.

"Luca?" she choked out, but he just ignored her, his eyes hard, his mouth set in a thin line. He swept her gently aside to get to her assailant.

"Get up," Luca hissed, and although Hazel had heard him angry before, she'd never heard him sound quite so *cold*.

The boy did as he was told, scrambling to his feet. The hallway had begun to fill with people from downstairs, watching with interest. "What the hell, Cawley," he said angrily, holding the side of his face. "What was *that* for?"

Luca's eyes flashed dangerously. "You know *exactly* what it was for, and you're never going to do that again, not to anyone. Are we clear?"

The boy stared defiantly up at him as if he couldn't believe anyone would have the audacity to tell him what he could and couldn't do. Especially not Luca, the boy who treated blending in like it was an art form. Hazel wondered if Luca was drunk—she knew he'd had a couple of beers at the party and probably a couple at Hunter's before they'd arrived, but he didn't look drunk. He looked like he knew exactly what he was doing.

"I said, *are we clear*?" Luca repeated calmly when he didn't answer, and the boy shifted uncomfortably, aware that every pair of eyes in the hallway was focused on him.

"Yes," he muttered eventually, lowering his eyes to the floor. "We're clear."

Luca gave him a curt nod, apparently satisfied. He turned

around and fixed his gaze on Hazel. "Are you okay?" he asked, sounding genuinely concerned. "Did he hurt you?"

Hazel shook her head, but her hand went instinctively to her shoulder. She could still feel his fingers there, digging in and leaving bruises, but she'd live. "Can we go and find Red, please?" she mumbled instead, suddenly embarrassed at the way everyone was staring at her.

"Sure," Luca said gently. He offered her an arm, which she took gratefully as they started down the hallway. Hazel ducked her head as they passed the boy. She couldn't bear to look at him. All she kept picturing was his hands on her skin, remembering the smell of his breath on her lips. She hated how weak he'd made her feel.

"Dickhead," Hazel heard him mutter at Luca once they'd passed, and when Hazel looked back at him incredulously, she saw that he was about to swing his fist at Luca's head. She opened her mouth to warn him, but Luca was way ahead of her—he whirled around, deftly blocking his fist, and pushing him away before he could get close. The boy stumbled backward, but he didn't give up; teeth bared, he launched himself at Luca again, fists flying. This time, Luca delivered one smooth punch to his jaw, and the crowd erupted in noise as the boy's eyes rolled back in his head and he crumpled to the floor.

21

TEN MINUTES LATER, HAZEL, LUCA, AND RED were crammed into the back of a taxi, sitting in awkward silence. After the incident upstairs, they'd hastily found Hunter and Maddie to say goodbye and then rushed out of the party.

"Well," Red said finally, "*that* was a complete disaster."

Luca snorted, and Hazel glanced over at him. He had his face pressed against the glass of the window, staring angrily at the world that whizzed past. "That fucker deserved it."

"Jesus, Luc, you can't just go around punching everyone who pisses you off! That's not how it works!"

"So what would you rather I did? Let him continue forcing his tongue down Hazel's throat?"

"You could have tried pulling him off her first!"

Hazel winced, the memory of that boy's mouth on hers still uncomfortably vivid. She knew that Red was only angry because he was worried—worried about her, and worried about his brother. But she also knew that he was glad Luca had stood up for her. The fact that he'd done it with his fists wasn't great, but even so, they all knew that Luca wasn't the one in the wrong here.

"Oscar Whitely's an asshole," Luca added vehemently. "Someone should have knocked him out a long time ago."

Red met Hazel's eye and half-smiled. "Not gonna argue with that."

The taxi fell into silence, and no one said a word for the rest of the journey. When they finally pulled up outside the Cawleys' house, Luca disappeared inside while Red paid the driver. Claire was still at work, so Red ordered Hazel to sit on the sofa while he scrounged some cookies from the cupboard and made them tea.

"Do you think he's okay?" Hazel said finally.

"What, Oscar? He's fine. He was only out of it for like two seconds."

"I meant Luca."

"Oh. I . . . don't know," he said, placing a tray with cookies and two mugs of tea on the coffee table.

"Is he drunk?"

"Not badly. Not like last time."

"But you're worried about him," she said.

"He punched one of the most popular guys in his year in the face. *Twice*."

"He was protecting me, Red."

"Maybe I should check on him."

"Go," Hazel said.

Red shot her a grateful smile and disappeared upstairs, and she'd barely had time to lean back into the sofa when he returned.

"Everything okay?"

"Yeah, Luc's fine," he said, sitting beside her. "But he wanted to speak to you."

"To me?"

"For some reason."

"Okay," Hazel said, and stood up from the sofa. She could only imagine how weird this must look to Red; as far as he knew, she and his twin barely had anything to do with each other beyond the interactions they had because of Red himself. "I don't mind. He is my knight in shining armor, after all."

Red grimaced. "Hazel, I'm sorry. I should have been there to look out for you."

"It's okay."

"I'm glad Luca was, though."

"You and me both," she said. "I'll be right back, okay?"

Hazel headed up the stairs. She walked to the very end of the hallway, past Red's room and Claire's room and the bathroom, until she reached the one door she'd never seen open. Luca's.

She took a deep breath and pushed on it. The room was completely dark, just like the hallway at the party.

"Luca?" she said, fumbling for a switch.

Light flooded the room, and she stood there for a moment, taking in her surroundings. Luca was standing in the middle of the room, wearing a pair of running shorts and a T-shirt.

"Hey," she said softly. "Red said you wanted to talk to me?"

"Yeah, I . . . just wanted to say sorry."

"Why? It wasn't your fault."

"I shouldn't have hit him, though."

"Probably not. But I'm glad you did. Thank you, by the way."

"I couldn't let him hurt you."

"That's . . . honorable," she said with a wry smile. "But I'm not completely fragile."

"More than you realize," he told her firmly. He stepped forward, placing his hands gently on either side of her face, his touch feather-light—and, okay, he was *definitely* a little tipsy. "Sometimes you gotta let other people look out for you for once."

Hazel didn't know how to respond, so she shook her head. "Good night, Luca."

"Night Hazel," he murmured back, and closed the door behind her.

Dear Mum,

I remember the time you were called in for a meeting with my English teacher at school. She was angry with me because I spent more time writing in my diary than I did listening to her talk. You nodded when you were supposed to and promised her you'd give me a good talking to.

When we left, you asked what I wrote in my diary. I told you I liked to write stories, and it was what I wanted to do when I grew up. You just gave me a hug and told me to follow my dreams.

That's not my dream anymore, but I'll never forget the faith you had in me. It meant so much.

I miss you, Mum, but I remember.

Love,
Hazel

22

DESPITE THE DRAMATIC EVENTS OF FRIDAY night, everyone wanted to stick to their plan to spend Saturday together—even Luca decided to join them in the end. Hunter was going to give them a personalized, off-duty tour of the waterfall, and Hazel was excited to put last night behind her and focus on enjoying herself.

They agreed to meet at the end of Hunter's road at midday so they could catch the bus to the waterfall together. Hunter was the only one there when Hazel arrived, and he waved enthusiastically, his wild blond hair scraped back off his face with a colorful bandanna.

"How're you doing?" he asked as she approached.

"I'm fine," she said, and she was. After all, it could've been a lot worse. "How were things after we left?"

"Honestly? A bit anticlimactic. Everyone was pretty impressed that Luca stood up for you like that, though."

"Hopefully Oscar will think twice before doing that again."

"Hopefully," he agreed. "I can't believe he tried to force himself on you. What a dick."

"I think he got his comeuppance."

Hunter laughed. "He sure did."

The others arrived not long after, and they headed toward the bus stop. The sun was already high, and now that Australia was in the middle of spring, the heat was sweltering, especially pressed up against one another in the aisle of the packed bus—but Hazel didn't mind. Everyone was in a good mood, and she was glad to be out of the house.

Hunter led the way through the rainforest to where the waterfall began, reeling off his tour-guide spiel as they went. The waterfall itself was smaller than Hazel had imagined—it couldn't have been more than five meters tall.

"Okay," Hunter said as they came to a stop at the edge of the pool at the bottom, which was already filling with tourists. "Ready to go up?"

"*Up?*" Hazel echoed, horrified—because although it was small, it wasn't *that* small.

He grinned. "Of course. What did you think we were here to do? Stand at the bottom and just look?"

"Actually, that sounds like a really good idea. You guys go ahead, and I'll stay here with the bags."

"Nice try," Maddie said brightly, linking her arm in Hazel's. "This is a group bonding exercise, which means everyone has to do it. No exceptions."

Hazel looked over at Red, begging him silently with her eyes to back her up, but he just smirked at her. "Come on, Hazel, it'll be fun!"

"If I fall . . ."

Red rolled his eyes. "You won't fall."

"Promise?"

He crossed his heart solemnly. "On my life."

Hazel surveyed the others. They were watching her expectantly, even Luca, waiting for her answer. Was she going to join them, or was she going to chicken out and miss what might be the experience of a lifetime?

"Fine," she caved, and everyone cheered.

Fifteen minutes later, the five of them were making their way slowly and carefully across the rocks. Hunter and Maddie were at the front, followed by Luca and then Hazel, with Red bringing up the rear. They were already high enough that Hazel's head was starting to spin.

Ahead, Hunter had picked up speed—but just as Hazel started worrying about keeping up, her foot slipped on an algae-covered rock and she lost her balance. Her arms started to flail but before she could fall, Luca whirled around and caught her, big hands firmly on her shoulders to help steady her.

"You okay?" he asked.

"I'm fine. Thanks."

Luca nodded curtly and let go, turning around on the rock and carrying on after the others.

"He's got a real thing about protecting you at the moment, huh?" Red teased quietly from behind her. Hazel turned to pull a face at him, took a moment to gather herself together, and then followed Luca.

By the time they reached the top of the waterfall, she'd just about gotten the hang of scaling the rocks with ease, but it was still a relief to be able to sit down and catch her breath without worrying about falling. They sat in silence, admiring the view of the rainforest. The rushing of the water was surprisingly calming; it was beautiful and peaceful, and Hazel was so glad she'd made the climb.

"I'm too hot," Maddie complained after a while, tugging at the neck of her T-shirt. "It's like seven hundred degrees up here."

"You know an easy solution to that?" Hunter said, scrambling to his feet.

"No, I . . . Wait! No, no, no, Hunter *don't*!"

He ignored her protests with a grin, wrapping his arms around her and jumping off the side of the rock. The two of them plunged down toward the bottom of the waterfall, a mess of screaming and flailing limbs as they broke the surface of the water. They both emerged again a moment later, spluttering and laughing, their clothes sticking wetly to their bodies. Maddie clung on to Hunter as he waved up at them.

"Come on!" he yelled. "The water's lovely, and it's safe, I promise!"

Luca turned slowly to look at his brother, who was watching him with a smirk. "Redleigh, don't you dare—" he started, but Red had already shoved him off the edge. Luca went down a little more gracefully, save for the yelp he gave as he left the rock, and even managed to cover his face before he hit the water.

Red turned to look at Hazel. He held out his arm to her, his smirk replaced by a soft smile. "Together?"

She looped her arm through his, holding on tight. The two of them made their way to the edge, Hazel took a deep breath and let it out, and then they were jumping, they were in the air, and they were falling, and as the wind whipped around them Hazel looked down and felt her heart soar.

No matter what happened next, her friends were right there at the bottom, waiting for her.

Monday night. *Three hundred and forty-five days.*

Hazel and Luca were back on the track running laps. Or, rather, he was running laps, and she was sitting patiently on the sidelines timing him. That was one of the things that had surprised him most about her: how understanding and imperturbable she was.

That evening, they got down to thirteen minutes and thirty-eight seconds. It didn't sound like much—to shave nine seconds off his time from last session—but it meant a lot. Nine seconds closer to his goal. Nine seconds closer to being back where he was before.

When he had finished his cooldown, they set off from the field and walked in silence for a while. Luca liked how if there was nothing to say she just said nothing, and that she wasn't constantly looking over at him to see if he was okay, which meant he could relax a little. He was going to miss that when she left—having someone around who *got* it. He and Redleigh had never talked about the specifics of Hazel's plan for going back to England—Redleigh refused to speak about it behind her back, which was annoyingly admirable—so Luca didn't understand exactly why she'd want to go back to London if her mum wasn't there anymore. Was it just about returning to the familiar? Was that really enough to warrant leaving behind the life she'd started to build here? Her new friends? Her dad?

"So," Hazel said finally. "You're doing great time-wise lately. I think you'll be at your target pretty soon."

Luca just shrugged. "I don't know about that. We're making progress, though."

"Lots of progress."

"*Some* progress," he corrected.

"Lots," she argued, and he turned to glare at her. "Don't look at me like that, Cawley, I know what I'm talking about. I'm not an idiot, you know."

"Could've fooled me, Coach," Luca said, and Hazel just grinned at him.

They soon arrived at Graham's gate. Luca wondered whether Hazel knew that this had become the part of the training sessions he least looked forward to, leaving her at the gate. He hoped not.

"Thanks for walking me back," she said.

"You're welcome. Thanks for training with me."

"Anytime." She raised a hand in farewell and headed through the gate toward the house. Luca waited until she'd let herself safely inside before turning around and walking home.

When Luca got back to his house, he snuck into the kitchen to get a drink. Red was there, sitting at the table and staring at a stack of photographs. He jumped slightly at the sound of Luca's footsteps, whirling around to face him.

"Oh," he said when his eyes landed on Luca. "Hey, Luc."

Luca reached into the fridge for a bottle of water. "Hey."

"I thought you were in your room. Have you been out?"

"No," he lied automatically, and then caught himself. "I mean, yes. I have. I was helping Hazel with her math."

"Oh, yeah," Red said. "She said you offered to tutor her. That was . . . nice."

"It's not a big deal."

Red nodded slowly, but he was still watching Luca closely, like perhaps he didn't entirely believe him. Luca was so grateful that he was just wearing normal shorts and a T-shirt—if he'd been in training gear, he'd have been caught out in a second.

"Well, thank you, anyway," Red said, getting to his feet. "For being cool with her."

"I didn't do it for you," Luca said quietly, but his brother was already out of the room.

23

AT DINNER THE NEXT EVENING, EVERYTHING
was going fine until Claire announced cheerfully that Marc
had called and was expecting to be back in Port Sheridan by
the weekend. For the rest of the meal, Luca spoke only when
spoken to. He excused himself from the table as soon as he'd
finished eating.

Red and Claire shared a look of concern as he left the room.

"Do you think he's okay?" she asked quietly, as they listened
to Luca's footsteps making their way upstairs.

"I'm sure he's fine. Probably just tired. Don't worry about it."

She smiled faintly since they both knew that was an impossible task, that worrying about Luca came as naturally to
her as breathing did.

"Do you want me to go talk to him?" he offered, and she nodded.

"Maybe take him some dessert?"

Red dished up a slice of the apple pie from the fridge, heated it in the microwave, and headed upstairs. Luca's door was shut, but when Red knocked there was no answer. He eased it open; the room was empty.

Red shut the door again and made his way to the other end of the hallway, where the big bay window was propped open. Luca was sitting out on the garage roof.

"Hey," Red said, climbing through the open window and out onto the flat surface.

Luca didn't look up. His arms were wrapped around his legs where they were drawn up to his chin. "Hey."

"Mum told me to bring you this." Red handed him the bowl. Apple pie was Luca's favorite—or, it *had* been at least, before. Was it still? He wondered how much Luca had changed in the last year, how much about Luca he no longer knew.

Luca took the bowl, looked at it for a moment, and then placed it on the roof beside him. "Thanks."

"No problem."

Luca fixed his eyes back on the horizon, expression carefully blank, and Red found himself studying the side of his face. He looked the same as he always had on the outside, with no sign of his inward struggles etched into his skin. He and Red were just versions of each other when it came down to it, even despite their differences. Luca 2.0. Red thought it was funny, really, how he still found the concept of having a twin so strange when he'd lived with it for seventeen years. *I am you, and you are me.*

"So," Red said finally. "This is about Dad, right?"

When Luca didn't answer, Red bumped his shoulder with his own. "Hey. Maybe this time will be different."

Luca looked over at him. "Have you heard from him since his last visit?"

"Yeah, of course. A few e-mails, some texts. We even Skyped last—"

"I haven't."

Silence.

Red felt a surge of anger toward their father. Did he even *know* what he was doing to Luca? When he didn't call him, when he pretended like nothing had happened but still couldn't look him in the eye? Couldn't he *see*?

After Ryan died, their mum smothered Luca in motherly love, keeping him close as if that would somehow stop the hurt from reaching him. Their dad, on the other hand, just slowly pushed him away.

When they lived in Sydney, the family was split down the middle, but in a good way. Their dad *got* Luca, in a way he never got Red. Luca's whole life was running back then. He lived it, breathed it. Marc Cawley ran track himself when he was a teenager, and he was the driving force behind Luca's involvement in the sport, always pushing him forward, helping him train harder.

Luca never minded, though. He loved it. He and Ryan and Dad would spend hours out on the beach, practicing sprint starts and honing their technique. Sometimes Red would go down there too with his mum, and she would read, and he would draw. Dad went to every race and only missed a few training sessions. When Luca wasn't running, the two of them were always talking about it, scheming, and once the scouts from the University of Sydney started recruiting Luca with the promise of a full track scholarship, there was no stopping them.

It wasn't as if their dad didn't love Red, or that he loved him any less, but he certainly loved him in a different way. Luca was his protégé, and Red was just his son. His mum would take Red out instead, to art galleries and to buy canvases and other art supplies. At dinner, the table would be split too—Dad and Luca down one end so they could talk running to their hearts' content, Red and his mum down the other. Not that anyone was bothered back then. That was just how things were.

When Ryan died, Red thought for a while that things would stay the same. That Dad would continue to be the light of Luca's life, the one person he looked up to. At first, things were normal—as normal as they could be under the circumstances. But then, after just a few weeks, their dad started suggesting that Luca go back to training, kept trying to get him to race again. He was so frustrated and angry when Luca told him he couldn't. He didn't understand it, wouldn't accept it, and kept trying to get Luca to change his mind—but he wouldn't. Red wasn't sure if it was even a choice; all he knew was that Luca hadn't set foot on a track since Ryan's death, because it reminded him too much of his best friend.

Dad hadn't known what to do. Their whole relationship was built around their shared passion for a sport Luca was now refusing to participate in. When he got dropped from the track team, Dad was furious. He told Luca to get his act together before he lost everything.

What he didn't realize was that Luca already had.

Their father worked for a consultancy firm for digital analytics based out of Sydney, and his job had always required travel and time away from home, but before Ryan died, he had turned down the long-distance business trips to Canberra or Hong Kong so that he could always be there for Luca's races. When Luca stopped running, and the house became such a difficult place to live in, he began accepting more of the offers. Just a trip or two at first, and then volunteering himself for more.

Since moving to Port Sheridan, Marc split his time between working from home, traveling to visit clients overseas and around Queensland, and living in an apartment the company rented for him in Sydney and working from his old office there, even though the latter wasn't required of him and none of the other senior associates did it. That hurt, more than Red would ever admit—that his dad would choose to stay away more often than to be at home. This weekend would be the first time Red had seen him in over three months, and honestly, he'd started to think that Marc was never coming back. Three months was a long time to be without a dad, but even when he *was* home it was as if he wasn't really there. Red didn't think his father understood that Luca's depression was hard for all of them, not just him, and that if they stuck together then maybe they'd have more of a chance of getting through it.

"I'm sorry," Red said eventually, because he'd let the silence stretch out between them.

"I wish people would stop saying that," Luca muttered.

"Why?"

"Because people always apologize. That's the first thing they say—as if them saying sorry will change anything. It doesn't change a fucking thing. He's still *dead*, Redleigh. He's . . . He's still dead."

And suddenly Red was sorry about that too—sorry that Luca felt so trapped, that he felt like things would never get any better. But sorry wasn't something Luca wanted to hear. Sorry wasn't something he *needed* to hear. Red wished he could argue with Luca about this, tell him he was wrong, and that he didn't know what he was talking about, but he *did*. He *did*, and Luca was right, and there was nothing Red could do or say to make him feel better.

Dear Mum,

I remember the time I was picked on at school by a group of girls. They told me I was useless, and that I didn't have a dad because he didn't love me, and that no one ever would.

You held me tight that night while I cried, and you told me I was the most perfect person in the world, and anyone who told me otherwise was just too blind to see what was right in front of them. I believed you, and it kept me strong next time they started teasing me.

I miss you, Mum, but I remember.

Love,
Hazel

WHEN RED ARRIVED BACK AT THE HOUSE ON
Sunday after spending the afternoon at Hazel's, there was a
sleek black Audi in the driveway: his father's pride and joy. Marc
was sitting at the breakfast counter when Red walked in,
perched on the stool that lately Luca had adopted as his own.

"Redleigh!" he cried when he caught sight of Red, jumping up and crossing the room to smother him in a huge bear
hug.

"Hey Dad," Red mumbled into his shoulder, hugging him
back just as tight.

"How you doing, kiddo?" his dad asked when he finally let
Red go.

"I'm great, thanks."

"Glad to hear it. Have you grown again?"

Red shrugged. "An inch or two, maybe. Trying to overtake you."

Marc let out a laugh and pulled him in for another hug, ruffling his hair affectionately. "I've missed you, son."

"Could you go and tell Luca that dinner's ready, please, love?" Claire said from where she was cooking at the stove. "I'm about to dish up."

Red nodded, leaving the kitchen and making his way up the stairs. Luca's bedroom door was ajar. Red could hear his music playing from the other end of the hallway, a loud, heavy rock song. He peeked his head around the door. Luca was sitting at his desk, his head in his hands as he studied the computer screen intently. Red knocked on the door, and Luca looked up.

"Hey."

"Hey." Red hovered in the doorway. "Dad's home."

"I heard the car."

"He hasn't been up?"

Luca didn't have to reply—the answer was obvious from the hurt in his eyes—and *Christ*, Luca shouldn't have to deal with this.

"Well, dinner's ready," Red told him quietly, and turned on his heels.

"This is so great," Claire said a little too brightly. "All of us finally back together."

The four of them may have been back together, but they were still sitting around the kitchen table acting like it was perfectly normal that Dad was the only one actually eating his food.

"Come on, boy," Dad said suddenly. Red looked up to see him glaring across the table at Luca. "Stop with the sulking and eat, will you?"

Luca raised his head in surprise and looked helplessly over at their mother like he didn't know what to say, how to answer.

"Marc," she said quietly, but there was a warning in her eyes. *Shut up*, she was saying. *Shut up before you make this so much worse than it already is.*

Marc held a hand up to silence her, eyes still trained on Luca. "Did you hear me?"

Luca nodded, lowering his eyes back to the table.

"I don't think you did," his father pressed. "Because if you had you'd have wiped that look off your face."

Luca stood abruptly, his chair scraping back across the tiles. "Please may I leave the table?" he asked his mother.

Mum nodded, but Dad wasn't finished yet, wasn't ready to let him walk away without having the last word. "No, you can't. You've barely touched your food."

"I'm not hungry," Luca replied stiffly, pushing his chair back under the table and slipping out of the room.

For a moment, no one spoke. The air was thick with tension, the sort that made the hairs on the back of your neck stand up.

"What?" Marc finally exploded. "Why are you looking at me like that? Don't you dare make this out to be my fault. That was all him."

"He has a name," Claire said wearily, and Red realized that since he'd been back, his father hadn't used it once. "For God's sake, Marc, he has a name. Luca. Your son's name is Luca."

"Claire, don't—"

"Luca," she repeated, ignoring him. She got to her feet too, still saying his name as she followed in his footsteps out of the room as if it were a mantra, a spell that might just make things right. *Luca, Luca, Luca.*

Red sat frozen as his father eyed the untouched plates around the table, the meal just as incomplete as everything else. "Christ," he hissed, slamming down his glass. "That was not my fault."

He wasn't looking at Red, probably wasn't even talking to him, but Red found himself shaking his head in disagreement. Of *course* it was his fault; his fault for failing to see what kind of damage he was doing by treating Luca like a child he was tired of raising.

"It's not my fault," he said again as he stormed out the back door, but Red wasn't sure he was even convincing himself.

25

LUCA HAD TO GET OUT OF THE HOUSE. HE HAD
to get the hell out of there before he broke something.

He'd been better than this lately, was the thing. He'd been
so much better than this, and that just made him even angrier
at himself. It had been weeks since he'd felt the urge to punch
something or someone—and that Oscar guy from the party
last week didn't count because he was asking for it and really
all Luca was doing was protecting Hazel anyway.

Shit. Luca hated that he wanted to protect her, hated that
she was so small, so gentle, so trusting. Hated how many times
he'd thought about how different things would be if he'd met
her before everything with Ryan, back in Sydney, back when he
wasn't so screwed up. Not that there was any point thinking

like that, not when it was already too late and this was the only version of him that she was ever going to know.

He found himself on the road, without really remembering how he got there. He was just glad to be out in the open air. He started running the second he arrived at the stadium. He ran around and around the track, and he didn't keep count of the laps because for once he wasn't trying to reach a goal. He was just running. Not for his dad, not for Hazel, not to prove he could. He was running, finally, for himself.

Red closed the sliding door behind himself as he stepped out on the veranda to join his father. "I thought you gave that up," he said to Marc when he lit a cigarette with shaking fingers.

"I did." Marc rubbed his forehead as if what he'd really been suffering from all this time was a headache, not the heartache the rest of them were dealing with.

They both watched the smoke start to rise upward in silence. His father breathed it in, savored it, but didn't once lift the cigarette to his lips. Red figured that, at forty-four, his dad didn't need a lecture on secondhand smoke. He wished he had his camera right now. This would make a great picture for Hodgkins's stupid assignment that he still hadn't finished. The silver of the smoke, his father silhouetted against the pink sky. It was the most obnoxiously perfect composition.

Here's my fucking family, in all its honest glory. Mum in tears inside the house, Luca God knows where, and Dad here, passive smoking like a stressed-out teenager. How's that for honesty?

"Sometimes," Marc said eventually, "I wonder why I bother coming back."

"Dad . . ."

"Your mum has been telling me how much better things seem to be, but now I'm here . . . You're all better off without me, that much is obvious."

Red balled his hands up into fists, resisting the urge to punch them as hard as he could into his father's chest over and over and over, because it was too much and every time Red thought it was getting better it just *didn't*.

"You're not the problem, Dad," he muttered. "You just don't help."

Marc raised an eyebrow. "What's that supposed to mean?"

"You're too hard on him."

"Too hard?" he echoed. "I've barely said a word to the boy."

"Yeah," Red said flatly. "I think that might be the problem."

Marc narrowed his eyes at Red. "Are you giving me lip?"

"No, Dad. I'm just saying it's been almost a year now and—"

"Nearly a year, *exactly*!" he said. He wasn't angry at Red; Red knew that. He wasn't even angry at Luca, although he did a good job of pretending otherwise; he was just angry at the world. "I thought things would have been back to normal by now!"

"Just because things aren't normal doesn't mean you can't

love him like you always have," Red said sharply. "Just like the fact that he isn't running doesn't mean you can't be proud of him. Can you not see how hard he's trying? Can't you see you're not helping by pretending he doesn't even exist?"

"I want him back. Is that so wrong of me? To want the old, happy Luca back? To want my *son* back?"

"He's still right here," Red said. "You just stopped looking."

He met his father's eye.

"You might miss him," he added softly, "but I guarantee that Luca misses you more."

Marc didn't speak for a long, long moment. "You're right," he said then, dropping his cigarette on the ground and stamping it out with his foot. "I need to fix it."

When Luca was done running, he began to walk home slowly, feeling drained, vulnerable. There had been moments in the past couple of months where he'd had hope, usually on the track with Hazel. Moments when he didn't feel lost, when he felt like he wasn't floating in limbo, when he could really *feel*, and it wasn't the end of the world.

But the moments were just that, only moments, and he always came right back to here no matter how hard he tried. He'd been buried in bubble wrap and suffocated by his mum and Redleigh—and now his dad was back and full of that same old disappointment.

When Luca saw that his father's Audi was still in the

driveway, he almost turned and walked away again. He let himself into the house anyway, bracing for the fallout from dinner.

"Luca?" his mum called from the kitchen.

He froze in the hallway. "I'm going to bed. Don't feel well."

"Can we talk for a minute? Please?"

Luca closed his eyes and took a deep, steadying breath before opening them. He walked into the kitchen, where his mum and dad were sitting at the counter. Claire eyed her son warily like she was trying to ascertain whether or not he was likely to detonate right there in the middle of the floor.

"I'm sorry," Luca said finally when no one spoke, voice cracking.

"Luca," Claire said firmly. "It wasn't your fault."

"I wasn't talking about dinner."

Her face fell as she realized what he was apologizing for: not just for tonight, but for every single day since Ryan died. For every family meal he had missed. Every conversation he wouldn't have. Every time he got in a fight or missed school or refused to take his meds. Every time he shut them out and pushed them away and buried himself in his grief. "Sweetheart . . ."

He shook his head, because this was something he had to say. "I'm sorry that I can't just get over this, and I'm sorry that I can't make everything go back to normal. I wish I could. I really, really wish . . . I'd do *anything*. I would. But I don't know how."

"You lost your best friend, Luc," she said softly. "No one is

180

expecting everything to be like it used to. We just want to know that you're okay."

"And if I'm not?"

His mum didn't answer, just held his gaze from across the counter like she was scared of what might happen if she tried to speak. Luca turned to look at his father. Marc looked ashamed, and sad, and scared all at once.

Marc wet his lips. "You'll get past this."

"How do you know that? You don't know anything. You haven't even fucking *been* here."

"Language, Luca," his mum said absently, but her voice was still soft, still careful, with none of the bite she used when she reprimanded Redleigh for cursing in front of her. And that was it, that was the thing that Luca hated most: how she and Redleigh were always handling him with kid gloves, like if they made one false move he might explode and destroy everything. Luca knew they were doing it with the best intentions, giving him space and treating him gently to protect him and let him heal, but he was so tired of it. So tired of it being just Hazel, of all people, who was the only one in his life who wasn't afraid to talk to him straight or call him out on his moods or hold him accountable for his actions.

That's why he liked training with her so much—not because she was particularly good at it, but because she didn't treat him like the poor, broken boy with the dead best friend.

Luca stepped toward his mum until he was standing right in front of her, eye to eye. "Shout at me," he said.

"What do you—"

"Shout at me!" he repeated. "Tell me off! Send me to my room for swearing, *punish* me. Shout at me, Mum! Treat me like you'd treat Redleigh, treat me like you would have treated me before. Pretend you don't think I'll fall to pieces if you do. Just *shout* at me!"

"Luca—"

"Please," he begged, tears glistening in his eyes, and he was so, so tired. "*Please*, Mum. I don't want to feel like this anymore."

Claire pulled her son against her chest, folding him into her arms and holding on tight, holding him together, and he finally let himself cry.

By the time Luca and his mum had stopped crying, the light outside the kitchen windows had faded to black. After being assured repeatedly by Luca that he was okay, Claire excused herself from the kitchen and disappeared upstairs.

Marc, who had been mostly quiet during the conversation, hesitated for a moment and then stood from the counter. He gestured awkwardly toward the kettle.

"Do you . . . ?"

"Please," Luca said. Now that the tears had stopped, he felt . . . lighter. Calmer. He'd been totally honest with his parents about how he was coping—or how he *wasn't* coping, rather—and it was fine. The world hadn't collapsed. He hadn't exploded, and nothing was destroyed. The relief was over-whelming.

His dad set about making tea and then brought two cups over to the counter, sliding one across to Luca. Luca thanked him quietly, took a careful sip, and waited.

"Well," his dad said finally.

"Well."

"Your brother gave me a very stern talking-to while you were out."

Luca smiled wryly despite himself. "Sounds like Redleigh."

"He shouldn't have had to, but I think I needed it." Marc hung his head, eyebrows drawn like he was struggling to find the right words. "Look, Luc. Your mum was right. I know I haven't been around much lately, but that isn't your fault. That's all on me, all right? That was my choice. My mistake."

"I . . . Okay?"

"The truth is that I was scared."

His stomach dropped. "Of me?"

"No, Luca. Of *losing* you. I could feel you pulling away, and I didn't know how to help you so I just . . . I stayed away. I stayed away, and I'm sorry."

"Dad—"

"No. *I'm sorry.* You went through something horrible, and instead of being supportive I pushed you away."

"Because I *made* you. I was difficult."

His mouth twisted upward. "You're my son, Luca, you're supposed to be difficult. That's what families are—difficult and complex and imperfect. But if nothing else, they're supposed to be there for each other. And I wasn't there for you. And if I could go back and undo that, I would in a heartbeat." He met Luca's eyes again and held his gaze, and Luca swallowed past the lump in his throat. "But I can't. So I'm sorry."

Luca exhaled shakily, fighting the urge to start crying again. His father looked as close to tears as he felt, but Luca knew that he'd needed to say that as much as Luca had needed to hear it. "Thank you. That really . . . Thank you."

Marc's shoulders sagged with relief, like he'd been afraid that Luca would reject his apology. Once upon a time, he might've done—but not anymore. An apology wasn't going to magically fix or change anything, but it was a start. It was a step in the right direction.

"I'm going to be better," his father promised then, reaching over to squeeze his shoulder. "I'm going to try my hardest."

"I know," Luca said, but what he really meant was, *Yeah, me too*.

Dear Mum,

I remember the time you bought me my first pair of heels. They weren't very high, barely even an inch, but I felt so grown-up. You spent hours teaching me how to walk in them, how to stand up tall and be proud of myself.

You told me to be careful and to only wear them around the house until I was used to them. I didn't listen. I wore them out to the shops. I fell over a rock, twisted my ankle, and fell flat on my face, but you didn't tell me off. You just tended to the cuts on my chin and my hands and told me that it would come with practice.

Several years later, it finally has. You were right, Mum. As always.

I miss you, Mum, but I remember.

Love,
Hazel

26

THINGS HAD BEEN SO WEIRD AT HOME SINCE
his father's return the day before that Red couldn't wait to get out
of the house and meet Hazel on the beach Monday night. Not
uncomfortable weird, just different. Luca had assured him before
school this morning that everything was okay, but you wouldn't
know it from the way everyone was tiptoeing around one another.
This tentative peace was better than the alternative, though.

Hazel was already there when he arrived, climbing to her
feet to greet him. "Hey, you."

Red didn't say anything, just drew her into his arms and
nestled himself into her neck, holding her tighter than ever before. She held him back just as tight and didn't ask any questions until he'd pulled away.

"Everything okay?" she asked him softly.

Red nodded. "It's been one of those days."

"Well, if it's any consolation there's only about three minutes of it left."

He smiled gratefully and sank to the sand. Hazel followed suit, and they sat in silence for a while, her head resting on his shoulder.

"My dad's home," he said after a few minutes had passed.

"Yeah?"

"Yeah," Red said, the corners of his mouth tugging downward. "It's just that having him back has thrown everything off, you know? He hasn't been around for so long and now that he *is* it feels weird. It's like we're all back in the past or something, back in Sydney after Ryan—"

He stopped suddenly, eyes wide. Shit. *Shit, shit, shit,* Hazel wasn't supposed to know about Ryan. That was Luca's secret to tell, and now he'd gone and opened his big mouth and Luca was going to—

"It's okay," Hazel said hastily. "He told me."

Red blinked at her. *What?* "He did?"

"Yeah. He didn't mean to, I don't think, but he did. When he was drunk at Kayla's party."

"Did he tell you everything?"

"He told me Ryan died, yeah, but not how—and he doesn't remember telling me, so I never said anything. I figured that if he wanted me to know, he'd tell me again. Sober. That's why you moved away from Sydney, wasn't it? Because of Ryan. So that Luca could have a fresh start."

"That place was killing him," Red said. "Everything there reminded him of what he'd lost. So we left."

"And what about you? Didn't you have a life there?"

He shrugged. "Of course I did. So did Mum and Dad—but that's the thing about the people you love, isn't it? You'd do anything in the world to make them happy, fuck the consequences. You know that better than anyone."

Hazel turned her gaze out to the ocean. "I guess I do," she said. She swallowed hard. "Speaking of which, there's something I really need to talk to you about."

"To do with your mum?"

"Kind of. And also to do with Luca."

Red shifted to look at her. She looked nervous, or upset, or maybe both. "What is it?"

She wet her lips. "It's . . ."

"What, Hazel?"

She shook her head; she couldn't do it. "Never mind. It's nothing."

He studied her for a moment, trying to get a read on her expression, but she'd closed herself off. He knew better than to push her; she'd talk when she was ready. They sat in silence for a while, just listening to the waves.

"Do you ever get mad at her?" Red asked then. "Your mum, I mean. Even though none of what happened to you both was her fault, even though you don't blame her. Do you ever get mad anyway?"

Hazel nodded. "I get frustrated. By the situation."

"You do?"

"I wouldn't be human if I didn't."

"It's like everyone knows how painful it is to lose someone, but no one ever talks about how hard it is to watch someone you *love* lose someone. To have to watch them grieving and not be able to help. And now Dad's back, and Luca says it's fine, but . . . what if it's not?"

"He'll get better, Red."

"I know. Doesn't make me any less of a shitty person for thinking it, though."

Hazel found Red's hand and gave it a squeeze. He squeezed her hand back, and then let go. "I used to be so jealous of him," he admitted.

"Of Luca?" said Hazel.

"Of Ryan."

She raised an eyebrow but didn't say anything, waiting.

"Being a twin is special," he explained. "It's not like having a brother. It's like being two halves of the same whole, having a person who's preprogrammed to be your best friend. Except I was never Luc's best friend. Ryan was."

Red hung his head. "I could never compete with him. He and Luc had so much more in common than we ever did, and Ryan was such a genuinely nice guy, which made it worse. Mum and Dad loved him too. He was like part of the family, and I hated sharing them with him. I spent so much time when I was younger wishing he would just disappear so I'd get my twin back."

"And then," Hazel said quietly, "he did."

Red still remembered it now: the moment Claire had told him what had happened. His first reaction had been flat-out denial. *No, don't say that. You're wrong, Mum. You're wrong. He can't be dead.*

"I never wanted him to *die*," he whispered. "I just wanted Luc to like me as much as he liked him."

"He *does*," Hazel said. "Luca loves you."

"And I love him," he said, raising his head to look at her. "I'm just worried that that's not enough."

"What do you mean?"

"Dad promised to try harder, but I'm worried Luca's going to go back to shutting us all out now that he's home." He paused, one side of his mouth turning upward into a wry smile. "And just when I thought he might have gotten himself a secret girlfriend, too."

"Girlfriend?"

"He's started wearing aftershave and styling his hair again. In Sydney he only used to do that when he fancied someone."

"Oh," Hazel said.

"Maybe it's Maddie," Red said thoughtfully. "Do you think he might fancy Maddie?"

"Maybe?"

"I'm pretty sure Hunter would kick his ass if he went near her," he said.

"You really think he has a girlfriend?"

"Well, he disappears for hours at a time." He shrugged. "He

sneaks out and thinks no one notices. I don't know where else he'd be going."

"Maybe he's just going to get some fresh air?" she said.

"Maybe," he agreed. "I was hoping he *was* seeing someone, though. That would be a big step back to normal."

Hazel said nothing, just smiled down at the sand.

AFTER REALIZING THAT CRICKET WASN'T HIS
sport of choice, Hunter had finally decided that the next one
he was going to try was tennis. Maddie offered to give him a
quick lunchtime crash course in it before the practice after
school on Tuesday so he wouldn't make a complete idiot of
himself, and Hazel joined them at the court to watch.

Hazel knew Hunter wasn't especially athletic or graceful,
but she thought—wrongly—that he might have been able to
grasp the basics of tennis. He was hopeless, although Maddie
managed to do a pretty good job of convincing him otherwise.
He didn't have a single iota of hand-eye coordination, and every
time Maddie prepared to serve the ball, he fumbled with the
racket, complaining that he couldn't hold it right.

Within ten minutes Maddie had given up on trying to

explain the rules of the sport and decided to concentrate instead on getting him to actually hit the ball *at all*. After what felt like a hundred serves, he finally managed to hit three in a row in a rally, even if none of them landed inside the white lines. He was trying so hard, though, that Hazel found herself jumping up and down on the sideline in excitement whenever the racket and the ball connected.

After a quick break to eat lunch, Hunter and Maddie swapped sides on the court and carried on practicing, with Hazel continuing her cheerleading from the sidelines. They were just getting into the swing of it when Luca appeared, hovering on the edge of the court like he wasn't sure if he was welcome. Hazel had texted him at the beginning of lunch to let him know where they were, but she hadn't expected him to come—this was hardly their usual quiet, relaxed lunchtime setting.

"Hey, Luca!" Hunter said cheerfully to him, waving his racket about precariously in greeting.

"How's it going?" Luca asked.

"He's doing great," Maddie said. "We've got a good twenty minutes yet; that's loads of time to master the backhand."

"Backhand?" Hunter echoed, his frown deepening. "Which one's that again?"

Maddie shook her head almost imperceptibly. "Don't worry about it. The names aren't important as long as you can hit the ball."

"Preferably over the net, though, right?"

"Preferably, yeah. Are you *sure* tennis is the right fit for you?"

"Only one way to find out," Hunter said.

He and Maddie went back to practicing, and Hazel moved next to Luca to watch, where they stifled their laughter every time Hunter swung for the ball with his racket and missed horribly or hit the ball outside the court. To her credit, Maddie remained as patient as ever, calling out words of reassurance and not even blinking when he asked her for the fifth time which of the lines were the boundaries of the court.

Finally, the bell rang, signaling the end of lunch, and it was time for them to give up and head to their classes.

"Hey Hazel," Hunter said as they walked toward the main building. "Are you ready for the Math test tomorrow?"

Hazel sighed heavily. Her teacher, Mrs. Williams, was giving the class another test, and would be using Hazel's results to decide if she needed to be moved down a level. She was already nervous. "Please don't remind me."

"Oh yeah," Luca said suddenly. "I was going to ask if you wanted me to come over after school to run through some equations one more time?"

"You don't mind?"

Luca shrugged, and Hunter shook his head in amusement. "I'm surprised your brain is still intact. I feel like crying every time he attempts to explain even just *one* equation to me."

Luca shoved him in the shoulder. "Yeah, right. I'll remember that next time you're begging me for help."

"Ha!" Hunter scoffed. "And *I'll* remember *that* when I'm a professional tennis player and getting paid a million dollars a day to model Adidas gear!"

"You do know if that ever, ever happens, you owe me everything, right?" Maddie cut in. "Seeing as I've been the one suffering through all of this for you."

"*Suffering?*" he said. "Suffering? Is that all this has been to you? And there I was, calling it the best time of my life . . ."

She shoved him in the shoulder too, and he let out a booming laugh and pulled her against him, holding her tight. Hazel couldn't help but glance over at Luca to see what he thought of their play fighting; he was already looking at her, eyebrow quirked upward in amusement.

Less than half an hour into the tutoring session that afternoon, Hazel's head ached from the sheer amount of work her brain was being forced to do, and her eyes hurt from staring at the textbook trying to make sense of the numbers. It wasn't that Luca wasn't a good teacher, because he was—she was just sick of math. They'd crammed in a whole load of quick tutoring sessions in the last couple of weeks, be it on the field after training or in their free periods at school, and if it wasn't enough to help her show Mrs. Williams that she could handle the topics she was going to cry.

"Hazel?" Luca said loudly, tapping her on the arm to bring her back to the sum at hand. She looked down at the paper and the number there; it began with a four and ended in a stupid amount of zeros. "Come on. You can do this. Just tell me what the number is in scientific notation."

She chewed the end of her pen in frustration. "You say that like it's so easy."

"It is," he said. Then, gently, "Go ahead."

Hazel shot him a glare, because even though he was only there to help her, it felt as if he were killing her slowly. That was how it had been every time they'd sat down for a tutoring session: the calmer he stayed, the more stressed she got. "Right. So now there's four, and if we count the zeros up after it, we get . . . eighteen."

"Exactly!" he said, and for a split second, she actually felt pleased with herself.

"So that's four times ten to the power of eighteen?"

He nodded again, giving her an encouraging smile as he moved to shield the sheet with his palm. "Right. Which is how many zeros?"

She let out a groan. "How am I supposed to know? You've covered it up!"

"You're supposed to know because we've *literally* just done this!" he pointed out, still managing to sound surprisingly cheerful. Perhaps he enjoyed her pain. The sadist. "You know how to work it out backward. You just convert it, remember? Like when we did five times ten to the power of three?"

"Five thousand," she said automatically.

"See? You *do* get it! This is exactly the same principle, just with more difficult numbers." He held his hands up in front of her. "If it makes it easier, you can use your fingers—if you don't mind feeling like a preschooler."

"Okay, okay," Hazel said gruffly, swatting his hands away. "You've made your point."

She took a deep breath and closed her eyes for a moment, trying to visualize the sum in her head. "Okay," she muttered, more to herself than to him. "So it's four, to start with. Four and . . . and eighteen zeros?" She opened her eyes to peek at him. ". . . I think?"

He just smiled. "Correct."

She gave a sigh of relief. "Jeez. This is way too difficult."

"But you're really getting the hang of it now!" he said. "So if it's a four and eighteen zeros, what number does it make?"

She stared at him. "Seriously?"

"Seriously."

She heaved another sigh, rubbing her forehead with the palms of her hands. "Okay. Let's think this through logically. Six zeros is a million, so twelve is a million million which is a trillion. And then eighteen is three sixes so three times a million is a million million million, which is . . . a quintillion? So four times ten to the power of eighteen is four quintillion?"

He broke into a grin. "Correct again. Probably. Although

you could just be a million or a million million or a million billion trillion short. Who knows at this point."

"Hilarious," she said, but he just smirked back at her. "You know what? You're just jealous I can count that high."

"Because *that* makes sense when *I'm* the one teaching *you* math."

"This is scientific notation, it's not *math*."

"Pretty sure it is, Coach."

She gave him her sternest look. "I've told you a million billion trillion times, Luca. Coach on the field, Hazel off of it."

"Okay," he said. "I get it. Sorry, Coach."

"Screw you." She slammed her book shut. "I never have to deal with this sort of crap from your brother."

"That's because he thinks you're an angel," he said with another smirk.

"Right," she said. "Except he doesn't, at all."

"So you say—but you also claimed you studied this topic back home, so . . ."

"Don't blame me, blame my teacher," she said, and Luca narrowed his eyes at her.

"I can only work with what you've already got, Coach. It's just a shame you haven't got very much."

"Just because you're Red's brother doesn't mean I'm above hitting you."

"I'd like to see you try," he teased back, and so she raised her hand in a fist, swinging it toward his arm. His reflexes were fast; he caught her hand in his, his strong fingers closing around her fist like a cocoon.

"Nice try," he said, and let her go.

"Come on. I need to pass this test tomorrow, or I'll have to sack you."

"I'm not sure you can sack someone you're not even paying."

She rolled her eyes at him. "Just get on with it, Cawley."

They studied for almost another hour until the doorbell rang just after six. Hazel opened the door to find Maddie and Red standing on the doorstep.

"Hi guys," Hazel said. "What's up?"

"This is an intervention," Maddie announced. "We've come to save you from the deathly throes of mathematics."

"And, more important, we brought food," Red added, holding up a huge cardboard boxful of what smelled like Chinese takeout. "Because food makes everything better."

Luca appeared behind Hazel. "What's going on?"

"We're saving her from your terrible teaching skills." Red grinned at him. "And just in time, by the looks of it. You look like you've been to hell and back, Hazel."

"Thanks." Luca snorted. "We were basically done, anyway."

"Get bored of torturing her?"

"I'm *helping* her, you moron. Which is more than you've offered to do."

"In case you forgot, I'm in *art* school. Where I study *art*."

199

"Yeah, but that's only because you're—"

"Enough!" Maddie cut them off with a fond roll of her eyes. "Let's dish this up before it gets cold."

The twins traipsed ahead into the kitchen, but Hazel stopped Maddie. "Where's Hunter?"

She just sighed. "Practice ran over, he just called."

"And?"

"And it doesn't sound like it's going all that great."

"Poor Hunter."

"I just wish I could help him, you know? Make him happy."

"Maddie, you *do* help him," Hazel said. "You know how much he appreciates your support."

"I know, I know." Maddie sighed. "I just wish one of the boys was more into sports so they could help him too. He *really* wants to find a place to fit in."

"He'll figure it out," Hazel said lightly, and they followed the others into the kitchen.

Hunter turned up on the doorstep soon after, along with Graham, and they joined them for Chinese food.

"Tennis," Hunter declared as he collapsed into the kitchen chair next to Maddie, "is *not* my thing."

"You didn't enjoy the practice?"

"Not even remotely." He shook his head in annoyance, making his curls bounce. "Too many balls flying everywhere, it's a safety hazard. It's okay, though. I guess it just wasn't the right sport."

"Hunter," Luca said carefully, "I'm not trying to be funny, but are you sure there is one?"

"Yes!" he said indignantly. "And I'll find it to prove it."

"What about swimming?" Hazel suggested. When he wasn't working at the waterfall, he was constantly at the beach. "You love the water, don't you?"

"I do, yeah, but the swim team's really competitive, and it's already filled up—even for next year. Coach said I could have a place on the synchro team for next year if I wanted it, but I told him to get screwed."

"A little more politely than that, I hope," Graham said without looking up from his plate.

"Of course."

"What's so bad about the synchro team?" Maddie asked.

"Callum would have a field day. It's the only sport in the whole school that's worse than doing nothing at all. I'd probably have to wear a stupid flowery swimming cap and prance around in a pink costume . . ." He shuddered. "Nope, my masculinity is too fragile. I'll just find something else."

"Are there many sports left that you haven't tried?" Hazel said.

"Coach said I could go along to a fencing practice in a couple of weeks." He sighed.

Maddie just leaned over to squeeze his shoulder reassuringly. "It'll be okay."

As Mrs. Williams handed out the test papers in Math the next day, Hazel's heart was racing, and her palms were clammy. As soon as Mrs. Williams gave them permission to start, Hazel took a deep breath and opened the first page, eyes focused on the numbers written there. She smiled, nerves dissipating; she *knew* this. She put her pencil to the paper and scribbled away as if her life depended on it.

She finished with time to spare, even after she'd checked through her work twice to make sure she'd answered all she could. The test wasn't easy by any stretch of the imagination, but it wasn't just blurry numbers anymore; it actually made sense.

When the bell rang for the end of class, Mrs. Williams asked Hazel to stay behind.

"I know you've been struggling, Hazel. Would you like me to grade this now so we can see how you did?"

Hazel nodded and took a seat at one of the desks in the front row, waiting quietly and hoping with all she had that she'd at least managed to *pass* this test. It only took Mrs. Williams a few minutes to grade the paper, and then she was beckoning to Hazel, her face unreadable.

Hazel approached her desk slowly and took the paper she was holding out. She almost didn't want to look at the grade scrawled in red at the top, because she was scared, but then she had to and . . . *wow.*

She'd done more than pass. She'd gotten a big, fat B+. She exhaled in relief.

"Happy?" Mrs. Williams asked, although Hazel was pretty sure she could tell from the way she was beaming. "Congratulations, Hazel. You deserve this—you've obviously been putting in a lot of hard work."

She just nodded dumbly. Those sessions with Luca had been intense. She owed him big-time.

Mrs. Williams waved her off. "Go on then, go eat lunch. And Hazel?"

Hazel paused in the doorway. "Yes?"

"Keep up the good work."

Luca was the first thing Hazel saw when she walked out of the classroom, leaning ever so casually against the lockers, waiting for her. He looked up at the sound of her approaching, and she crossed the hallway to him, ready to hand him the paper, but instead she found herself throwing her arms around his neck and hugging him tightly.

For a fleeting second he was stiff in her arms, unyielding, but then something changed, and he was hugging her back, laughing into her ear and spinning her around. It felt so carefree and natural and normal. The moment was brief, and it vanished as soon as they pulled apart, but it had been there, and it took her breath away.

"I take it the test went okay?" he asked then.

"Mrs. Williams graded my paper early," she said.

"And?"

Hazel showed him her test. "And I got a B+!"

"Well done, Hazel!"

"Thank you," she told him sincerely, and hoped with all her heart he knew just how much she meant it.

28

THAT WEEKEND, CLAIRE HAD INVITED HAZEL
and Graham over to the house for a proper sit-down meal with
the whole family. Red had told Hazel that his dad had arranged
with work to stay in Port Sheridan for good, which she knew
was going to be a really positive thing for the family. She'd spent
the last few days avoiding the Cawley residence, figuring it was
best to let the family settle back in with one another first.

Marc was nothing like Hazel expected—he was younger,
warmer, more friendly looking. His entire face lit up when he
caught sight of Graham standing in the hallway, and he crossed
the room in three strides to pull him into his arms. "Graham!"
he barked, clapping him on his back. "Good to see you!"

Graham hugged him just as tightly. "You too, Marc. It's
been too long—when was the last time I saw you? July?"

"Just before you jetted off to London." He looked past Graham for the first time, and when his eyes landed on Hazel his whole face changed. His eyes softened, and the corners of his mouth turned down.

"Christ," he murmured. "You look just like her, don't you?"

Hazel's breath caught in her throat, but before she could say anything Red instinctively stepped forward between her and his father. "Let's get some drinks, shall we? Hazel? You want to help me?"

Hazel nodded, glancing briefly back at Marc—who was watching her closely—before following Red into the kitchen.

No one brought up England or her mum after that, which Hazel was thankful for. They ate in the dining room, with Hazel and Graham on one side of the table, the twins on the other, and Marc and Claire sitting at either end. It was strange, seeing how comfortably Graham interacted with Red's parents. Strange but nice.

After they'd finished eating, Hazel and the twins excused themselves from the table and headed up to Red's room to watch a movie. Hazel paused in the dining room doorway, looking back at Graham over her shoulder. He was laughing, his head thrown back, green eyes sparkling. He looked so relaxed, so at home. He looked *happy*, truly happy, for the first time since she'd met him in the lawyer's office in London. It was a nice sight; she hadn't realized how much his happiness had started to mean to her.

"You coming?" Red called from down the hallway, where he and Luca were waiting at the foot of the stairs for her.

Hazel tore her eyes away from Graham. "I'm coming," she said cheerfully, and went to join them.

Luca's newest running goal was to get below thirteen minutes before the end of November—just a week and a half away. A couple of months ago, the idea would've seemed impossible to Hazel, but she knew now that Luca was more than capable.

"Okay," she said as he stretched out his hamstrings, "How's this? If you get under thirteen minutes and fifteen seconds to-night, I'll buy you a muffin from the cafeteria for breakfast tomorrow."

"Is that bribery?"

"It's incentive," she corrected. "Blueberry or double choco-late?"

"Always blueberry."

"Come on then," she said, nudging him in the shoulder. "Show me how it's done."

Luca grinned at her and climbed to his feet, gathering himself ready to start. Hazel counted him in like always, and then he was off, running around and around the track. He was making great time and was well on target to beat his last session when, halfway through his eighth lap, he lost his footing and stumbled. He gave a yelp of pain and tumbled to the ground, hands clutching at his ankle.

"Oh my *God*," Hazel said, breaking into a run. She didn't slow down until she was beside him in the middle of the field. "Luca? Are you okay?"

"Peachy," he said through gritted teeth.

She crouched down beside him on the grass. "What happened?"

"I twisted it, I think. I just . . . I was running, and I just felt it *go*."

"How much does it hurt?"

Luca moved his foot slightly and winced. "Not too much," he said.

Hazel frowned at him. "Don't be a martyr. Let me have a look."

"I don't know if that's—"

"I'll be gentle," she promised, and knocked his hands out of the way.

She began carefully unlacing his shoe, making sure not to touch his ankle, and when the sneaker was loose enough, she eased it off his foot and set it down on the ground beside her.

"It looks a bit inflamed," she said absently, running a fingertip across the slight swelling. When he didn't answer, she glanced up at him.

He was leaning back on his elbows, watching her closely

with an unreadable expression. Their eyes met. Hazel became acutely aware of the way her other hand was resting on his knee, of the feel of his skin beneath her palm.

"What?" she said, removing her hand hastily. "What are you looking at?"

He watched her for a moment longer, then shook his head slightly. "Nothing."

"Do you think you can stand?"

Luca nodded. Hazel stood up herself and helped pull him carefully to his feet. He kept his foot lifted off the ground and wobbled slightly, reaching out to her for support. She steadied him.

"All right?"

Luca nodded again, but his jaw was set, teeth clenched in pain.

"Can you walk?"

"I can probably hop," he said.

She offered him her shoulder, and he leaned on it carefully. "Shall I call your mum or dad?"

"It's date night. They're at the cinema."

"What about Red? He's got his learner's permit, right?"

Luca shook his head furiously. "He can't drive without an adult in the car. Besides, I don't want him to know."

"You think he won't figure it out when you're limping around the house?"

"I'll tell him I twisted it walking home," he said, grimacing. "He doesn't have to know about the running."

"Fine." She relented, reaching for her phone, but she was so tired of hiding. "We'll call a taxi."

After over two months of struggling, Red had finally started to take some photos that he was happy with. Pretty damn happy, actually, and pretty damn proud too. They weren't perfect—the lighting and focus were a bit off on some of them, and the compositions left a lot to be desired, but Red knew that didn't matter. When he saw them like this, all laid out across the kitchen counter, he knew he was beginning to nail Hodgkins's theme. This was his family, in all of its ugly, honest, wonderful, still-healing glory—and it might be scary to see them so exposed and vulnerable, but Red was dealing with it. He didn't have a choice; ignoring their problems wouldn't make them go away. Their dad had already found that one out the hard way.

So from now on, Red was going to apply Hodgkins's assignment advice to his entire life and strive to seek the truth in every moment. Honesty was the best policy, right? It had to be.

He heard a car door slam and when he looked out the window, he saw Luca and Hazel climbing out of a taxi. He quickly put the photos away in his portfolio and went to meet them at the door. Hazel was helping Luca walk, and it looked like he'd hurt his ankle.

What's going on here, then?

"Well," Red said, leaning against the door frame as he watched them hobble up the path. "This is . . . unexpected."

His brother just glared at him, and Hazel shook her head in warning. "Could you give us a hand, please?"

"I'm fine," Luca said.

"Clearly." Red snorted but went to help them anyway. He shifted Luca's weight carefully onto his shoulder and half-carried him into the house and through to the living room. He dumped him unceremoniously onto the sofa and then reached instinctively for his camera.

"*Really*, Redleigh?" Luca snapped. "For fuck's sake."

Red took the shot anyway, grinning, and hung his camera around his neck. "All right, all right, keep your pants on. What do you need? Some painkillers? Ice?"

"Anything. Everything."

Red looked at Hazel. She looked . . . *guilty*. What did she have to be guilty about? He eyed the two of them curiously. He had about a hundred questions right now, but they'd have to wait. He left Luca in Hazel's capable hands and went off to collect some emergency supplies, returning to the living room a few minutes later with a bottle of ibuprofen, a glass of water, a bag of ice for the swelling, and a cushion to elevate his ankle. He waited until Luca had taken the tablets and positioned the ice before speaking.

"So. You want to tell me what happened?"

"No," Luca said.

Red narrowed his eyes at him and turned to Hazel. "What about you?"

"He hurt his ankle."

"I figured that much, funnily enough. How did he hurt it? Doing what? And where was he? And why were you there with him?"

She glanced at Luca, who hesitated and then shrugged. Perhaps he was tired of hiding too. "We were at the track," she said carefully. "And I was there because I've been helping him. With his running."

"Running?" Red echoed, and what? *What?* "Luc, are you—"

"No," Luca cut him off flatly. "I'm not."

"But you're—"

"I said *no*, Red."

Red clamped his mouth shut. *Shit, this is huge.* He sat back in his chair, arms folded across his chest, and watched his twin from across the table.

"Well. I don't know what to say."

"Then don't say anything."

Red was too happy right now that Luca was running again, in whatever capacity, that he couldn't even bring himself to care about the fact that Luca and Hazel had apparently been going behind his back to do it. How long had they been training together for? A few weeks? Longer?

"So this is where you've been sneaking off to?" he said finally. "You don't have a secret girlfriend?"

Luca looked mildly horrified. "*Girlfriend?* No!"

"Interesting," Red murmured. *Very, very interesting.* "What are you going to tell Mum and Dad?"

"I'm not."

"Luca . . ."

"Redleigh," he countered. "I swear to God, if you tell them anything about this I'll never forgive you."

"Why, though? Why don't you want them to know?"

"Because."

"Because why?"

"Just *because*, all right?" Luca snapped. "Because it's not a big deal and if Dad finds out it'll get his hopes up and I don't want to disappoint him all over again."

Red felt his chest tighten. "Luc, that's—"

"Please don't say anything to them. Not yet."

And it was that, the *not yet*, that made Red nod. Because *not yet* wasn't *never*, it was *let me figure this out first*, and Red could do that for his brother. He looked over at Hazel instead, who was sitting on the edge of her chair—perhaps in case the conversation turned bad and she needed to make a hasty exit. "How is his running, then? Is he any good?"

Hazel turned to Luca with an expression that was suspiciously fond, and Luca cocked an eyebrow back at her.

"Yeah," she said softly. "He's good."

LUCA'S ANKLE, IT TURNED OUT, WASN'T AS badly injured as they'd initially thought. After he'd told his parents that he'd twisted it walking home from school—which neither of them questioned—Claire and Marc went with him to the doctor, who assured them it was just a mild sprain that would be easily treated with anti-inflammatory medication and a few days' rest from physical exertion.

By Thursday, though, Luca was restless and eager to get back to his training, worried he would fall behind if he took a day off. He cornered Hazel after school and practically begged her to un-cancel their session later.

"Absolutely not. The doctor told you to rest."

"He told me to take it easy," Luca corrected. "And I've *been* taking it easy. I'm sick of sitting on my ass all day doing nothing."

"If you start running on it too soon, you'll hurt yourself even worse," Hazel said firmly. "And then you'd *really* screw up your progress. Just give it a few more days, all right? We'll train again on Monday."

He sighed heavily. "Fine, whatever. Let's do something else tonight then. Let's . . . I don't know, let's go to Bluehill. It's got some great views. Come on, I'm going out of my mind. Mum keeps fussing over me like I'm a kid. We can catch a bus."

Hazel considered it for a moment, studying Luca's face as he waited patiently for her response.

"Okay," she said finally. "We'll go."

He broke into a smile. "I'll meet you at seven outside your house?"

"Seven it is," she said.

Bluehill, Luca had decided, was a very misleading name for a place that was neither blue nor small enough to be a hill. It was, however, the most popular lookout point in town, particularly with tourists during the dry season. The sun had already set by the time he and Hazel arrived at the foot of the towering mount, and the night had sunk into twilight, leaving the sky a canvas of pink and blue. They had to walk up a winding dirt track from the bus stop, using just a flashlight to guide their way—which took them a while because of his ankle—and when they reached the top, they found that they were the only ones there.

"Want to sit?" Luca said.

Hazel nodded. "Sure."

He took a plaid rug from his backpack and laid it out near the edge of the hill, and the two of them sat down on it. Below, the lights of the town were sprinkled about, the glow of the harbor and the pier spilling out onto the black sea. The sky above was alive with stars, thousands upon thousands of brilliant white pinpricks.

It was so quiet Luca could hear Hazel breathing. He wondered if she knew how attuned he'd become to her every movement these past few months, how closely he listened to every word she said. If she realized that he noticed every smile, every laugh, that he'd begun to catalog them away in the back of his mind without even meaning to. Without even *wanting* to. He hoped she didn't realize. He hoped she'd never realize.

"You haven't seen stars until you've been to Bluehill," he murmured then, to break the silence, to divert his thoughts.

Hazel tilted her head to stare up at the sky in wonder. "It's really beautiful, Luca."

"Redleigh used to say that the stars are spy holes for heaven," he said. "So the people we lose can still watch over us, even when they're gone."

"I like that."

"So do I. It . . . helped a lot, after."

"After?"

"After Ryan," he said heavily. Hazel said nothing, and suddenly Luca wanted to tell her everything. He was sick of hiding. "Back in Sydney. He was my best friend since before I even knew what that meant, and we were inseparable all the way through school. Just me and him. But then last year he . . . he died. Sudden cardiac death. We were in the middle of a training session. Coach had us running laps, the whole team together, and one second he was sprinting past me and yelling at us all to catch up, and the next . . . *bam*. He just dropped straight to the ground. And we thought he was messing around at first, playing a joke—classic Ryan, never taking anything seriously—but then he didn't get up and . . . and I knew something wasn't right, so I went to him, but I couldn't get him to respond and we tried to resuscitate him but we . . . but I . . ."

He exhaled. "By the time the ambulance arrived, he was gone. He died. Ryan died, and it was really, really shitty, and I haven't . . . I don't know how to—"

"Luca," she cut him off. "I knew. About Ryan, about what happened, I already knew."

He stared at her. "Did Redleigh tell you?"

"No—*you* told me, at Kayla's," she said. "You were drunk, and we were outside. You told me about him, and you asked me not to tell anyone. So I didn't."

"You knew?" he said. "All this time, you knew?"

"Luca, I'm so sorry," Hazel said, suddenly on the edge of tears. "I should have said something. You have every right to be angry with me."

"Angry?" he echoed. "Why would I be angry?"

"Because I knew and I never told you what happened at the party?"

"Hazel," Luca said slowly. "You knew, and you still treated me like I was normal. Christ, you made me *feel* normal. Why would I ever be angry about that?"

"I figured you didn't need the fuss," she mumbled.

"Thank you," he said. "And thank you for not telling Maddie and Hunter. I couldn't do it again, you know? I couldn't be the guy with the dead friend, not here too. I had to try and be myself. You're the only one who knows what that's like, Hazel. You just get it."

"Luca, wait—" Hazel began, but Luca cut her off.

"No, no, you understand, and that means I don't have to feel so alone."

"You're not," she promised him.

He smiled gratefully and then shook his head. "What is it about the truth we're so scared of anyway? How bad can it really be? It's not like we haven't both been to hell and back already."

A movement on the blanket caught Luca's eye. He glanced down and watched as Hazel slowly, gently inched her hand across the ground until it covered his. He stared across at her, eyes widening slightly. She looked at him, and he looked back at her. Hazel lowered her gaze first, a slight smile playing on her lips.

Heart racing, Luca turned his attention to the stars again. A few moments later, without saying a word, he threaded his fingers through hers so that their hands were well and truly intertwined.

* * *

When Luca woke up on Friday morning, he lay in bed for a long while, staring up at the ceiling. *Three hundred and sixty-five days.* A year. It had been one whole year since the day that Ryan died. It felt more like months, though, still. Weeks. Days, even, since it happened.

Three hundred and sixty-five days. That was eight thousand, seven hundred and sixty hours. That was five hundred and twenty-five thousand, six hundred minutes. That was more seconds than he was even willing to contemplate.

After Ryan died, Luca was surrounded by people telling him there was no right way to mourn, that he could cry, and he could get angry, and he could point-blank refuse to believe Ryan had even died, because all of that was normal. But that had just made it worse, somehow, because Luca didn't know *how* to mourn. He didn't want to cry, and he didn't want to get angry, and he couldn't kid himself into thinking that Ryan was still around because he *wasn't* around and everywhere Luca looked he was reminded of it.

He hadn't known what to do. He *still* didn't know what to do. He and Ryan used to have their whole lives mapped out together: college and traveling and racing and their future families. And then suddenly, without warning, he was gone. That had hit him hard, realizing that out of everything he'd ever planned for himself in life, everything he ever thought he wanted, there wasn't a single scenario that didn't have Ryan in it.

The thing about remembering Ryan was that once Luca started, he couldn't stop. It was all he could think about, like his mind was set on punishing him for still being alive. Lazy days at the beach, running together, goofing off in class . . . even the *bad* memories were good.

They were going to travel in Europe. They were going to break a Guinness World Record. They were going to climb Mount Everest, go on safari, see the northern lights. When Ryan died, Luca forgot about all that. He forgot about everything he ever said he wanted from life, because suddenly none of it mattered—and he thought it never would again. He put his life on hold because it didn't seem worth living without Ryan.

But it was, and Luca needed to start remembering that. He needed to start remembering all the things he wanted to achieve. He needed to start remembering how to live his life the way he had when Ryan was still in it. He needed to let go and start *living* again.

Luca marked the day off on the calendar with an *X*, the same way he'd marked off all the days before, and put it back in his nightstand. Out of sight, out of mind.

"Three hundred and sixty-five days since I lost you, buddy," he murmured as he kicked back the covers, ready to face a brand-new day. "Reckon it's probably time to stop keeping count now, don't you?"

*   *   *

School that day was easy, because to everyone else it was just another Friday in late November. Luca went to classes, keeping his head down and focusing on the page, but his mind never really drifted far away from Ryan. He kept asking himself questions he didn't want to know the answers to: Where would Ryan be now if he hadn't died? What would he be like? What would their lives be like? What would *Luca's* life be like?

Home was harder. His mum and dad knew what today was; Ryan had been as much like a son to them as he'd been like a brother to Luca. Dad had definitely been making a concerted effort since the apology the other day, but that evening both of his parents were more careful, more gentle, as if they were scared he might suddenly shatter into a thousand pieces all over the kitchen floor. Luca wished he could reassure them otherwise, but he wasn't even sure himself whether he could hold it together.

Red didn't say anything about it, but he didn't have to. He said hello casually enough as they passed each other in the hallway after dinner, but then he grabbed hold of Luca and pulled him in for a tight hug. Red might not have been as well built as him, but he was a good few centimeters taller, and when his arms wrapped around him Luca couldn't help but feel that Red was trying to hold him together too, in his own way.

There was a candle on his desk when he went upstairs. Just one single cream candle in a glass jar. Luca took it to the track, because that was where he felt closest to Ryan, where he felt Ryan was looking down—if he was looking down at all. Luca walked to the very middle of the grass, illuminated by the floodlights. He lit the candle, watching as the flame flickered slightly in the evening breeze, and took a deep, shuddering breath.

He had a thousand things he wanted to say. There were so many ways he wanted to remember Ryan, to memorialize him, but for some reason he couldn't. He couldn't find the right words, couldn't figure out how to do him justice.

"I miss you, buddy," he whispered instead, and somehow that was enough.

He sat down cross-legged on the grass and placed the candle in front of him. He watched the flame, and he pictured Ryan's face in his mind during his last seconds, those green eyes and those curls and those dimples. Then Luca pictured his laugh, wild and reckless and untamable—so inherently alive even in the face of death—and he replayed it over and over and over again in his mind until the wax melted down into a hot puddle and the flame dwindled into darkness.

Dear Mum,

I remember the Christmas you took me ice skating at Somerset House. Neither of us was very good, I thought, and so we clung to each other as we made our way slowly around the rink. We spent almost the entire hour teaching ourselves how to move our feet properly on the ice, but we still had a great time.

When the hour was up, you led me off the ice and then told me to hang on while you did one more lap. I was confused, but I did as you asked.

Without me, you skated around the rink like a professional. You glided across the ice like you'd been there all your life.

You could've let me learn on my own, but you didn't. You took it slow for me, and I never told you just how much I appreciated that.

I miss you, Mum, but I remember.

Love,
Hazel

LUCA TURNED UP ON HAZEL'S DOORSTEP
without warning on Saturday evening. "Are you busy?" he
blurted out before she even had a chance to say hello.

"Just clearing away dinner, what's up?"

"I just . . . I'd really like to talk. If that's okay. I need someone to talk to."

"Of course," Hazel said, pulling the door shut behind her.
"Let's go."

She took him to the stretch of beach behind Graham's house,
and they sat down on the sand, facing out to sea.

"I was supposed to have a scholarship," Luca began. "For

the University of Sydney. I was only sixteen, so it wasn't an outright offer, but the scouts said it was as good as."

"A scholarship for what?"

"For running." He was silent for a moment, gathering his thoughts. "The scholarship was a big deal, even if it was unofficial, because they're so difficult to get over here. But I screwed up. When Ryan died, I stopped racing, and when the university found out, they cut me off. I *wanted* to run, at first. I tried, I just . . . It felt wrong. I didn't—I couldn't do it, not without him. We'd always done it together, and knowing that we never would again just . . . It made me miss him too much. So I gave up, in the end. Not just on the running. On everything."

Hazel said nothing, waiting for him to continue, but he didn't. Just looked out to sea.

"Us training," she said finally. "You being so focused on getting back your time. Was that a way to come to terms with it?"

"Partly—because it was something we always did together, even when we weren't training, and it makes me feel close to him somehow. But also partly because running has always been the only thing that clears my head, even before that, and I thought that maybe if I could just get back up to the standard that I was at when . . . when he . . ."

Hazel reached out to touch his arm, and Luca shuddered, hard, before raising his eyes to hers. "I thought it would *fix* things, you know? That it would make me feel better. That it would make it not hurt."

"And it hasn't?"

He smiled ever so slightly. "No, it has. Somewhat."

The thought of being a part of the reason why Luca felt better—however marginally—made Hazel feel good. He deserved that. He needed that. They *all* needed that. She thought back to that night when she'd first found him at the track, sitting with his head in his hands, and how he'd been such a mystery; she remembered trying to piece together the few things she knew about him and failing to turn those fragments into a person. People didn't work like that—they weren't the sum of a handful of unconnected facts, they were the sum of *everything*, and now that Hazel knew so much more about him and what he'd gone through he wasn't a mystery anymore. He wasn't an enigma or a riddle to be solved; he was just human.

"It was a year ago yesterday," Luca said then. "A year ago that Ryan died. One whole year."

"I'm sorry," she said automatically. "If I'd have known, I would've—"

"It's fine," he said. "I just wanted to be alone, you know? To think things through."

"Did it help?"

He nodded. "I think so. If nothing else, it made me realize how afraid I am that if I let myself move on I'll start to forget about him. *That's* what terrifies me the most."

Hazel thought back to her own mum, about all the times she'd told herself the exact same thing. *I remember, I remember,*

I remember. "Then you just . . . you have to keep remembering. Every day."

He was quiet for a moment. "Is that how you survived losing your mum?"

"Luca, my mum isn't—" she started, and he looked at her, his eyes wide with the hope that there was a way out, that she was living proof that there was light at the end of the tunnel.

"She isn't what?"

"Yes," she whispered. "Yes, that's how I survived."

He let the words sink in. "How long has it been since you lost her?" he asked eventually.

"A long time," she said, and that wasn't even a lie, not really. "Years."

"And it gets better?"

"It gets numb," she said softly.

You learned how to get up every day and survive, and you kept on moving forward even when you didn't want to, and eventually, finally, the pain started to fade to something bearable.

It was almost one o'clock in the morning by the time they decided to turn in, which was incredible considering a few months ago she and Luca couldn't even sustain a conversation for a couple of minutes.

Instead of disappearing back through the hole in the

undergrowth, Hazel let Luca walk her around to the front of Graham's house the way he did when they trained together.

"Well," she said, stopping at the gate.

He shifted on the pavement to look at her. "Thank you for tonight. It means a lot."

Neither of them spoke for a moment. Hazel studied his face—thinking once again how different it was from Red's, despite all the DNA they shared, how his eyes seemed to burn, even in the near darkness—and Luca watched her back.

"I'll walk you to the door?" he offered, and Hazel nodded. The air between them seemed suddenly thick, perhaps with all the things they were both thinking but not saying.

"So," he said when they reached the porch. "Here you are."

She rocked up on her tiptoes to pull him into a hug, wrapping her arms around his neck like she would Red or Hunter or Maddie. At first, he seemed to freeze like he had in the hallway at school, but then after a moment he hugged her back.

He smelled good, warm and musky. He started pulling away, but not completely. He stopped when they were face-to-face, his hands still at the bottom of her back, holding her. He swallowed hard, looking right into her eyes.

Hazel remembered how he'd looked in the moonlight on the beach earlier, and suddenly she had the strangest urge to lean forward, to close the space between them and put her lips on his. Just quickly. Just to know what it would feel like. But then the moment passed, and she had stood for too long just looking at him and not saying anything. She dropped her arms and took a definite step backward, putting distance between them.

He rubbed his neck. "I should probably go."

"You probably should."

She met his eyes, and he looked away first. Did he know what she'd been thinking?

"See you," he said then, and before she could answer, he ducked his head and walked down the path without looking back.

part three

31

THE BEGINNING OF DECEMBER BROUGHT A
shift in the heat. The weather in Port Sheridan had gotten
steadily warmer as Australia headed toward its summer, but
now that it was here, it had changed from a dry heat to a more
humid one, which everyone kept telling Hazel was because
of the "wet season."

When Hazel had arrived in the country back in August,
she'd hoped that she would be home by Christmas, but with
each day that passed that was seeming less and less likely. She
still hadn't heard anything from England, but instead of letting herself dwell on it the way she would have a few months
ago, she focused on other things instead—like the fact that
there were three weeks left in the school year and everyone at

Finchwood was gearing up for the final push before the six-week-long summer vacation.

Hunter was taking Coach up on his offer to join a fencing practice at lunchtime today—something that Maddie was apprehensive about.

"Are you sure about this?" she asked him. "You do realize that fencing is just a bunch of people sticking each other with swords, right? It's *dangerous*."

Hunter waved a hand dismissively. "I'll be fine. I'm a natural-born warrior."

Maddie patted his arm. "If you hurt yourself, don't come to me expecting Band-Aids and sympathy."

"You know you won't be able to resist kissing me better, Mads." He grinned back at her.

She rolled her eyes. "You are delusional."

When Hazel, Luca, and Maddie caught sight of Hunter emerging from the gym as they were on their way to class at the end of lunch, he just shook his head.

"Fencing," he said as he approached them. "Is definitely—"

"*Not your thing!*" Maddie and Hazel chorused back at him, and fell into a fit of laughter.

Hunter sighed, nursing his elbow. "You know, this isn't even funny anymore. I'm a failure."

"Hey." Luca put an arm around his shoulder. "Sports aren't for everyone. It just means you have another calling."

"You think?"

"Oh, definitely. Knitting, maybe?"

"Oh, screw you," he said. "I sincerely hope you burn in hell. All of you."

"Love you too," Luca said with a smirk.

"You know, I liked you more when you didn't talk."

"He's joking," Maddie said quickly. "Hey, Hunter, does this mean you don't want kisses and Band-Aids and sympathy ice cream after school?"

Hunter beamed at her. "You know I love you, right?"

"Yeah," she said, smile slipping slightly. "I know."

In the end, they all wound up going around to Maddie's house to comfort Hunter—not that he needed it, since he was over the whole fencing debacle before the end of the school day. Instead, he was focused on the fact that he hadn't yet tried any track-based sports.

"There's loads of them!" he said excitedly. "Sprints, relays, hurdles, and that's just the ones that involve running. There's gotta be something there that I'm not terrible at, right?"

"Not trying to be a killjoy," Maddie said carefully, digging her spoon into a tub of Ben & Jerry's. "But when was the last time you ran more than ten meters without getting a stitch or cramp?"

"Irrelevant."

"Relevant," she argued. "You're the slowest runner I know."

"Then I'll do long-distance!" he countered. "That's all about stamina, not speed."

"Do you realize how many laps of the running track that is?"

"I don't know . . . like, five?"

"Ten," Luca corrected him automatically, and they all turned to look at him. "Well, that's a 4K race, anyway. Some are longer."

"Dude," Hunter said, horrified. "Ten? I'd *die*."

"Long-distance is anything over 3K, but you could try mid-distance. That'd only be seven and a half laps, or fewer, which would still require some anaerobic training, but considerably less than long-distance."

"Interesting." Hunter helped himself to some more ice cream, sucking on his spoon thoughtfully. "Didn't know you knew anything about sports."

"I don't, really. About most sports, anyway." Luca paused. "But I do know a thing or two about running."

"Great! So you can take me through some of the basics before I go to a track practice?"

The expression that crossed Luca's face was so fleeting Hazel couldn't quite put a finger on it. Was it pain? Hope? Nerves?

"Well . . . ," he started, sounding uncertain.

"Please? Pretty please? I'll love you eternally."

At this, Luca caved. "Fine," he mumbled. "I'll—I'll try and help you. I'm not promising you anything, but I can try."

Hunter let out a huge sigh of relief. "You won't regret it."

Luca smiled at him and went back to eating his ice cream as if nothing had happened, but Hazel was amazed that he was willing to take his running out of the safe, secret bubble they'd created for themselves at the stadium.

Luca was in his room that night finishing up an English assignment on his computer when a loud knock came at his door.

"Come in," he called absently. "Hey, Red, what do you think about us all—"

He broke off. His father was standing in the doorway. In the weeks since he'd moved back, things between Luca and Marc had been civil. Luca knew that his dad was making a concerted effort, always taking the time to ask about school and friends.

"Luc," his dad said. "Are you busy?"

Luca shook his head. "What's up?"

Marc stepped inside and took a careful seat at the end of Luca's bed. He cleared his throat. "So."

"So," Luca said.

"How are things at school?"

"They're okay, thanks. I have an exam this week, but I think I'll do fine."

"Good, good."

They fell into silence. Luca wondered how long it would take for conversation between them to feel less forced. Even though they were both trying, it still didn't feel the same as it used to. He missed that so much. After a minute, his father stood from the bed and brushed down his trousers, heading for the door like that was all he'd come up to say.

"Well," he said. "Your mum's left me in charge of dinner, so . . ."

"Sure."

Marc was almost out the doorway when Luca said, "Dad?"

"Yes? What is it?"

"It's just . . . I've actually been doing some training."

"You have?"

"Yeah. With Hazel. Not competitively, obviously, but . . ."

"But you're running?"

"I am," he said. *I'm running, without Ryan, and it's not the end of the world.*

His dad studied him across the room for a moment and then nodded once. "Well, I'm glad," he said. "But you know the running isn't important to me, right? It's not what I care about. You're what I care about."

Luca smiled. "I know. But I'm enjoying it."

"You are?"

"I am," Luca assured him. "Did you . . . want any help making dinner?"

Marc's face lit up. "I'd love some."

238

32

HAZEL HAD NO PLANS FOR THE WEEKEND—
except sleeping and catching up on her homework—so when a
buzzing sound from her bedside table woke her from a dreamless sleep far too early on Saturday morning, she groaned loudly
before answering it. It was a text, from Luca.

Get ready, it read. I'll be outside in half an hour. Bring
swimming things. X

She glanced at the alarm clock: half past nine. What could
he have planned that she'd need swimming things for? Surely
it was too early to go to the beach? She read the text again. She
and Luca never hung out on the weekends unless everyone else
was there too, so this was a new development.

She typed out a reply—See you then x—and pressed Send,

smiling up at the ceiling for a moment before climbing out of bed and heading for the bathroom to shower.

Hazel was standing out in the front garden enjoying the morning sun when she caught sight of Luca riding his bike toward her. It took a moment for her to realize he wasn't on his own—Hunter was riding behind him.

"Hey," she said as the two of them approached. "Morning, Hunter. Didn't expect to see you today!"

"It's my fault." Luca came to a stop at the gate with a grim expression. "He heard what I had planned and decided he was coming too. Phoned in sick to work and everything. Red wanted to come as well, but he said he had to work on some project for school."

"Oh," Hazel said, laughing. "Okay. I feel privileged."

She mounted the bike she'd borrowed from Graham and followed the boys down the road. Fifteen minutes of leisurely cycling later, the three of them rode into the parking lot at a small marina. They chained their bikes to the rack, and Luca rearranged his huge rucksack on his shoulder.

"You ready?" he asked Hazel.

"What are we doing?"

"We're taking a boat out."

"Yeah, I figured that much—but to where?"

"The reef!" Hunter blurted out excitedly.

"Wait," she said slowly. "The Great Barrier Reef?"

"Well," Luca said, "Red says you've never seen it—and we *are* in Australia."

Hazel looked around at the sparkling sea, the palm trees, the white sand, the blue sky. "So we are."

Luca had rented the boat for the whole day so that the three of them could explore the outer reef at leisure. Both he and Hunter had marine licenses, so they were going to take turns driving. Luca had barely driven them out of the harbor and into the open water when Hunter started getting impatient and begging for a turn at the wheel. Luca rolled his eyes and swapped out of the driver's seat, making his way to the back of the boat to sit with Hazel.

It took about three-quarters of an hour for them to find a spot above the reef that Hunter was happy with before he cut the engine and lowered the anchor. As far as Hazel could tell they were literally in the middle of nowhere—all she could see in any direction was bright, clear water. The sun was beating down hard now that they were no longer moving, and everything seemed unnaturally still.

Luca unzipped his rucksack and pulled out a selection of accessories for Hazel to wear: a wet suit to keep the jellyfish at bay, some heavy, clunky black flippers, a snorkel, and a pair of fluorescent-green goggles. Hunter pulled his hair back into a ponytail and began stripping down to his blue hibiscus-print swimming shorts, and Luca followed suit, peeling his top off with slightly less gusto. Underneath, he was every inch the athlete, all toned, well-built muscles and tanned, smooth skin.

Hazel realized that she was staring. She tore her eyes away, cheeks flushing hotly, and focused on pulling on her wet suit as the boys put on theirs without meeting anyone's eyes. By the time she was suited up and had struggled into her flippers, Hunter was already in the water, using his strong legs to swim away from the boat in just a few easy strokes. Then he was swimming downward under the surface until she could just see the spout of his snorkel. Luca waited until she was ready and then he helped her put on her goggles.

"Okay?"

"I'm nervous."

He squeezed her shoulder. "You'll be fine. All you have to do is climb in."

He tossed the ladder over the side of the boat, and Hazel listened to his snorkel instructions as he guided her into the water, which felt refreshingly cool even through the thick material of the suit. Once she was submerged, he jumped in too, right over her head, and then turned back to grin at her. "I'll see you in a bit," he said, holding his mouthpiece ready. "Prepare to be amazed."

By the time Hazel had her own snorkel sorted and had gotten used to using it to breathe under the water, Hunter and Luca were nowhere to be seen. She found it was, strangely, a relief. This was new to her; this was something completely out of the ordinary, and knowing how comfortable they were out there in the water was a little unnerving. Hazel forced herself to stop thinking about it, about *anything*, and just put her head under the water to really look at what was down there.

If they'd left one world behind by coming out into the middle of nowhere on the big wide ocean, Hazel found a whole new one below the waves. The sun cut through the glassy surface and shone in beams of golden light through the water. She could see the seabed, but it wasn't the sort of floor she'd imagined, not just sand or pebbles—it was alive, an explosion of colors and shapes.

There was coral everywhere, some vivid orange and piled high so that it was within arm's reach, some pale pink and lying low, tendrils swaying slightly through the surprisingly shallow water. There were clams so large it would be impossible to pick one up, and flamboyant blue starfish dotted around, clinging to rocks with their pointed arms.

There were fish too, fish everywhere—halfway between her and the floor was a shoal of tiny silver ones, sparkling and glittering as they darted from side to side, in and out of the coral. Hazel could see bigger fish as well, types she had never imagined actually existed outside of movies, all bright and moving slowly and nonchalantly, as if they weren't fazed at all by the fact she was there.

It was surreal and utterly wonderful, and as time passed she let herself relax completely, just floating in the water. It was beautiful, serene, and . . . *What the hell was that?*

Hazel went rigid, every inch of her body frozen in fear. Directly below her, gliding out menacingly from under a rock, was a creature with a dark and thick but somehow still streamlined body, a broad round snout, and large silvery eyes. Fully emerged from the rock, it was huge—its fins seemed to slice through the water. A shark. It was so close she knew she'd only have to stretch slightly to touch it. It turned to look at her, and Hazel screamed on instinct. Her snorkel fell out and her mouth filled with bitter salt water. She shot her head up above the water, choking and calling out for the boys.

Luca appeared in an instant, and as soon as Hazel saw him, she burst into tears, still gasping for air.

"Shit," he hissed, propelling himself toward her, tearing off his own mask as he went. Hazel let him pull her against his chest, burying her face in his shoulder.

"Hey, it's okay," he soothed. "It's all right, Hazel. I've got you."

Hunter appeared in the water beside him. "What the hell happened?" he asked Luca.

Hazel felt Luca shake his head, treading water to keep them both afloat. She wanted to warn them about the shark, to let them know the danger they were all in, but she couldn't speak. "I don't know. I just heard her calling my name."

"Yeah. Me too."

"I think we should get her back on the boat."

"Good idea," Hunter agreed.

"Hazel, we're gonna move, okay?"

She nodded. Getting out of the water sounded like the best idea in the world. Hunter climbed the ladder first so he could be at the top to pull her up if she needed help, but she managed it on her own. Luca followed behind, and once on deck he took a towel and wrapped it around her, sitting beside her on the bench. Hunter handed her a bottle of water, which she took gratefully.

"Hazel," Luca asked then, after giving her a minute to collect herself, "what happened?"

"I saw a . . . a *shark*."

Hunter burst into laughter before he could stop himself. "Are you *serious*?" he spluttered. "All that for a shark?"

Luca glared at him and then turned back to Hazel. "Ignore him. It's fine. How big was it?"

"Big."

"Thirty centimeters?" Hunter asked, holding his hands apart. "Half a meter?"

"No, I—I don't know. At least a meter, probably more?"

This wiped the smirk off Hunter's face. "It can't have been."

"Well, it was." She looked at Luca, and Luca nodded back. *I believe you.* "It was wide, really wide, and it had a white tip on its fin, the big one on its back."

"That's the dorsal fin," Hunter said absentmindedly, his face creased with concentration now. "Luca, you know what that sounds like, right?"

". . . No?"

"*Carcharhinus amblyrhynchos*," he told them proudly. "Or, grey reef shark. It's really rare to see one, especially here."

"Are they dangerous?" she asked.

"Reef sharks generally aren't. But I *have* heard they can get extremely aggressive when they feel threatened. They're supposed to have this incredible threat display. I guess you got lucky."

"I guess I did," she agreed, but somehow she didn't feel it.

"Are you okay now?" Luca asked her, and she forced a smile.

"I'm fine."

"Maybe this was a bad idea. Do you want me to take you home? We can eat the picnic onshore if you don't feel like—"

"I want to stay," Hazel said firmly. Luca didn't look convinced, but she just smiled at him again, this one not forced.

"Okay," he said after a moment, smiling back. "Good."

That night on the beach, Red laughed without stopping for a solid five minutes when he caught sight of her heading across the sand toward him.

"Is this about the shark?" she said when the chuckles finally ceased.

"I'm sorry. But only you would come face-to-face with a shark the first time you go into the ocean."

"It's really not funny," she said. "I was terrified!"

He managed to compose himself. "Yeah, Luca did say that, actually. I think he was worried about you."

"He worries too much."

"I think it's nice for him to be stressing over someone else for once. So what did Graham think about you finally seeing the reef?"

"He was pretty happy about it. He wants us to go out together sometime."

Red was quiet for a moment, studying her closely. "He really likes having you around, huh?"

Hazel's chest tightened. "He likes having *someone* around. He was lonely—it's not personal."

"You don't really believe that, do you?"

She hung her head. She didn't know what to believe anymore. Everything she ever thought she'd understood about having a dad—or *not* having one—had been turned on its head these past few months. Things with Graham were . . . complicated, and the longer she stayed in Port Sheridan, the more complicated they became. Now her feelings about him had gotten tangled up with her feelings about going home to England, and with the weight of her grief, and the pain of missing her mum too, and she didn't know how to separate them anymore. Didn't even know if she should.

"I don't know," she admitted.

"You're his *daughter.*"

"That doesn't mean anything," she said. "Being family isn't something you get automatic rights to—you have to earn it. It's about choice. And he didn't choose me."

Red's face fell. "Hazel . . ."

"Well, it's *true*, isn't it? He chose not to be a part of my life, like he chose to let a child take care of the woman he was supposed to love. That was his decision. And I'm not going to forget that after a few months. I never had a dad, and I don't need one now just because I've got no one else."

Red looked at her, concerned, and Hazel took a shaky breath and exhaled slowly. There were tears in her eyes, threatening to spill, and a lump in her throat. That first day in the lawyer's office in London, she'd hated Graham so much that she'd felt sick with it; hated him for all the years of her life he had missed, for all the moments he hadn't been there for, for all she had had to go through alone. As she'd gotten to know him, that hatred had lessened and faded, but it didn't make things any easier. Hating him was something she was used to—she'd resented him for his absence all her life—but caring about him was not.

"He loves you," Red said finally. "Unconditionally. That much is clear as day to everyone. He loves you today, he'll love you tomorrow, and he'll love you every single day after that too, for the rest of his life. And I know it doesn't change anything, but I'm sure that he's loved you *all* these years, even if he wasn't around."

Hazel didn't know what to say, but she thought he was right. Graham was family. He always had been and always would be. It wasn't his fault he was all Hazel had left.

"He loves you," Red repeated, squeezing her hand, and Hazel finally let herself nod in agreement.

33

HAZEL SPENT THE NEXT FEW DAYS MULLING over her conversation with Red, thinking about what he'd said about Graham loving her unconditionally the way only family could. She knew she owed Graham the same courtesy, and it was about time she started making an effort.

On Wednesday, he'd worked the daytime shift, so he was there at the house when she got back from school, doing paperwork in his office. He looked up in surprise when he caught sight of her standing in the doorway.

"Everything okay? How was school?"

"It was fine, thanks!"

He set down his pen. "What can I do for you, then? These can wait until tomorrow if you need me for anything."

"No, it's nothing like that," she said. "I was just . . . I was wondering if maybe we could sit together in the kitchen at dinner tonight? So we can talk and catch up and stuff?"

"I think that's a lovely idea, Hazel, but I'm not sure there's enough food on hand to make a proper meal."

That was a very good point. Graham had taken to leaving out cash on the counter in the kitchen for Hazel to buy groceries with when they ran out of fresh fruit and other basics, but she hadn't been to the store in a couple of days, and they were running low on pretty much everything.

"I think we have bread?" she said. "And maybe three eggs?"

"Do we have any cheese?"

"Only those orange burger slices."

He pushed himself away from the desk and stood up from his chair. "You know what? I think I can rustle something up out of that."

"On second thought, let's just get takeout," she teased.

Graham turned to look at her, amused. "I'm sorry, is my world-famous grilled cheese not good enough for you?"

"I'm just saying—a fresh meal at home every once in a while wouldn't kill either of us."

Graham broke into a huge, goofy grin.

"What?" she said warily. "What did I do?"

"You said *at home*."

"So?"

"So it's the first time you haven't called it just a house. You called it a home. Like it's *your* home."

Hazel felt the blood rushing to her cheeks and she knew she must be flushing a deep red. "I'm sorry, it was a slip of the tongue. I wasn't thinking."

"Please don't apologize," Graham said. "I like hearing it."

She didn't say anything; she couldn't. Suddenly, there was a lump in her throat, one she couldn't swallow. It was true, what he'd said. All this time she'd refused to look at Graham's house as anything other than a halfway house, a place where she could gather herself back together before continuing onward. But there had been no continuing, no moving on, and she supposed it made sense that somewhere along the way she'd started looking at that stupid big white house as a home. It made sense, it really did, it was totally logical—so why had it come as such a shock to her?

"Look," he said then. "Maybe I can't cook anything decent with those ingredients—but I *do* happen to know a place where every chef learned their five-star skills from me."

"To the Anchor?" said Hazel.

"To the Anchor," he agreed.

Half an hour later, the two of them were walking wordlessly along the beachfront, the bright lights of the restaurant glowing before them. It was funny—coming here felt completely different with Graham than it did with her friends. With him there she didn't just think of it as a restaurant; it was his baby, his pride and joy, the one thing in his life he'd truly loved and nurtured.

"You never told me the story of how you got this place," Hazel said to him once they'd taken their seats.

Graham looked surprised. "You really want to know?"

"Of course. This place means a lot to you." *And you mean a lot to me*, she finished silently.

"Okay, well, let's see. I opened the Anchor when I was twenty-four. I'd dreamed of having my own restaurant since I was a little kid, so when it finally happened it felt like a miracle. At first, business was tough, because I was new and young and people doubted I'd be any good. Months went past where I was so close to throwing in the towel and becoming an engineer or something, but I stuck at it, and eventually people started to realize that for someone so young and so new, I was actually a pretty awesome chef."

A waitress, who Graham introduced to Hazel as Arisha, stopped by the table with some water and the menus, which neither of them had to look at before they ordered their food. Once the waitress had gone, they talked some more, Hazel shooting off any random questions about the restaurant that entered her head, and Graham answering them.

When their food arrived, Hazel asked Graham if Claire was working tonight. He nodded. "Yep. We'll pop into the kitchen afterward and say hello if you like."

"She's a pretty good chef too, huh?"

"One of the best. Which is why I'm so interested in making her my business partner."

It took a moment for the implications of what Graham had said to sink in, but when it did Hazel's mouth fell open. "Wait, you want her to *co-own* the Anchor?"

"I do, yes. Why do you sound so surprised?"

"I thought this restaurant was your baby?" She frowned.

"Oh, it is!" he said earnestly. "But babies grow up into bigger things. I've had a handful of offers to expand the Anchor into a chain. They've wanted one up in Tamoya Bay for a couple of years, but I just don't have the time. With Claire, though . . ."

"And she hasn't said yes? Why not?"

"Luca," he said, and then shrugged. "She doesn't want to sign up to something so huge until she knows that Luca's going to be okay."

"But he's been getting better," Hazel pointed out.

"He certainly has. Every time I bring it up lately, she seems more and more interested. I don't want to push it, but I just wish she knew how perfect she would be. I mean, this is a good thing I've got here, isn't it?"

Hazel looked around the restaurant, feeling suddenly overwhelmed with pride. "Yeah," she breathed. "It's a really good thing."

"You have no idea how much it means to hear that from you," he said. "And you know if you ever want a job, there'll be a place for you here, right?"

Hazel laughed him off. "I'll bear that in mind."

"I'm serious," he said. "You and Red could work some shifts over summer vacation if you'd like."

She considered it carefully, tried to picture her and Red pulling long shifts together. "That would be . . . fun."

"How are things going there, anyway?"

Hazel's eyebrows shot up. "Oh, no, Red and I aren't—"

"I know," Graham said with a smile. "You're not exactly his type, I hear."

"Not exactly," she agreed.

"Besides, I've seen the way you look at each other—you and Red are more than friends, you're family. And that's just as important."

"But boundaries do get blurred, don't they?" Hazel asked, and she wasn't talking about Red anymore. "Sometimes? Between friendship and . . . something more?"

"Of course." Graham nodded. "*All* the time."

"How can you tell? That things have shifted? That you've crossed over from being friends to being something else?"

"You'd feel it when you looked at them." He placed his palm flat against his chest. "In here."

"Oh God."

"I'm serious. Falling for someone is . . . is all somersaults and cold sweats and bolting upright in the middle of the night because you want to be asleep, but you can't think of anything else but them."

"Sounds all-consuming."

"It is. But it's beautiful. And you won't stop smiling. That's the best thing; that's how everyone around you will be able to notice it. You'll be doing something completely stupid like washing dishes or checking your e-mails and you won't be able to take this silly smile off your face."

Graham was smiling now just thinking about it. Hazel knew without a doubt he'd felt it all before, felt the all-consuming and beautiful feeling of falling in love—but that wasn't something she wanted to think about right now.

When the two of them had finished their meal, they headed to the kitchen to say hello to Claire. She hugged Hazel tightly and gave her a quick tour of the kitchen.

"All good?" Graham said as they walked back out onto the beach.

"All good." She nodded. "But I was thinking—not that the meal wasn't delicious, because it totally was, and takeout is fine sometimes too—that maybe I could start cooking at home? I know the last thing you want to do after a long day of cooking is more cooking."

"You really want to cook?"

"I really want to try," she corrected him. "I'm not very good, but that's okay, right? Seeing as I've got a pretty amazing teacher."

Graham just smiled down at her, those fine lines reappearing around his green eyes. "Come on," he said. "It's been a busy day. Let's get you home."

This time Hazel didn't balk at the phrase. As she followed him across the sand and back toward the car, she even let herself consider for the first time the possibility that she could have *two* homes, somehow. Her real home, back in England, and her new home, here.

Could that really happen?

34

THE FUNNY THING ABOUT TRAINING WITH
Luca was that the closer they drew to his goal, the more on
edge he became. When they'd first started training months
back, twelve minutes had seemed like an impossible goal. Now
that they were probably only a few weeks away from making it
a reality, the stakes were suddenly raised.

"Redleigh thinks I should look at joining a track team,"
Luca said after their session on Thursday night. He'd been un-
usually quiet for the whole hour and a half, and Hazel was
glad he was talking now—especially about this. "Get into competitive running again."

"Yeah? Are you going to do it?"

"I don't know," he admitted. "I've been thinking about it

myself for a while, though. I think subconsciously this training was always about racing."

"You wanted to give yourself the choice to go back," she said gently. "It makes sense."

"Does it? The thought of competing without him still makes me feel sick."

She studied his face. "Luca, just because something scares us doesn't mean we shouldn't do it. If anything, it means we *should*. It scares you because it means something, and that's good—it means you care."

Luca held her gaze, uncertain, and then swallowed hard. "Yeah," he said, nodding. "Yeah, I know."

"Just don't underestimate yourself, all right? If you want to join a team, join a team, and if you don't, don't. But don't hold back because you're afraid of moving on. You have the choice, and that's what counts. It's up to you. You can do anything you want."

He didn't answer. The two of them walked on in silence. It was a lovely night out, not too cool and not too warm, the stars in the sky particularly bright. Hazel could feel Luca's eyes on her as she tilted her head up to look at the stars as she walked.

"We are all made of stardust," he said suddenly. "Did you know that? I read that somewhere—that everything we are, everything we know is made from the ashes of decayed stars. All we are is the remnants of explosions that happened a billion years ago."

Hazel said nothing, just kept walking.

"Stardust," Luca said again, after a while. "A whole galaxy destroyed so we could exist. Where's the sense in that? Entire solar systems dead so that *we* can live, and for what? For us to just die too?"

"Everyone dies eventually, Luca."

"Yeah," he said lightly. "But most of us get the chance to live first."

Hazel knew he was still thinking about Ryan, and that was fine. He was allowed to feel down and angry sometimes. He *should* feel down and angry sometimes; God knew she did. It was all part of the healing process.

"Hey," she said, slowing to a stop on the pavement. "Do you know *how* they know we're made of stardust?"

Luca stopped too. "No, how?"

"Because both us and the stars are made up of the same elements. Carbon and oxygen and nitrogen, things like that. The elements are recycled the same way water is. It's not some romantic notion about the circle of life. It's just science."

"So?" he said.

"So instead of looking at it as destruction, why don't you look at it as *creation*? Focus on the fact that when we die, we're reborn as stars. Everything we've been and everything we've known is shaped back into galaxies and constellations and supernovas. *That's* a nicer thought, isn't it?"

Luca just stared at her, brown eyes a little wide. "Yeah," he said finally, as they started walking again. "That's a much nicer thought."

* * *

As the summer vacation drew closer, so did Red's deadline for Hodgkins's assignment. He'd made really good progress and he was happy with how it was coming together, but he was still nervous as he waited for his final tutorial with his teacher before he handed the project in on Friday afternoon.

"Redleigh, come on in," Hodgkins said when he arrived, ushering Red into his office. They sat opposite each other at his desk, and Hodgkins found Red's portfolio from the stack on the floor. He stared at it for a moment, expression unreadable, and then raised his head to look at him.

"Well," he said, handing it over to Red. "Where do I start? It's like looking at a completely different project. I'm really impressed."

Red looked down at his folder and then back up at Hodgkins. "Really?"

"Don't sound so surprised. You show a lot of maturity in your work, and there's a lovely balance in there between the candid photographs and portraits. Your captions are carefully thought-out and elicit a powerful response, and with a bit of tweaking, your presentation and composition will both be excellent—you've captured your family beautifully."

"I . . . thanks."

"Have you thought about submitting any of these photos for the end-of-year competition?"

"Oh, no, that's not—"

"Redleigh," Hodgkins cut him off firmly. "You should. You really should."

Red blinked. "Okay."

Hodgkins reached into his desk and pulled a flyer out of the top drawer. "The winning photographs will be displayed in the gallery by the pier. It's a great opportunity to get some exposure for your work, and it will look good on your CV when you apply to university."

The thought of his photos getting exposure—the thought of anyone outside of his immediate family and friends seeing them at all—both terrified and exhilarated him. University too. He'd always had some vague dream of going on to study art full-time, pursuing it as a real career, but it had never been a concrete plan. While all his classmates had spent this year thinking about college, Red had spent it thinking about Luca. For a long time, it hadn't seemed like Luca was going to go to college—he didn't give enough of a shit about his future to start planning for it—which meant that Red hadn't thought about going either. He was staying wherever Luca was staying because they were twins and that's what twins did: stayed for each other.

If you stay, I stay. If you go, I go.

And Red had always been fine with that, with sidelining his plans and his dreams and his *everything* to be there for his brother, because that was what he had needed to do for the family to survive.

Not anymore, though.

Luca was running again—and Red wasn't so naïve as to

think that it was going to fix everything, or even *anything*, but it was a start. It was Luca choosing, finally, to draw a line between his past and his future and move on. It was Luca choosing hope.

And if Luca could think about his future again, then maybe Red could too. Maybe Red could submit his photographs to Hodgkins's competition. Maybe he could show people his artwork. Maybe he could apply to art school and start a new adventure in a new city, safe in the knowledge that his brother would survive just fine if he did.

"I'll look into it," he promised, and Hodgkins handed him the flyer like he'd known all along that he would.

35

WHEN HAZEL JOLTED AWAKE EARLY SATURDAY
morning, the room was still dark, and the air was so muggy it
pressed down on her chest. Even the light breeze coming in
through the window didn't touch the heat.

Her sheets were pooled around her feet at the end of the
bed, and she was damp with sweat. So *this* was what sum-
mertime in Australia felt like. She willed herself to lie back
against the pillow, wondering how she was going to survive
another three months of this oppressive humidity.

There was a sudden knock at the balcony window, followed
immediately by three more in quick succession. Hazel started
in surprise and looked at her clock. It was four thirty in the
morning—who could be at her window at this hour? She

climbed out of bed and tiptoed across the room, carefully pulling back the corner of the curtain.

"Christ," she muttered, letting the curtain fall back into place. She unlocked the balcony door and pulled it open. "Hey, Luca."

"Wow." He whistled, stepping over the threshold and into her room. "You look . . ."

"A mess?" she offered.

"I was going to say hot."

"Thanks," she said, closing the door after him. "What are you doing on my balcony in the middle of the night?"

She peered out the window—it was pretty high up, far too high to warrant climbing. "Which was completely idiotic, by the way. You could've gotten hurt."

"Well, I could hardly ring the doorbell, could I?"

"This couldn't have waited until the morning?"

"Nope," he said firmly. "Can't you feel it?"

"Feel what?" she grumbled, tugging at the neck of her pajama top in a futile attempt to cool herself down a little.

"The heat." He grinned. "Are you ready?"

Hazel knew she should kick him out and crawl back into bed, but truthfully she was curious. Whatever it was Luca was taking her to see had to be pretty amazing to warrant him waking her up at this hour.

"All right." She sighed. "What do I need to wear?"

"Something you don't mind getting wet. And a change of clothes, and possibly a towel."

Hazel narrowed her eyes at him, but grabbed yesterday's swimsuit and beach dress from the back of the chair and took them with her into the bathroom to change, ordering Luca not to touch anything while she was gone. Once she was decent, she found some clean clothes and a spare towel from the bottom of the dresser and stuffed them into a bag. "Okay, I'm ready."

"Let's go. We've got to be quick." He went to open the balcony door again, and Hazel yanked him backward.

"Luca, for God's sake!" she hissed. "We can take the front door. Don't be an idiot."

"Yes, Coach." He smirked.

Ten minutes later, the two of them arrived on their bikes at the sandy bank of a lake. Outside, the air was even thicker and heavier, if that was possible, which had made cycling there uncomfortable. It was utterly silent too, as if the wildlife was having trouble breathing as well.

"Okay," Hazel said, eyeing the tiny rowboat floating on the water in front of them, which Luca was in the process of untying from the jetty. "Whose boat is this?"

"Don't worry, we're not stealing it," Luca said. "It's our next-door neighbor's. He lets Redleigh and me borrow it whenever we want. Come on then, hop in."

She used his shoulder to balance as she climbed inside and took a seat at one end of the rowboat. Luca tossed the rope onto the bottom and stepped in too, taking the seat opposite her.

He stowed their spare clothes safely underneath the bench, and then picked up the oars and began rowing away from shore in quick, powerful strokes.

"Wow," Hazel said. "Are we in a rush or something?"

"Yes, actually."

"An adventure! How *exciting*!"

Luca rolled his eyes. "Why don't you talk me through the constellations while I row?"

"Fine." She laughed, turning her gaze to the sky. "Okay, there's . . . Wait. I can't see any."

"No?"

"Nope. The whole sky's black."

"It's cloud," Luca said smugly.

"Cloud?"

"The darkness," he explained, rowing faster. "The whole sky is full of clouds."

"*What?*"

"I told you it would be coming, didn't I?"

"Told me what would be coming?"

"The first storm of the wet season," he said, and just then a drop of rain landed on her cheek.

"Luca?" she said uncertainly, and he slowed to a stop, resting the oars on the floor of the boat. "Should I be scared?"

"No, Hazel. I'm right here."

He took hold of her hand and held it tight, and they didn't say anything else as the rain began to fall, big fat drops of water plummeting from the dark sky. The rain became heavier, coming down in sheets and waves, and within minutes they were drenched to the bone. "Luca!" Hazel shouted over the noise of the rain drumming against the surface of the lake. "It's warm! The rain's *warm*!"

"I told you it was different!" The rain was falling so fast now that Hazel had to keep blinking just to be able to see. When Luca had said that the rain in Queensland was nothing like the rain in Sydney or England, she'd thought he was exaggerating. She'd never expected *this*. Suddenly, somewhere in the distance, a flash of silvery-white light forked through the black sky, leaving a purple smear across the horizon. It was followed a few moments later by the low growl of thunder.

"Should we be on the water?" she yelled at him.

"It's fine!" he answered. "I've been out here in storms before, and the lightning never comes this far over!"

Another fork of brilliant white light, another clap of thunder. "Luca, it's getting closer!"

"Hazel! I won't let you get hurt, I promise!"

The raindrops ran down their cheeks like tears, but they weren't crying, they were *laughing*. Both of them, in a tiny boat in the middle of a lake, laughing and laughing. The sky flashed again, and this time the thunder followed immediately, the rain still pounding relentlessly down. The lake around them was alive, dancing and shimmering as the drops beat the surface.

"Scream!" Luca said then, leaning across the boat so his face was inches from hers.

"Scream?"

"Scared someone will hear you?"

"No!" she said, throwing her head back and letting out the loudest, longest scream she could manage. Then Luca did the same, letting himself go entirely and bellowing up at the angry sky. It felt incredible, releasing so many pent-up emotions with no one around to witness it but each other, safe in the knowledge that they were the last people on earth who would judge.

By the time the rain finally began to stop, Hazel was exhausted—exhausted, but completely and utterly calm. As the drizzle faded to nothing, she and Luca sat and watched the sky turn hues of pink, crimson, and orange with the sunrise, watched the last of the clouds lighten and disappear entirely.

"Well," Luca said finally.

"Well."

He leaned over, wiping her cheek gently with his thumb. "You're a little bit wet, Hazel."

She glanced down at her sodden beach dress and grinned. "I should probably get changed."

"Right." He studied her closely for a moment, then picked up the oars and began to row as if nothing had happened since he put them down. "Good morning, anyhow."

"Good morning." She beamed.

"I don't know about you, but I'm starving," he said. "How does a hot breakfast sound?"

"It sounds perfect."

BY THE TIME THEY ARRIVED AT THE CAWLEYS'
house, the rest of the family was awake. Claire sent Marc off
to the store to pick up some fresh strawberries and began preparing the biggest breakfast Hazel had ever seen, while she
and Luca sat at the counter and Red paced around the kitchen
sipping on a smoothie.

"Let me get this straight," Red said. "You took Hazel out
on Mr. Langley's boat to the middle of the lake during a thunderstorm?"

"Yep."

"And how do you feel about this, Hazel? That he recklessly
risked your life for an adrenaline rush?"

"A, I would never risk anyone's life," Luca said. "B, you
know just as well as I do that the lightning never usually

reaches the lake, and C, why don't you just shut your mouth for once?"

"Did you hear that, Mum? He told me to shut my mouth."

Claire turned around from the oven. "Luca," she said wearily. "Please don't tell your brother to shut his mouth, it's not polite. Redleigh, please stop winding things up."

"But *everyone* knows you should avoid water in a thunderstorm," Red pointed out. "So what he did was dangerous."

"Actually," Claire conceded, "it *was*, Luca. Please don't do it again."

"Christ. I won't."

"So Luca," Red asked then. "Are you, like, a legitimate storm chaser now? Is that going to be your new hobby? Chasing thunderstorms and purposely trying to get people hit by lightning?"

"I wasn't trying to—"

"Maybe next time you could take Hazel out on a boat at Port Douglas," he suggested. "Isn't that where they get the most cyclones?" He turned to Hazel, his brown eyes impossibly bright. "Oh, Hazel, you'll just *love* cyclones. They're so big and bad and dangerous . . ."

Luca stood up angrily off his stool. "If you don't shut up, I'll—"

"Mum! Quick, where's the stress ball?"

"Don't *push* me," Luca growled.

"Oh, here it is." Red plucked a green ball out of the fruit

bowl and threw it to Luca who, naturally, caught it perfectly. "Luca's little gift from our tactful father. See, apparently Luca suffers from anger problems."

"I swear to God, I will knock your skinny little ass out," Luca warned.

"Now, now," Red said. "Don't get angry. Squeeze the stress ball."

"If you don't shut up about this fuc—"

"Language!" Claire snapped.

"Sorry," Luca said, throwing the ball as hard as he could at Red's face. Red let out an indignant squawk and ducked just a moment too late, but even with a red welt on his forehead, he was still grinning.

"Stop messing around, Redleigh, and set the table, please. Luca, you can sort out drinks for everyone."

"Is there anything I can do, Claire?" Hazel asked.

"No, no. You just sit tight, young lady, and let the boys run around for you."

Hazel settled back to watch Red and Luca bicker their way through their chores.

Marc returned from his trip to the store, and the five of them sat around the kitchen table and ate together. After filling Marc in on the storm debacle, Red started talking about a discussion he'd had with one of his counselors at school about his plans for when he graduated next year. He and Claire discussed it for a few minutes before Marc turned the conversation around to Hazel.

"What about you, Hazel?" he asked her. "What are your plans? Will you work with your dad, or will you go to college instead and study something else? And will you go out of state?"

Hazel just stared at him, hands balled into fists on her lap. She didn't know how to answer. She could feel Red and Luca watching her, feel their eyes boring into her head.

"Because I know we've got some decent enough local universities here," Marc continued, oblivious, "but places like Deakin or Macquarie are really great if you don't mind being a bit farther from home. You know what I mean?"

Hazel opened her mouth and then clamped it shut again, standing abruptly. "I'm sorry, I need some air," she said, and walked out of the room.

Relax, Hazel told herself as she sat on the stairs of the veranda outside, but Marc's words kept repeating themselves over and over in her head. *Will you go out of state? Will you go out of state? Will you go—*

—No, she thought. *I can't.*

She couldn't think about that. She couldn't think about a future here, not with how she'd left things in England. When she had first arrived, she was desperate for that call; she was constantly checking in with Graham to hear if he'd had any updates about when she could go back. But then a month passed, then two, then more, and the call didn't come—and the worst thing was that there was a part of her that was *glad*. A part that wanted the call to wait just a little longer so that she could have just a few weeks more in Australia before she had to leave. It wasn't that she didn't want to go—she was just terrified that the moment she left Port Sheridan, she would go right back to being the girl she was when she left England all those months ago. Hazel didn't like that girl. She didn't like how unhappy she was. She didn't like what that girl had to go through.

At the sound of the back door opening, Hazel jerked around. Marc was standing in the doorway, looking across the veranda at her with concern.

"Everything okay?" he said.

"Yes. Sorry. Everything's fine, thanks."

He shut the door behind him and came to sit down beside her on the deck.

"Did Claire ever tell you how we met your dad?" he asked after a few minutes, and Hazel shook her head. "We were in the same year at Finchwood, but we didn't get to know one another until we were in our senior year. All three of us got roped into helping with a drama production, and we just clicked. Nothing really changed when we graduated, even when we all went our separate ways—I went off to college downstate, and Claire and your dad both went to cooking school. Even with our hectic schedules we still found the time to keep in touch. Then we all got jobs, and Claire and I got married, and then that's when your mum showed up."

You look just like her, Marc had said the first time they met. Hazel had assumed he'd seen photographs of her mother and that was how he had recognized the resemblance; she had no idea that he and Claire had actually *met* her. Hazel found herself leaning forward, listening closely, desperate to hear this side of the story.

"I was out of town when the two of them first met, but when I came back a few weeks later, he was absolutely smitten. From the first time I met her, I knew just how badly he'd fallen. I don't know how, since your dad was ever so coy about the whole thing, but I knew."

"Did you like her?"

"*Like* her?" he echoed, and then he laughed, a warm, booming sound that seemed to come from deep in his chest. "Oh, sweetheart. Of course I did. We all did. We all totally loved her to pieces. She was just that kind of person, you know? This little ray of absolute sunshine."

Hazel smiled at that, because it was good to hear—even if it wasn't exactly how she thought of her now.

"You really are her spitting image," Marc added thoughtfully, and Hazel knew his words weren't supposed to be insensitive. Just honest. "It's funny, isn't it? Everything coming full circle like this. Us coming back home. And you and the twins too . . . It's just funny."

And it *was* funny, really, but she also couldn't help but find some comfort in it too. Marc knew her mother. He knew her back when she was young and healthy. He knew her when she

274

was still the woman Hazel now struggled to remember. He knew her when all she did was smile and laugh and fall in love and make new friends and just *live*.

As she and Marc went back inside the house to finish up breakfast, Hazel thought to herself not for the first time how she would give anything and everything to have that version of her mother back. Even just for a day or a minute.

Even just for long enough to tell her that she missed her.

Dear Mum,

I remember the time I had my tonsils out. I was in hospital overnight, and I was put in a room without a spare bed for visitors. I was old enough for you to leave me and go to sleep back at the apartment, but you didn't. You went to sleep in the creaky wooden chair in the corner with your coat as a blanket. It can't have been comfortable, but you didn't once complain.

In the middle of the night, I woke up in pain. You awoke wordlessly and slid into the bed beside me, curling your body around mine. There in your arms, I fell back to sleep.

You always knew how to make me feel better, Mum. I just wish I'd learned to do the same for you before it was too late.

I miss you, Mum, but I remember.

Love,
Hazel

37

LATER THAT AFTERNOON, HAZEL, RED, AND
Luca left the Cawleys' and went to meet Maddie and Hunter
on the beach outside Graham's house. Red had been going on
for weeks about camping out together for the night, and after
much protestation about the possibility of another storm and
the sand and the insects, everyone had relented.

They'd come prepared with bundles full of food, drinks,
and sleeping bags, and as soon as they'd decided on the right
place to camp, the boys set about lighting a campfire while
Maddie and Hazel organized all their supplies neatly to one
side. Once everything was assembled, the five of them sat
down around the fire to watch the sun sink beneath the line of
the horizon.

It was a great night, filled with chatter and laughter and

stories. They managed to stay up past midnight, eating s'mores and sharing bottles of beer. Maddie fell asleep first, nestled into Hunter's side, and—careful not to wake her—he wrapped a sleeping bag around her and pressed a kiss to the top of her head.

"What?" he said when he looked up and saw everyone watching him. "I was just tucking her in."

Red lifted up his camera from around his neck. "Do you think she'd mind if I . . . ?"

"Go ahead," Hunter said.

He snapped a few shots of her sleeping peacefully, before turning the camera on Hunter, who protested and shielded his face. "It's like being stalked by the paparazzi when you're around, you know."

"Sorry," Red said, sounding not very sorry at all. "It's for something I'm working on."

"What is it? A project on future athletic superstars?"

"Nah. It's a collection of photographs of people who look like dogs."

Hunter narrowed his eyes at him, and Red winked, snapping a couple more shots. He started taking photos of the others too, their faces glowing orange from the flames of the fire.

"Hey," he said then, lowering his camera and turning to Hazel. "Maybe we could print all these out for you before you go back. Then you could have them to pin up on your wall when you get home to remember us by."

In that moment the thought of leaving made her chest ache,

but Hazel just smiled. "That'd be good. Not that I'll ever be able to forget any of you."

They didn't talk much after that, each of them listening to the crackling of flames from the campfire instead. Hazel looked around, letting her eyes settle on her friends one by one. Red—the first person in this country to truly make her feel at home, even before Graham. Hunter—funny and charming and endlessly positive. And Maddie—fiercely loyal and so hardworking and caring.

Hazel looked across the campfire to where Luca was sitting, his head turned to the side slightly as he looked out to sea. Luca was the most surprising of them all. When Hazel first met him in the Cawleys' sunny kitchen, she never would've imagined they'd end up on talking terms, let alone here, like this.

"Take a picture," Red murmured from her other side, and she started, turning to face him.

"What? I wasn't—" she began, her cheeks flushed, but he just smiled at her.

It wasn't long before Hunter fell asleep too, his head resting on top of Maddie's. Red followed suit soon after, wrapped up tight in a sleeping bag, and then it was just Hazel and Luca.

"This is nice," Luca said quietly, after a while. "I've never really done this before."

"What, camped out?"

He shook his head. "Had a whole group of friends. It used to always just be Ryan and me."

"I never really did either," Hazel said.

"Because you just had one best friend?"

"Because I didn't really have *any* friends. It was my own fault. I just . . . I was so busy looking after Mum. Someone had to be there for her basically 24/7, and we didn't have anyone else, so . . ."

"You have us, now."

"I know," she said softly.

They were quiet for a moment. Hazel wondered if Luca was thinking back to the years he'd spent with Ryan in Sydney the same way she was thinking about the years in London with her mum. She'd always known she was lonely there, but it hadn't really hit her just *how* lonely she'd been until she found herself here, with more friends than she ever could have hoped for.

"He'd have loved this," Luca said then. "He loved camping out and building fires and getting his hands dirty. And he *really* would've loved you guys."

"I bet we'd have loved him too. He sounds wonderful."

"He was." Luca smiled, craning his neck to look at the stars above them. "And now he's up there watching over me. Maybe he and your mum have found each other up there. Maybe they're watching over us together."

"Maybe," Hazel agreed, ignoring the wave of nausea that passed through her at his words.

They were quiet after that. Hazel was so tired she could hardly keep her eyes open, but she felt too on edge to go to sleep. Eventually, the flames of the campfire started to dwindle, the wood almost gone, until all that was left was a pile of burning embers that glowed red in the darkness. Hazel stretched out on her sleeping bag, lying beside the remnants of the fire. Luca stayed sitting, sleeping bag wrapped around him, and rubbed his hands together.

"Are you chilly?" she asked. It wasn't at all cold out, but the temperature had definitely dropped in the last hour or so.

"A little."

Hazel scooted over on the sand to make room. "Here, come closer to what's left of the fire."

"Are you sure? I don't want to steal your space."

"Get over here."

Luca stood up, gathering his sleeping bag and making his way carefully around the fire toward her. He lay down next to her. Hazel suddenly realized what she'd been getting wrong this whole time when she'd been so focused on going back to England; home wasn't a country, or a place, or even a person. Home was *this*. Home was wherever you felt happy and comfortable and fulfilled and safe and loved. And if home was here, with Red and Luca and Maddie and Hunter and Graham, then why on earth would she ever want to leave?

"Night, Hazel," Luca said from beside her, cutting off her train of thought.

"Good night, Luca."

There was a pause, a beat where no one spoke.

"I'll miss you when you go," he mumbled then, and when she finally shifted around to face him, he was already asleep.

* * *

Hazel woke to the gentle rush of waves, the distant chatter of seagulls, and the sound of Hunter and Red bickering loudly about breakfast. She gave herself a moment to enjoy the comfort of her sleeping bag and then pulled herself upright. The sun was burning its way through the early-morning wisps of cloud. Luca was still beside her, sitting up, and Maddie was on the other side of the fire ring, both of them watching the squabbling unfold with unbridled amusement.

"What's going on?" Hazel asked.

"Red reckons we should try and catch some fish for breakfast," Luca said. "Says he can catch them with his bare hands from the water." He paused, head tipped to one side as he watched his brother gesticulating wildly. "Christ, he's so full of shit."

"Did you sleep well?" Maddie asked.

"Not too bad," Hazel said. "You?"

"Until Hunter started trying to smother me in his sleep, yeah."

Hunter halted his argument to turn around indignantly. "*Hey!* I was being affectionate!"

"Is that what you call attempted murder now? Being affectionate?"

"What*ever*." He scowled, brandishing the bag of leftover marshmallows as he addressed the others. "What do you guys think, then? S'mores for breakfast?"

Maddie let out a yawn and stretched her arms. "God no. I never want to eat another s'more again."

"Until next time we camp out."

"Yeah. Until then."

"Well, we can't cook anything until we get the fire going again," Red pointed out, kneeling next to the pile of ash and digging around in it to see if there was any coal or wood left. There wasn't. "All right, who's on driftwood duty? Luca?"

"Piss off."

"Fine, we'll all just *starve* to death then . . ."

"There are some rolls in one of the bags that should still be edible," Hazel said. "Or we could just go to the Anchor for brunch. Dad said he'd save us a table."

Red let out a whoop of triumph, and the rest of them murmured their agreement.

"Your dad's officially the best, you know that, right?" Hunter said.

Hazel just smiled down into her lap. "Yeah. I know."

38

IT WAS DURING LUNCHTIME ON THE FOLLOW-
ing Monday, at the beginning of their last week of school, that
Hunter's search for a sports team to join finally came to a close.
He'd been quite positive about exploring running, but although
Luca thought he showed some promise in their lunchtime
practices, Hunter still didn't think it would be enough to ever
actually get him on a team. He'd been surprisingly chipper
about it when he broke the news, and Luca had assumed it
was because he'd already moved on to preparations for his
next sport. It turned out there wasn't going to *be* a next sport.

"What made you decide that?" Luca asked him.

"I guess I realized that I don't need to prove myself to Callum or anyone else, and I don't need to be part of a team to be
proud of myself."

"So you're giving up?" Maddie said.

"I am. Are you angry? That you wasted so much of your time on something that never went anywhere?"

"Hunter," she said. "Time spent with my best friend will never be wasted—and if nothing else, it's been fun! Right, guys?"

"Right," Hazel and Luca agreed in unison, and Hunter's face flooded with relief.

Luca was sitting on the ground at the stadium when Hazel got there on Thursday evening, waiting for her. "Hey, Coach."

"Hey," she said. "Are you ready to go?"

"As ever." He stood up. "What time are we on?"

"Twelve minutes and eleven seconds."

He shook his head slightly. "Christ, that sounds like such a small number, doesn't it? *Just eleven seconds left to go.* But each time it's harder, you know?"

"I know. But it's still totally doable, Luca."

He nodded slowly. "No, I know that. I do. I'm just half-expecting to get down to twelve minutes and one second and then *really* break my leg or something and not be able to run for six months."

She nudged him with her elbow. "Hey. Don't even think about it. Let's just get started, okay? Concentrate on getting rid of a few more seconds tonight, and we'll keep going from there."

Luca aligned himself behind the start line as he always did, and when he was crouched down into a comfortable stance, he fixed his gaze straight ahead, waiting for the command.

"Three. Two. One. *Go.*"

Luca lifted his front foot off the ground on her command and launched himself forward down the track. It took him a moment to get properly into his stride, but then he found the perfect pace and the rest followed naturally. Hazel shouted out his time every time he passed her until he was on the final stretch of his last lap.

When he finally reached her, she was standing up, a funny look on her face. Luca collapsed on the ground by her feet, exhausted. He lay on his back, staring up at the dark sky, his chest heaving as he caught his breath.

"Hey, Luca," she said eventually.

He squinted up at her. "Yeah?"

"You did it."

It took a moment for her words to sink in, but then Luca jolted upright. "*What*? I did it? Are you serious?"

"Yep. Eleven minutes, fifty-seven seconds."

"Christ." Luca was smiling so hard that his face ached. "Hazel, I—I can't even tell you how grateful I am. This meant so much. This is such a milestone and you just . . . well. I couldn't have done it without you."

"Hey," she said, sitting beside him. "I can't take the credit. This was all you."

He sighed happily and lay back down on the ground. He couldn't quite put his finger on what it was, but something felt different—like something had shifted, or a weight had been lifted.

"We should go out for a meal," he murmured after a while. "To celebrate. I owe you a dinner at the very least, to say thank you for all this."

Something unreadable flashed across Hazel's face. "No, it's okay. You don't have to do that."

Luca knew he didn't have to—knew Hazel would never expect anything from him—but that wasn't the point. The point was that he *wanted* to. He wanted to let her know how much the past few months had meant to him, and how much he appreciated her help and support. How much her friendship had changed him. "But Hazel, I—"

"Really." Hazel cut him off, her voice clipped. "You don't owe me anything. You reached your goal, so we're done here. That's all there is to it."

He looked up at her in surprise. "Sorry, what just happened? Did I do something wrong?"

She ignored him. "I need to be getting home."

"Well, can I walk you?" he asked, confused and a little hurt. "I don't think so."

"Hazel, *wait!*" he called after her, but she just turned and hurried away.

Red knew something was wrong when Luca got back from training with Hazel. Lately, Luca had swapped hiding out in his room for joining the rest of his family in the living room to watch some television, but tonight he slammed the front door behind him and went straight up to the garage roof.

Marc and Claire shared a look and then both turned to Red, who nodded.

"I've got it," he said, and left the room, stopping by the kitchen to grab a couple of beers from the fridge. Luca hardly seemed to notice as Red joined him.

"Brought you a beer," he said.

"Thanks."

He waited for Luca to open the can and take a sip. "So what's up? Haven't seen you out here in a while."

"Not a lot."

"Luc."

"It's nothing." He sighed. "I just . . . I think I screwed it up with a girl I might like today."

Red cocked an eyebrow—because of all the things in the world he'd have guessed his brother was upset about, that seemed the most manageable. What a relief. "Yeah? What happened?"

"I asked her if she wanted to grab something to eat and she sort of freaked out."

"I'm sure it wasn't as bad as you think."

"Yeah? She *literally* ran away from me."

"Oh."

Luca shook his head. "It's fine. I wasn't really expecting anything else. I knew she'd never look at me that way."

"Why did you ask then?"

"Because I'm a complete masochist?"

"Maybe she just really had to be somewhere."

Luca let out a snort and took a swig of his beer. "Yeah. Maybe."

Red studied the side of his brother's face for a moment and then looked across the garden to the beach. Sitting up here, he had the most perfect view of the sea—he'd have to come back up one day with his camera and take some pictures.

"You know what?" Luca said eventually. "I think I'm kinda glad she freaked."

"You *are*?"

"We're probably better as friends."

"Cliché."

"*True.* I mean, we're *good* as friends. *Really* good. She's good for me. I don't want to screw that up."

"Going out for a meal with the girl isn't going to screw anything up, Luc. It's just dinner."

"Falling for her would, though, huh?"

"Well. Yeah. That'd probably do it."

"She's just . . . She's *awesome*, you know? She's just the best. She's so funny, and she's smart."

"Cute?"

"Beautiful."

"Accent?"

"I could literally listen to her talk for hours."

"There's definitely something cool about the British, huh?"

Luca froze. "Wait, what?"

Red just shook his head, amused. "I'm not an idiot, Luc."

"I don't know what you're talking about."

"But *I* know who *you're* talking about. Come on. Give me some credit."

"How . . . How did you know?"

"Well," Red said slowly. "When you think no one's looking, you kind of *stare* at her."

"Okay, now you're making me sound like a creep."

"It's *true!*" He laughed. "But not in a weird way. Just—you look at her like she hung the moon, all right? Like she's the only thing in the world you see because she completely eclipses everything else, and nothing and no one will ever come close."

"Shit," Luca said.

Red just grinned at him again. "Yeah."

"I feel like a tool."

"You shouldn't. She's kinda special."

"And you don't think she knows?"

"Positive."

Luca was quiet for a moment. "Do you think it could work, me and her?"

"I think it's worth a try, don't you?"

He stared down at the can in his hands for a long moment and then took a swig. "Yeah," he said finally. "I think it's worth a try."

"You okay?"

Luca nodded. "I think so."

And Red believed him. For the first time in ages, Luca was okay, or he was well on his way to getting there. They'd moved to Port Sheridan to help him survive, and he'd done just that. Survived.

"Look, just don't overthink it, all right?" Red said. He climbed to his feet, patting Luca on the shoulder as he headed to the window. He paused halfway through the frame, turned back to face his twin. "And you're wrong, you know. About her. She does care about you."

"How do you know?"

"You remember all that stuff I said about you looking at her like she hung the moon?"

"What about it?"

"Well," Red said, "when she thinks no one's looking, she looks at you the exact same way."

39

HAZEL DECIDED ON THE BUS TO SCHOOL THE
next day that she was going to save herself the humiliation and
avoid Luca, and by the time she arrived in homeroom she'd
already evaded him a few times, pretending she didn't see him
when she passed him at the school gate and steering clear of
her locker so he couldn't find her.

Luca turned up a few minutes later and tried to catch Hazel's eye, but she ducked her head. When she looked up again,
he'd taken a seat on the other side of the room.

"What was that about?" said Hunter, looking back and
forth between them in confusion. "Are you two fighting, or
what? Lovers' tiff?"

Maddie elbowed him in the side, but she looked concerned
too. "Did something happen? He looks pretty upset."

Hazel shook her head, watching Luca out of the corner of her eye. He was avoiding eye contact, conveniently fascinated by his phone. She felt another hot stab of humiliation in the pit of her stomach, recalling his words from the night before. The way he'd said *I owe you* and *to say thank you*, like all the time they'd spent training together had been part of some business transaction. Just a favor, an obligation.

Because that wasn't what it had been for her. Not at all.

"No," she lied. "Nothing happened."

"Sure?"

No, she thought, but thankfully they both let it go.

Hazel spent the rest of the morning rushing between classes to avoid bumping into Luca in the hallway, and at lunch he was oddly silent, staying out of the conversations. It reminded her of how things had been back when she first arrived, and she hated it. She was angry at herself too, angry at how disappointed she'd felt and how much she'd let it affect her. It wasn't Luca's fault that at some point in the last few months she'd started having feelings for him.

She made it through the day, but it was a relief when the last bell rang, and she got on the bus home with Hunter and Maddie where she could finally relax.

She was walking through the door when Red rang. "Hey! Want to come over for dinner? Mum's making burgers to celebrate the end of term."

Hazel hesitated, glanced at the fridge, at the timetable

Graham had drawn up for her of his shifts. He was on a late. "Is Luca in?"

Red was quiet for a moment. "Haven't seen him," he said eventually. "Why?"

"No reason."

"You're coming then?"

She took a deep breath, exhaling slowly. "On my way."

Sure enough, Luca was nowhere to be seen when she arrived at the Cawleys' house. She and Red helped Claire and Marc in the kitchen, preparing the salad and making the burgers from scratch. She let herself relax and enjoy the cooking and the company, and she'd just about stopped worrying about Luca when she excused herself to use the bathroom and saw him coming down the stairs.

"Hazel," he said. "Can we talk?"

"Actually, Red needs me to—"

"No, he doesn't."

He moved toward her, and she took a step backward. He was so close she could count his eyelashes. "Red really is waiting for me. I need to—"

"Look, I just want to apologize about last night. That's all."

Hazel did a double take. "You do? For what?"

"Well, I—I'm not sure," he said, running a hand nervously through his hair. "Crossing the line, I guess? I shouldn't have asked you out for dinner."

She felt her stomach drop in disappointment. "You shouldn't?"

"It wasn't right," he said. "I don't want you to think I was trying to take advantage of you because of the running thing, because I really wasn't. I wouldn't. I know it made you uncomfortable, but please don't be mad at me."

"*Mad?*" she echoed. "Luca, what are you talking about?"

"You've avoided me all day!"

"You avoided me too!"

"Well, you avoided me first!"

"Yeah, but not because I was *angry* at you!" she said. "I thought—I didn't think you'd want to spend time with me anymore now we're done with the running. It's not like you have a reason to."

"A reason? Does being your friend not count?"

"Is that what we are?" she said. "Friends?"

Luca seemed to flinch. "What else would we be?"

"I used to think you hated me."

"Hate's a strong word," he said.

Hazel smiled despite herself, but it faded quickly. "I just . . . I didn't want this to end."

"Why does it have to end?"

"Everything ends, Luca."

"God," he said, digging her lightly in the ribs. "Way to lighten the mood, Coach."

"Hey, I told you to stop calling me that!"

"Make me."

"Is that a challenge? Did no one ever tell you we English never back down? We're all extremely stubborn."

"You're all *crazy*," he said.

"Maybe, but you totally dig it."

"Well, there's no accounting for taste."

"See?" Hazel said. "I'd *miss* this! I'd miss you rudely insulting my heritage."

"I'm endearing," he said.

"Hardly."

"You think it's cute."

"I think you're worse than your brother!" she said, laughing, and Luca laughed too, and then they were both laughing in the hallway, laughing until Hazel felt dizzy with it. Until, suddenly, they weren't laughing anymore. They were just standing there, staring at each other.

"Loser," she murmured, and he leaned forward and kissed her. His lips were pressed softly against her own, his hands cupping her face. The kiss was painstakingly slow and sweet, and then suddenly he was pulling away.

"Had to shut you up somehow," he mumbled. "Right?"

"Right," she echoed dumbly. She leaned back against the wall, heart pounding.

"That was stupid," he said.

"Yeah."

"Really, really stupid," he added, his brown eyes finding hers again.

This time it was Hazel who leaned in, but Luca responded

immediately. When they pulled apart for the second time, they were both breathless.

"Luca—" she started to say, because *what the hell just happened* and *how are we going to make this work*, but he cut her off by pressing his lips briefly against hers again.

"Don't," he whispered. "Let me have this."

She nodded and stepped closer to him, her hand on his chest. He smiled down at her, warm and relaxed and happy, and it was such a beautiful sight that she couldn't help but rock up on her tiptoes to kiss him once more.

That night on the beach, Red kept glancing over at her, looking like he'd just won the lottery.

"Would you *quit* that?" Hazel said eventually. "You're creeping me out."

"I'm just happy for you!"

"Don't make me regret telling you."

"What, you think he'd have managed to keep it a secret? He's spent the entire last month mooning over you. I bet he's lying in bed writing you poetry as we speak."

"Shut up," she said. "Did you know?"

"What, that he liked you?"

"That I liked him."

"Yeah," he said. "It was obvious how much you care about him."

"So? I care about you too."

"Yeah, but not in the same way. So do I have to give you the talk?"

"What, the *sex* talk?" Hazel said, horrified. "No, thanks, I'm good. I had it in school."

"You—*what?* Gross!" he said. "Oh my God, *gross gross gross!* That's my brother! *Hazel!*"

She giggled. "What talk did you mean?"

"The *if you hurt him I'll make your life hell* talk!"

"Oh!"

"Yeah."

"I'd never," she promised, ignoring the way the words tasted bitter in her mouth even as she spoke them. "Anything else?"

"You just . . . You make him so happy," Red said. "So thank you."

"Anytime," Hazel said.

40

THE NEXT MORNING, HAZEL WOKE TO A TEXT
from Luca asking—rather tentatively—if she wanted to go back
to Bluehill with him that evening.

Like on a date? she texted back.

Like on a date, yes, he replied, followed immediately by, If
you want??

Hazel smiled stupidly, giddy. She'd never been on a date
before, but she wasn't nervous. What did she have to be nervous about? This was Luca. The boy with the gentle hands and
the careful heart.

I want, she answered, and buried her face excitedly in her
pillow.

* * *

Luca picked her up from outside Graham's house at just after six o'clock, and they rode their bikes side by side. Conversation between them was blissfully easy, which Hazel was glad about—the last thing she wanted was for what had happened yesterday to change anything about their relationship. Other than the obvious, of course. The new kissing aspect was completely fine by her.

Their date was simple, and casual, and perfect. Luca had packed a picnic for them to eat while they watched the sunset, and by the time they'd finished eating, the sky above them was dark. Luca packed up their empty things, and the two of them stretched out leisurely on the blanket. They talked about anything and everything—like Ryan, Red, Luca's running, and their plans for after graduation next year.

After a while, Hazel shifted so that she could rest her head on Luca's chest, reaching for his hand and tangling their fingers together. He ducked his head to look down at her, and he was quiet for a moment, fingertips tracing gentle patterns onto the back of her hand. He was so close, close enough that she could just about make out the curve of his Cupid's-bow and the scattering of faint freckles across the bridge of his nose.

"Hey," he said finally.

"Hey," she murmured, closing the distance between their lips. He kissed her back tenderly, hands holding her carefully, like this was too precious to break.

Heart racing, Hazel broke away.

"Hey," she said, reaching up to hold on to his wrists. "What is this? What are we doing?"

"Does it matter?"

"Maybe. I'm leaving, Luca. I'm going home to England."

One day. Eventually. When the call comes.

"Not yet," he reminded her firmly, and this time when he kissed her, she didn't stop him.

Hazel had suggested that she and Luca get everyone together for Sunday brunch at the Anchor the next day to tell them in person how things between them had changed. She worried all morning about how she was going to explain that somehow, without even realizing it, she and Luca had crossed the border from being friends to being friends who kissed underneath the stars.

Fortunately, Maddie took one look at the way Luca guided Hazel through the restaurant to their table at the back and broke into a triumphant grin.

"Oh thank *God*," she said. "We thought you two were never going to get it together."

Luca and Hazel just looked at each other. Why had it taken the two of them so long to figure out what everybody else around them apparently already knew?

They took their seats at the table, and Hazel braced herself for some mild teasing, but thankfully no one said anything more about her and Luca; instead, they started talking about all the ways that Hazel had turned out to be nothing like they were expecting when they found out she was English. She hadn't had tea with the royal family, she wasn't uptight or overly sarcastic, and she had pretty great dental hygiene.

"Maybe it's because I'm only *half*-English," she said. "But still, I'm sorry to disappoint you."

"So does *no one* know the queen?" Hunter said.

"How small do you think England is?"

"Small enough." He grinned. "Can we come visit, once you move back?"

Luca's hand tightened in her own underneath the table-top. "I'd love nothing more," she said sincerely, squeezing his fingers.

"Did we live up to *your* expectations, then?" Maddie asked.

"No. None of you ride a kangaroo to school."

"Too difficult to tame," Red said, and Hazel laughed.

"Honestly, the only thing I was disappointed about was the fact none of you surf," she said. "Especially you, Hunter, because you look the part, like you just stepped off the board and—"

"*Surf?*" Hunter cut her off.

"Yes, surf! You know"—she stretched out her arms, demonstrating—"on a surfboard? Catching the waves out on the ocean? Isn't that what you lot are supposed to do? You do live right by the sea . . ."

"Hazel," he said, leaning over to plant a big kiss on her forehead. "You're brilliant."

She laughed. "Am I? Why?"

302

"For being the one to figure me out," he said happily. "Don't you see? This is it! This *has* to be it! It makes so much sense. I love the water, I love being in the ocean, and Hazel said it herself, I even look like one!"

"Hunter," Maddie said, "what are you talking about?"

"I'm going to be a surfer," he said. "I'm going to learn how to surf, and just you wait—I'm going to be a natural at it too."

"You?" Maddie said in disbelief. "A surfer?"

"Yeah. Don't try and convince me otherwise, Mads. I have a really good feeling about this one."

Maddie, Luca, Red, and Hazel exchanged glances, and then Maddie sighed. "Okay, Hunter. You're going to be a surfer."

THE FIRST FEW WEEKS OF THE SUMMER holidays passed in a blur of days at the beach and nights out with her friends and *Luca, Luca, Luca*. On Christmas Eve, Hazel and Graham went over to the Cawleys' for a barbecue manned by Red and Marc, which carried on into the early hours of the morning, the two families drinking cocktails together out in the garden underneath the stars. On Christmas day, she and Graham stayed in by themselves and cooked a traditional English roast and exchanged gifts over dessert. It was peaceful, and relaxed, and easy. It felt like home.

January had arrived, bringing with it an influx of gigantic, humid storms, and Graham went back to work full-time. He still made an effort to spend time with Hazel, though—whether that meant organizing his shifts to get some time off at the weekends, or taking a break from work to eat lunch with her at the Anchor before she went off to spend the afternoon with Luca or Red or the others.

When she got back from one such late lunch in the second week of January, Luca was sitting on her front porch reading a book. He jumped up when he caught sight of her walking down the path toward him. "Hey!"

"Hey," she said. "I was going to call you. Have you been here long?"

Luca tucked the book under his arm. "Not really. Thought I'd drop by and see if you wanted to watch a movie or something?"

Hazel arrived at the porch. She stood right in front of him and gazed up at his face. He was so, so lovely in every way.

"Hey," he said again, softly, kissing her.

"A movie sounds good," Hazel said when he pulled away, and Luca took her hand and led her into the house.

Graham had purchased a little television set for Hazel's room so she could watch movies in bed at night when she couldn't sleep. Hazel wasn't sure he'd intended it to be used with Luca present—not that he'd set down any rules about having boys in her room. She figured he was just happy to see her happy.

They watched one movie together, *Crossfire*, and then decided to put on another. They took a break in between to go downstairs to get drinks and snacks, and then set up camp on Hazel's bed.

"What's Red doing today?" she asked Luca as he sorted out the DVD player.

"He was in the garden painting when I left," Luca said. "He's still working on the bird piece."

"Is that the one with the—"

Hazel broke off midsentence as her phone started vibrating in her pocket. She pulled it out with a frown, and then her mouth fell open. She stared down at the screen. It was a London number calling her. *The hospital.*

She answered it hastily. "Hello?"

"Is that Hazel?" a familiar voice asked—Dr. Wilson. Her mother's doctor.

"Yeah, it's . . . it's me. How is she?"

Dr. Wilson coughed awkwardly. "Well, she's been stable these past few months, but we were asked to get in contact if and when her condition changed—"

"So it has? It's improved?"

"No, Hazel," he said gently. "You mum has taken a turn for the worse. There's really nothing more we can do for her now except make sure that she's well looked after."

It took a moment for his words to register, but when they did she felt like she'd been punched in the stomach. Time seemed to stop. *There's really nothing more we can do for her now.* Hazel had been waiting for this phone call since before she and Graham even left London—since she promised Dr. Wilson that she'd wait for him to get in touch with news that her mum's condition had changed, instead of phoning all the time for updates the way she wanted to—but this was the last thing in the world that she wanted to hear.

"Hazel?" Dr. Wilson prompted when she didn't respond.

"I have to go," she said. "Tell her I love her, okay? I love her."

"Hazel, we need to—"

She hung up before he could finish the sentence, even though she knew they had things to talk about, and slowly lowered the phone. Dr. Wilson's words were still ringing in her head, an endless mantra of *There's really nothing more we can do for her now, There's really nothing more we can do for her now, There's really nothing more we can do for her now.*

Behind her, Luca let out a strained laugh.

Hazel whirled around to face him. She'd forgotten he was there, but now he was staring at her, his eyes wide with confusion, and *oh God* he was never supposed to hear that. He was never supposed to hear any of that; he was never supposed to *know.*

"Hazel?" he said, voice wavering. "Who was that?"

"Luca, I can explain."

"That's not an answer," he said flatly. "Who was it on the phone?"

She could feel her heart pounding in her chest. She desperately wanted to lie, to deny everything, but she couldn't do that to him. Not now. Not after everything. "It was the hospital."

"Who were you asking them about?" he said, but from the look on his face, she could tell that he already knew. "It was your mum, wasn't it? But you—you asked if she was okay. Why would you ask that if she's dead?"

Her stomach dropped. "Luca . . ."

He was silent for a long, heavy moment. Then, finally, "*Is she dead?*"

"I . . ."

"Hazel, please don't lie to me."

"No," she said, swallowing hard. "She's not, but she—"

"I've got to go."

"Luca, *wait*, please just let me—"

He ignored her and stood from the bed, and Hazel jumped up after him as he headed for the door. She tried to stop him with a hand on the arm, to get him to stay for long enough for her to explain everything to him, but he shrugged her off like he couldn't stand the thought of her touching him and walked out of the room.

No. No, no, no, this can't be happening. Everything was falling to pieces around her, and she didn't know how to stop it, couldn't even *think* straight.

With shaking fingers, Hazel found the number Dr. Wilson had just phoned from and called it back. The phone rang and rang and rang until finally there was a click that had Hazel feeling like she was about to burst into tears.

"Hazel?" Dr. Wilson answered, clearly surprised. "Is everything okay?"

"No," she said. "Please, I . . . Can I just speak to her? Please?"

"Hazel, your mother isn't—"

"I know," she cut him off, and there were tears burning her eyes. "I know she's sick and I know she isn't going to get better but I *miss* her, and I just need . . . I need to hear her voice, I need to—"

"Okay, okay," he said. "Bear with me."

There were some muffled noises, the sounds of him making his way from his office down the corridor to her mother's room, followed by a murmured conversation, and then, "Hello?"

"Mum," Hazel said breathlessly, clutching the phone to her ear. "It's me. It's Hazel."

"Hazel?"

"Your daughter?"

"Hazel," she repeated, and Hazel might have been delirious, but she could have sworn that this time the name was colored with vague recognition. "Everything is . . . Everything's jumbled."

"I know it is," Hazel soothed. "I know you're confused, but it's going to be all right. You're going to be fine, Mum, I promise."

"I don't—"

"I'm going to be there, okay?" she continued. "I'm going to be there. I'm coming for you, so you just hang in there, all right? Mum?"

She was met with nothing but silence, a heavy, endless silence that seemed to stretch out between them.

". . . Mum?"

"Hello?" her mother said finally, and something had changed in her voice, something had shifted, and Hazel could feel her stomach plummeting down. "Who's there? Who am I speaking to?"

"Mum," Hazel said weakly. "It's *me*. It's Hazel."

"Hazel who?" she said, and Hazel closed her eyes, tears spilling down her cheeks.

Dear Mum,

I remember when they took you into the hospital. I was so scared, I didn't know what to do. You were scared too, I could see it in your face. You had tears in your eyes when you looked at me and promised me it wouldn't be forever. That you would come home and we would be a normal family again.

Did you know it was a lie even then? Were you saying it to make me feel better, or yourself?

Maybe you really did believe it. I know I did, for a short while. But naïveté doesn't last forever.

I miss you, Mum, but I remember.

Love,
Hazel

42

HAZEL WAS SITTING ON THE BOTTOM STEP OF the stairs when Graham got home from work, a packed suitcase by her feet.

He did a double take when he saw her, expression clouding with confusion as he scrutinized the suitcase. He met her eye. "Hazel? What's going on?"

"Dr. Wilson called," she said flatly. "She's gotten worse."

"Oh," Graham said. She didn't have to clarify. He pulled the front door shut behind him, dropped his keys in the bowl by the door, and then walked slowly toward her like he was afraid she might bolt at any sudden movement. He came to a stop in front of her and gestured toward the suitcase. "And you were, what, going back to England to see for yourself?"

She hung her head. "I spoke to her," she mumbled. "I spoke

to my mum for the first time in five months, and she didn't know who I was."

"Hazel . . ."

"And that's . . . that's okay, but I—I have to *go*, I have to—"

"You can't." Graham cut her off, sitting beside her on the step. "You know how sick she is."

Before she could stop herself, she burst into tears again. His arm went around her shoulder without hesitation, holding her tight, keeping her safe—but she didn't feel safe, not anymore. She just felt lost. Lost and muddled like her mother, all those miles away.

"You don't understand," she managed to say through her tears. "I've got to get back there. I have to be with her. I have to make things better. I have to make it *okay*."

"Hazel, you can't." Graham held her by the shoulders, turned her to face him, and looked her straight in the eye. "I'm so sorry, love, but you *can't*. You can't fix her."

The words of truth, finally spoken out loud, hit Hazel hard. *You can't fix her.* No matter how hard or how long you try, or how much you sacrifice, or how many times you pray. You cannot be the one to bring her back. You cannot be the one to make her better.

Hazel shrugged off his arm. She'd fought for this for too many years to give up now. "But I have to try."

"You have," he said softly. "Oh honey, you have tried. I know that, I see that, but this is out of your control. Out of *anyone's* control. She's ill, Hazel. There's nothing you can do for her now, over there or from over here."

She wiped away the tears with the back of her hand. "So I'm supposed to just stay here and pretend everything's okay?"

"No." Graham closed his eyes and shook his head. "Or maybe yes. I don't know. You don't have to do anything you don't want to do. I just think, right now, it's time you did something for yourself. Worried about yourself. I know you love her, but you deserve more than what she can give you. You deserve a real home. A real family. To live with someone who cares about you."

"*She* cares about me!" Hazel said furiously.

"You've just said yourself that she barely knows who you are!" he said. "What are you going to spend the next five years doing? Sitting by her bedside in the hospital letting your life pass you by as hers slips away?"

"It'd be worth it."

"No," he said gently. "It wouldn't. She wouldn't even know you were there most of the time. It would be a waste."

"All my life, it's been her and me. She was the only one I could rely on, and now she's all alone. That's not *right*! I can't let it be that way."

"What you had to go through in England was unfair and wrong, but—"

"Then where *were* you?"

Graham blinked at the sudden sharpness in her voice. "What?"

314

"Where were you when we were struggling? When we needed help?" He didn't say anything; he couldn't because he had no defense, not to this, and so she pressed on. "You were never around. I didn't even know your name until you were on the flight over! *That's* unfair! *That's* wrong!"

"Hazel . . ."

She shook her head and went to stand up, but he stopped her with a hand on her arm.

"I think it's time we talked," he said resignedly, his green eyes filled with sadness.

Hazel felt all the fight draining from her body. She was too exhausted to argue any longer. She took a deep breath and nodded once.

After ducking into his office to grab something, Graham followed Hazel to the beach, and they sat down on the sand side by side just like she and Red had done so many nights before. Neither of them spoke for a long time, despite his promise that they would talk. Maybe, like her, Graham was trying to form sentences in his head, trying to figure out a way to say seventeen years' worth of words.

"You had your bags packed ready to go," he said finally. "But you didn't leave. You could've taken a taxi to the airport, but you didn't. You waited for me. Why? Were you waiting to say goodbye? Or were you waiting for me to stop you?"

Hazel stared at her hands where they were clasped together

in her lap. Why *hadn't* she left? Five months ago she would've walked straight out the door without looking back, but things had changed since then. *She'd* changed since then. Five months ago she had nothing to leave behind.

"You know, people told me I was crazy for keeping the house after your mum left," Graham said then, and Hazel looked over at him, listening. "Because it was way too big for just me and the mortgage was a handful, and it had been *ours*. I kept meaning to put it up for sale, but life kept getting in the way." He looked wistfully over his shoulder. "I guess I just couldn't let her go that completely."

She followed his gaze to where his big white house stood tucked behind the foliage. "You and Mum lived here?"

He just nodded. "Your mother and I had been engaged for a year when we moved in. We were in way over our heads, both working long hours to make enough to cover the mortgage payments. She was doing extra shifts at the hospital, and things at the Anchor were just starting to take off, and we were in the middle of making preparations for the wedding. It was tough, but it was *fun*, too. I thought everything was going great, that she was as excited about building our future together as I was."

Hazel waited, listening for the *but* that she knew was sitting heavily on Graham's tongue.

"She wasn't," he said finally. "If we hadn't both been so busy, if I'd paid more attention, maybe I would have noticed something was wrong . . . but I didn't. I came home from work one day, and she'd gone."

"Gone?"

"Gone." He nodded. "She left her engagement ring on the kitchen counter with a note asking me not to follow her."

"So you didn't."

"No," he said gently. "Because that's what she wanted, and you do anything and everything for the ones you love."

"But what about *me*?" she said, but what she really meant was, *Did you not love me too?*

Graham's expression softened. "Hazel, I had no idea. I had no idea she was pregnant with you because she never told me. She never said a word, but I swear if I'd known . . ."

"Then what?" Hazel managed to say, because how was that *possible*? How could her mother have kept her a secret from her own father? All this time she'd thought that not being around was his choice, she'd blamed him for his absence, and it turned out it wasn't his fault.

"Then I would've followed her to the ends of the earth to find you," he said. "Anything and everything, Hazel. I'd have done anything and everything to keep you safe and happy and in my life."

Hazel swallowed hard, her eyes burning. "I thought—I thought you weren't around because you didn't care. I thought you didn't love me."

"Impossible." He fell quiet, studying her face, but then he reached into his jacket pocket and pulled out an envelope, handing it to Hazel. The envelope was pristine and sealed. She turned it over in her hands. Written on the front, in a sloping handwriting that she knew by heart, was her name.

"Go ahead," Graham said quietly when she made no move to open it. "Have a read. I think now's a good time."

Her heartbeat picking up pace, she began to unseal the envelope, careful not to tear it, and pulled out its contents. A piece of thick cream paper. A letter written by her mother's hand in smooth black ink.

My darling Hazel,

As I'm writing this, you are sitting in the garden. You are seven years old and you are beautiful. You are perfect. You are far too young to carry the burden I'm about to lay upon you—for that, I am eternally sorry.

Today is July 3rd. I've just returned from the doctor's office. I've been in and out for the last few months, having tests done. The news wasn't good. Dr. Wilson believes I have the early onset of a disease called Alzheimer's. He says I display several of the symptoms already, but that I am still in the early stages. He says at this point there is no reason to panic as no one can be sure of what will happen in years to come. I may be fine from here on in, in which case this letter will never make its way to you. I may deteriorate, slowly losing my memories until my mind has turned to pulp. In that case, this letter will find its way to you some years from now. Hopefully later rather than sooner. The purpose of me writing this is not, however, to tell you of the disease. I am sure you will be acquainted with it when you are old enough to understand the implications it brings, but for now I am keeping you in the dark. You do not need to feel the weight of my troubles. No Hazel, the reason I am writing this letter is to tell you that you are truly the best thing that ever happened to me. Truly. If, somewhere down this long road I start to forget that, or fail to tell you it every day, I need to know you will read these words and be reassured. Be reminded that I love you to pieces.

I will write again. I will write you every month until it becomes impossible. If and when that day comes. You are a beautiful girl, Hazel, and you will have a beautiful life. I cannot promise that I will always be in it, but know that wherever you are, wherever I am, you are in my heart. I love you, sweetheart.

Yours forever,
Mum x

Hazel reread the letter twice, savoring the words and the writing, and only stopped when there were tears in her eyes, and the ink on the page had started to blur beyond comprehension. She swallowed hard, wiping her cheeks roughly with the back of her hand until the tears were gone. Then, finally, she turned to look at Graham.

He studied her expression again with concerned eyes. "Are you okay?"

She gave him a watery smile. "Yeah. I think I am."

"There's boxes full of letters in my office, Hazel. She wrote one every single month until she couldn't. She loved you more than anything."

"She wrote it. She told me." Hazel carefully tucked the letter back into its envelope, keeping it safe.

"She sent me a letter of my own last year," Graham said. "Told me all about her illness. She asked if we could speak on the phone, so we arranged a time and made the call. She opened the conversation with your name. It was the first time I heard about you, that I even knew you existed. She said you had my smile and her everything else. I couldn't imagine anything more beautiful."

He shook his head ruefully. "Then she told me about the disease. Told me how fast it was progressing, how bad things were getting. She knew it wouldn't be long before Social Services got involved and found you somewhere else to live. Unless I wanted you, she said. Unless I'd take you in instead."

"And you did."

"Of *course* I did," Graham said. "It wasn't even an option not to. She arranged for the lawyer to call when it was time and asked me not to get in touch with you before then. She wanted you to stay with her for as long as you could because she knew she might not see you again."

"I . . . don't understand."

"Hazel, your mum knew she wouldn't get better," he said gently. "She wanted to give you a chance at a better life. One here, with me. She wanted you to find a new home and start over."

Hazel didn't know what to say. She couldn't seem to find any of the right words, her mind a blank. Her mother knew she would never get better, and she had *planned* this. She planned Hazel coming out to Australia, and she planned for her to build a life with Graham. She never planned on her going back to England, or for them to be reunited. She planned for Hazel to move on, but it was more than that. She planned for her to be *happy*.

"She mentioned you once," Hazel said then because she didn't know what else to say. "I didn't know who she was talking about at the time. She went missing one day, and the police found her thirty miles away at a train station that had been deserted for a decade. She spent all afternoon waiting for a train that never came because she wanted to see her Graham."

"Hazel," he said. "I'm so sorry."

She forced a smile. "She remembered you, that's all."

Hazel turned her head, looking out to sea. Neither of them

spoke for a long moment, savoring the stillness. She wished they'd sat down sooner and spoken about her mum—she knew they'd both avoided it because it was painful, but painful things didn't just go away because you ignored them. Hazel watched the waves as they rushed toward shore, just like she had that second night when she was fresh off the plane and broken into a hundred pieces, but she barely noticed them now. It may have taken a while, but she'd adjusted. She'd fallen in love with this place just like Red promised her she would.

"I'm sorry," Graham said finally, breaking the silence. "That you had to go through all that on your own. It shouldn't have been your responsibility."

"No," she agreed. "It shouldn't. But it was, and I'm glad I did it. I'm glad I looked after her."

"And you did it so well, Hazel. She was so proud of you."

"I just . . . I *love* her," she told him. "I love her more than anything in the world, but that's not enough, is it? It won't bring her back. It won't make things right."

"No," he said frankly. "It won't. She's only going to get worse."

"You've known that all along, haven't you?"

"Yes. I have."

"Why didn't you say anything?"

"Because you weren't ready to hear it," he said simply. "And I was afraid that if you knew that for sure, you'd never have left England in the first place."

Hazel exhaled slowly. "I can't just give up. Even if that's what she wanted."

"You want to return to England?"

"It's my home," she said, before realizing that wasn't quite true. "It's all I've ever known."

"Well, in a few months, you'll be eighteen," Graham said. "You'll be an adult, and you'll be able to go back to England on your own. I know that's always been your plan—staying here was only ever supposed to be temporary for you, or—"

"Or?" Hazel interrupted. "I can go back to England, *or?*"

He smiled. "You can do what your mum wanted you to do and stay."

"Here? With you?"

"With all of us," he corrected. "With your family."

"I can't," she said. "I'm sorry."

"But you want to?" Graham said. "You want to stay? You like living here?"

"I *love* living here. I love our big white house, and I love my school, and I love my friends. I love the Anchor. I love staying with *you,* I just . . ."

". . . love her more?" he finished for her.

Hazel nodded, swallowing hard. "She's my mum."

"It doesn't have to be a choice, you know," Graham said then. "It doesn't have to be your life here or your life there. There are other options."

Hazel lifted her head to look at him, hope blooming in her chest. "Like?"

"Like splitting your time between here and England? Traveling back and forth? Or we could see about getting your mum moved to a facility over here so she'd be closer?"

"We could do that?"

"I made some inquiries about it when you first arrived," he said carefully. "I didn't want to do anything about it until you were sure you wanted to stay here with me—that we could be a family together. It'll be complicated, but it's definitely doable. We'll need to make sure that she's got round-the-clock care, but there are facilities nearby. We could make it happen, if that's what you want. To stay."

"I want to," she said automatically. Oh *God*, she wanted to stay so much.

"You have no idea how much I was hoping you'd say that," he said, his shoulders slumping with relief. He rummaged in his pocket for a moment. "Here, open your hand."

She did as he said, offering up her flat palm. Graham placed a small silver key in the center, tied onto an emerald ribbon, and it was cold and surprisingly heavy and real. Finally, after nearly five months, he had given her a key to the house. *Their* house.

She raised her head to meet his eyes.

"Welcome home," her dad said softly.

43

HAZEL WOKE UP TO THE SOUND OF SOMEONE
pounding on the front door. She rolled over to check her clock:
half past three in the morning. Graham would be sound
asleep.

The knocking persisted. Begrudgingly, she climbed out of
bed, pulling a sweater on over her pajamas as she made her way
downstairs.

"All right, I'm coming!" she called, unlocking the door and
yanking it open. Red was standing on the doorstep, out of
breath and wild-eyed.

"Red? What's wrong?"

"Hazel," he said. "Is Luca here?"

She shook her head. "What's up?"

"He never came home."

"What do you mean he never came home?"

"I mean he *never came home*," he said, voice wavering. "We were supposed to meet Mum and Dad for dinner in town, and he didn't show. You haven't seen him?"

"Not since yesterday afternoon."

"Shit," Red said, running a hand through his hair. "Shit, shit, shit."

Hazel ignored the nausea stirring in her stomach, nausea and guilt and the feeling that something was very wrong. With all that had happened with Graham, she'd almost forgotten about Luca overhearing her conversation about her mum. "He's probably fine, Red. He's a big boy, what are you so worried about?"

"Because he . . ." He broke off, raised his gaze to meet hers. "It doesn't matter. I have to go find him."

"What are you going to do, cycle around the entire town?"

"If I have to."

"Christ," she muttered. "Let me get some proper clothes on. I'll come with you."

Ten minutes later, the two of them were riding along the side of the highway into the town center. Red hadn't said a word since they'd left the house, too busy scanning the streets and shadows for his brother.

"He'll be okay," Hazel said as they arrived at the pier. "Red, he's going to be absolutely fine. He'll just have lost track of time or something. He'll be all right."

Red shook his head furiously, his grip on his handlebars impossibly tight. "No. He doesn't do that, Hazel. He always comes back. No matter where he goes or what trouble he gets in, he *always* comes back."

She said nothing, and together they continued looking. Red rode almost painfully slow, slow enough to look down the side roads and alleys to check that Luca wasn't hiding out somewhere in the darkness. Once they'd canvassed the entire center and still found nothing, he slowed his bike to a stop at the side of the road. Hazel followed suit, watched in concern as he rested his bike against a lamppost, defeated.

"He promised me," he said. "After last time, he *promised* me."

Hazel frowned. "Last time?"

Red was quiet for a moment, hands balling in and out of fists by his sides. "The day of Ryan's funeral. Back in Sydney. All four of us went to the service, Luc and I and Mum and Dad, and then back to his parents' house for the wake. It was horrible—even for me, and Ryan and I had never been close. I don't know how Luca managed to hold it together so well. I would've lost it."

He shook his head. "When we got back home, Luca went straight to bed. Said he was tired. Mum went up later to check on him, but his room was empty. We figured he just needed some air, so we thought nothing of it and sat and waited for him to walk back through the door, waited and waited for him to come back, but he didn't, not until the next day."

His eyes seemed to glaze over and his hands stilled, palms flat against his legs. "Anyway," he went on briskly. "He'd gotten into a fight, and got messed up real bad. After that night he swore that no matter what he got up to, he'd always come home or call if he needed help."

"Do you think that's where he is? Looking for a fight?"

"Where else could he be? God, I just . . . I don't understand what's *happened*, what's changed. He's been doing so well. I really thought he was better. Where would he go?"

Hazel felt sick again, the guilt twisting her insides up. This was on her, this was because of her selfishness. *She'd* done this. Luca could be out somewhere on his own, getting beat up, getting hurt, and it was her fault.

"Red," she said finally, "I know what happened."

He looked at her hopefully. "Yeah? What?"

"Luca and I had a fight earlier."

"A fight? About what?"

"My mum."

Red's brow creased. "Why did you fight about her? Did he say something?"

"No, it wasn't him," she said. She took a deep breath and let it out shakily. "It was me, Red. I let him think she was dead."

"You . . . *what*?"

"It was a huge mistake, and I was—"

328

"You did what?" he said again. "You let him think your mum died? Why would you *do* that?"

"Because he made assumptions and jumped to conclusions and I—"

She broke off, eyes welling up. *I didn't want to hurt him.*

"I can't believe this," he said angrily. "He *trusted* you."

"I was just trying to help!"

"You call this helping?"

"I wanted to give him some support, and I knew I could do it through the running thing," she said. "It was so important to him, and he only let me help because he thought we were the same, and . . ."

She trailed off, turning back to Red with wide eyes. "Wait, I think I know where he might be!"

It took a moment for Red to catch on, but then it dawned on him all at once. He pushed away from the lamppost and mounted his bike, riding off at double speed.

THE FLOODLIGHTS WERE OFF WHEN THEY
pulled into the stadium parking lot, the track completely dark.
It looked so different to Hazel like this, so unfamiliar even after
all the nights she'd spent there. She jumped off the bike with
the wheels still spinning, let it clatter to the ground. Behind her,
Red put his bike headlights on to illuminate at least a little of
the grass, and she scanned the length of the field frantically.

Her heart sank. It was empty. She checked again, just to
be sure, and then headed back to Red.

"It's okay," he muttered as she bent to pick up her bike.
"We'll just start again in the morning, when it's daylight and
we can actually—"

"Wait," she said, catching sight of a movement across the
other side of the track. "Give me a minute."

She stepped onto the grass. Eyes trained on the shadows on the far side, where the beam of the bike's headlights didn't even come close to reaching, she crossed the width of the track. She came to a stop in front of the undergrowth.

"Luca?"

No answer. She moved closer, determined, and then finally she found him. He was sitting in a gap in the bushes, arms wrapped around his legs, his expression carefully blank. Relief flooded through her. *It's okay. It's okay, I've got you.*

"Luca," she said gently. "What are you doing out here?"

He kept his eyes fixed on the grass in front of him, and said nothing. She crouched down on the ground so that they were level. "We've been riding around forever trying to find you. We were really worried about you."

Still nothing. Luca stared defiantly ahead, jaw set.

"I'm sorry," she said. "God, I'm so sorry. I should've told you the truth."

"You think?" He spoke finally, his voice flat. "You *knew* about Ryan! You knew about Ryan and you still told me that your mum died like it was some sort of joke to you."

"No," she said, and she *hadn't*. She'd just let him draw his own conclusions the same way she'd let Maddie and Hunter— so that she didn't have to talk about it. "I didn't, Luca. It was you who put two and two together and came up with five, because that was what you wanted to believe."

"What's that supposed to mean?"

"You needed me to be like you, didn't you?" she said. "You

331

needed someone to understand what it feels like to lose someone you loved, and when I tried to tell you the truth, you didn't want to hear it."

Luca stared at her, face ashen. "How are you making this my fault? Hazel, if you really wanted me to know you'd have made me listen."

"I *know*," she said, desperate. "I know, all right? I should've told you from the start. I just thought it would be easier."

"What, to have no mum rather than a sick one?" he said, and she could hear the change in his voice, the way his words had suddenly turned hollow. It had taken her months to break down his walls, and now here he was, building them back up right in front of her, shutting her out. "Jesus, Hazel! I'd give the world to have Ryan in a hospital instead of no Ryan at all!"

"That's different," she said. "You don't know what it's like!"

"She's *alive*!" he snapped. "How hard can it possibly *be*? She's still here! You still have her!"

"I *don't*!" she said furiously. She reached forward, palms flat on the ground to steady herself. "I don't have her at all, Luca."

"She's in England, isn't she?"

"Yes, but—"

"No," he said. "No buts. If she's alive, then you still have her."

"Luca, she's not sick the way you think! She doesn't even know who I am. She's got Alzheimer's."

"Alzheimer's?"

Hazel just nodded, throat tight. "Early onset. She's had it for years, but she got much worse last summer. One minute she was there, she was Mum, and the next . . . I was lucky if she recognized me once a week. I did everything I could to hold us together, but it wasn't enough. *None of it* was enough."

She lifted her head. Luca was watching her with guarded, careful eyes.

"I'm sorry," she said again, gently. "I just . . . *I* needed it too, you know? I needed someone to understand just as much as you did. I needed *you*, Luca."

He shook his head like he didn't believe her, like that was a lie, but it wasn't. It *wasn't* and she needed to make him understand, to make him get it.

"I've been writing to her since the day I arrived," she said. "Every time I think of something worth remembering about her, about *us*, I write it down in a letter. All the good moments we had, even while she was sick. Even when they got rarer. I used to think I'd mail them, but then I realized there'd be no point; she'd have no idea who they were from. So they sit in my drawer. A whole drawer full of letters I'll never send. A pile of shared memories only I remember."

"Hazel—"

"She's not dead, Luca," she said, voice trembling. "But that doesn't mean I haven't lost her."

He said nothing, eyes lowered back to the ground so he didn't even have to look at her. They sat there for a moment in complete silence, Hazel fighting back tears.

"Will you at least go home?" she said. "Please? You don't have to do it for me."

Luca nodded once, curt. Hazel deflated with relief, standing up to give him space. He trailed behind her as she walked back across the track, never getting too close.

Red was waiting by the bikes, face set. As they drew closer, he unfolded his arms and stormed toward them.

"You idiot!" he spat, shoving Luca square in the chest. "You selfish little shit! What the hell were you thinking?"

"I just needed some space," Luca muttered.

"You don't get to *do* that to me!" Red said, shoving him again. "You don't get to do it, Luc, not after last time! You scared me to death, you absolute moron!"

"Redleigh, I didn't mean—"

"Just start walking." Red cut him off, voice flat.

They walked home in silence, Hazel and Red in front, pushing their bikes, and Luca hanging back behind them. Hazel resisted the urge to keep turning and checking up on him; she didn't know how she was going to fix this, what she could possibly do to make this right. The second they arrived back at the house, Luca went straight inside.

"You can sleep here if you like," Red offered quietly.

"Are you sure?"

He nodded stiffly. They followed Luca wordlessly into the house and into the living room. Hazel sat on the edge of the sofa while Red went to get her a blanket and pillows.

"Here you go," he said, handing them to her and turning to leave, but Hazel stopped him with a careful hand on his arm.

"Red?"

He turned back to her. "Yeah?"

"I really am sorry."

"I'm not the one you should be apologizing to, Hazel."

"He didn't want to hear it."

"Do you blame him?"

Hazel could feel tears prickling the back of her eyes. "No," she whispered. "I don't."

"Look, Hazel. I don't care that you weren't honest," he said. "I care that you weren't honest with *him*. After everything he's been through, he deserved more than that."

"I know," she said. "I know I should've told him everything, but I didn't think I'd be around long enough for it to matter. And then when I was, I was scared if I told him the truth I'd lose him, and I just . . . I didn't want him to have to be on his own anymore. I wanted him to know that he had *someone*."

Red crossed the room and pulled her abruptly in for a hug, wrapping his arms around her and holding her fiercely until she finally relaxed and let herself hug him back. She buried her face in his chest.

"Thank you," he murmured into her ear, and let her go. He paused in the doorway, framed by the light from the hall. "Sleep tight, Hazel."

Dear Mum,

I remember. I remember it all, Mum, every single second.
If only you did too.

45

WHEN RED WOKE UP LATER IN THE MORNING,
Hazel had already left, her blanket and pillows arranged in a
neat pile at the end of the sofa. He felt a stab of worry for her
as he put them back in the closet, but he pushed it down. Luca
was his number-one priority now.

After stopping by his room to find Hodgkins's portfolio,
Red went straight to the roof because he knew that was where
Luca would be.

"I'm sorry," Luca said.

"What for?"

"I wasn't thinking. I didn't . . . I didn't *think*. I should've
come home. I'm sorry."

Red didn't answer right away. He'd spent most of the early

morning tossing and turning, trying to figure out what to say to him, how to get him to understand.

"You don't know what it was like that night," he said finally. "After Ryan's funeral. Mum was distraught, and Dad was going out of his mind. We were all out searching the streets for you with flashlights. They phoned the police, but they couldn't do anything because you'd only been gone a few hours. We tried to tell them that we *knew* something bad had happened, that we could just feel it."

"Red—" Luca started to say, but his brother cut him off.

"No, wait. Let me finish." There were tears in his eyes, unshed and glistening. "Do you remember how mad I was at you when you turned up the next morning? You looked so pathetic standing in the hallway with all your bruises and cuts and blood all over your shirt, but I was so pissed at you. I *hated* you. I hated that you'd bottled up your pain instead of sharing it with me, and I hated that you'd handled your grief with such an obvious disregard for your own life. I hated that you'd let me stay up all night worrying myself sick wondering what happened to you. Because you know the one thing that was running through my mind that night? What runs through my mind every time you get in a fight? *If he goes, I go.*"

"Red," Luca said again.

"That's how it is," Red said flatly. "That's how I feel. Because you're my twin, Luca, but you're also my best friend and I really, sincerely, do not know what I would do without you."

Luca dropped his gaze to his lap. "We're nearly eighteen,

Redleigh. It's not your responsibility to worry about me all the time anymore."

"Don't be an idiot. You're my brother—it's *always* going to be my responsibility. So quit giving me things to worry about, all right?"

"It won't happen again, I swear. I'm better than I was back then."

"I know you are," Red said, reaching over to squeeze his brother's shoulder.

They sat in silence for a while. Red fixed his gaze on the sea. The view was something special, something so real and untouched and beautiful that it took his breath away. The world was a truly amazing place, even if it got hard sometimes to remember just how incredible it really was.

"Here," Red said finally, holding out his art project. Since getting it back from Hodgkins, he'd continued adding new photos to the collection, building and growing it. "I think I'm ready to let you look at this. It's that school assignment I was working on."

Luca looked a little confused at the abrupt shift in conversation, but he nodded anyway and took the book. He flipped open to the first page, bearing just Red's name and the project title: *Family*. He glanced up at Red, eyes questioning, and then turned the page.

The first picture was of their mum from that day in the kitchen after she and Red had talked about Luca's scholarships, looking equally lovely and disheveled. *My mother, the professional chef,* the caption read. *Stress-baking to distract herself from my brother's impending self-destruction.*

Luca exhaled and turned to the next page. Another picture, this one of Marc standing with Luca and Red on either side of him. An updated version of an old family picture hanging on the wall in the living room. In that one, Red and Luca were barely as high as their father's waist; in this one, Marc was the shortest. Marc had his head tipped up slightly to look at Luca, who'd long outgrown him, staring at him like he was the sun.

The next few pages were filled with shots of Hazel, Maddie, and Hunter from the last five months, all in bright, beautiful color—inspired by Hodgkins's reminder that family weren't just the people who had raised you, but the people you cared about most. *Hazel, Hunter, and Maddie,* Red had written at the bottom. *Best friends and honorary family members.* Luca touched the page lightly with his fingertips and then turned to the final double spread.

This one was filled with pictures of him.

One from the night he twisted his ankle, middle finger up, and one from that night they shared a beer on the roof. Luca, doing homework at the kitchen counter. Luca with his face glowing orange from the flames of the campfire. Luca smiling, Luca laughing. A collage of Lucas. An entire collection of stolen moments of hope, of happiness.

Red knew what the caption said word for word; it was the one he'd spent the longest deliberating over: *Luca Jayden Cawley. My twin brother, my other half, learning that life goes on.*

When Luca finally looked up from the album, his eyes were wet. "Redleigh, this is—"

"Sappy?" he offered lightly.

He shook his head, closing the book and surveying the landscape in front of them. "Port Sheridan's not so bad, huh?"

"It's not," Red agreed. He waited for a beat, before adding, "So you want to talk about it?"

"About what?"

Red just looked at him. "About Hazel, Luc."

"It's not about the stuff with her mum," he muttered. "It's really not. I wish she'd been honest with me, but only so that I could help her, you know?"

"What's it about, then?"

Luca stared at his hands. "I just—I don't understand why she'd want to go back there. She's *happy* here."

"I know," Red agreed.

"She's got her dad, she's got friends, she's got a lovely home, and she doesn't have anything to worry about here. She's got *you*."

"And she's got you."

Luca's cheeks flushed pink. "It doesn't make sense. She's built a life here, a good life, and she'd give it all up to go back there? To be with a mother who doesn't even know who she is? What kind of a life is that?"

"The only one she's ever known," Red said simply. These past months Hazel might have been given a glimpse into the kind of life she could've had, but that was all Australia had ever been to her—a *could've been*. A version of her life that could've existed, but didn't. She could've grown up here, her parents still together. She could've had a normal life. She could've had friends, and freedom, and a real family. She could've had help with her mum, a support system, someone to hold her while she cried.

But she hadn't.

Red couldn't fathom why Hazel would choose her life in England over the one she had with them here anymore than Luca could, but that was because they hadn't lived it.

"What do I do, then?" Luca asked finally. "About Hazel? About *everything*?"

"Well, first off you remember that we love you, and we care, and we're here to help," Red said. "And then you remember that Hazel might have made a mistake, but that she's hurting just as much as you are, if not more—at least with Ryan you had a clean break, but she can't move on or put her mum in the past."

Luca nodded slowly and then handed the portfolio back to his brother before scrambling to stand up. "I've got to leave," he said. "Redleigh, I've got to fix this."

"Go," Red said, and Luca did.

46

THE FEEL OF THE CONCRETE UNDERNEATH
Luca's feet as he began to run was soothing. There was a light
wind in the air, a breeze coming inland from the ocean. It
brought with it the salty smell of the sea. The smell of *home*.
Home here in Port Sheridan, but home back in Sydney too.
He felt a faint, familiar pang right in the center of his chest.

"Still missing you, buddy," he murmured, but that was
okay, that would be enough, because he *remembered*. All the
wishing in the world wouldn't bring Ryan back, but as long as
Luca didn't forget, he would never truly be gone, either. That
was all that mattered, in the end.

He put his head down and pushed his legs farther, his feet
faster, and eventually his mind started to clear. *It's okay*, he told

himself, although he knew it wasn't strictly true, not even nearly. Then, more honestly, *You'll be all right.*

He reached the end of Hazel's road, her big white house looming in the distance. He slowed to a stop at the gate, suddenly dizzy with panic. *Could* he fix this? All this time Hazel had grounded and moored and saved him, and since yesterday everything had felt out of focus and blurred and *wrong* without her around.

Luca realized the dizziness was real, that he couldn't quite catch his breath. He leaned forward on the gate, his chest heaving up and down, until he'd gotten himself together, and then he headed for the house. He didn't let himself hesitate, just knocked quickly on the door.

It took a few seconds for Hazel to answer, but then she did and she was right there in the doorway, and everything came back into focus, sharp and clear and beautiful. "Luca?"

"Hey," he said, giddy with relief.

She held on to the door. "I . . . hey."

"I'm sorry," he told her softly. "I'm so sorry about your mum and I'm sorry about what you had to go through and I'm sorry I wasn't more supportive. You've been nothing but patient with me this entire time, and you deserved the same."

Hazel was on the edge of tears, her eyes shining. "Luca, I—I should've been honest with you. That's on me, that's not on you."

"It's on both of us," he said firmly. "Can you forgive me?"

"Can *you* forgive *me?*"

Luca just smiled. "I already have."

A flicker of a smile crossed her face. "I . . . missed you."

"I missed you too," he said, and she was so close, close enough that he could reach out and touch her. He wished he knew if that was still allowed. "I really, really want this to work. Do you think we can make this work?"

"It was supposed to be temporary," she said. "All of it— Graham, school, you guys, it was never supposed to be something that would last. But that's not what I want anymore."

"What are you saying?"

She managed a watery half smile. "I'm going to stay here in Australia."

"But what about England? What about your mum?"

Hazel took a deep, steadying breath and blew it out. "We're going to try and bring her here. See if we can find her a place in a local nursing home so that she can be nearby and we can go and visit."

"Hazel, that's . . . that's great! That's great, isn't it?"

"She's sick, and she's not going to get better, and that's *not* great, that's not okay, but I—I'm dealing with it." She raised her head to meet his eyes. "I can't fix everything. I don't even want to try anymore. My life is far from perfect, but it's *mine*, and I don't want to waste it looking over my shoulder trying to undo what's already been done. I have to move forward, Luca, and I really, really want to do that with you."

"Hazel, I—I don't know what I'm doing," he said. "I don't

know how to be everything you deserve. I only know how much better I am when you're around."

Hazel surged upward onto her tiptoes, throwing her arms around Luca's neck and kissing him fiercely. He looped his arms around her waist and pulled her flush against him, holding her tight. Hazel felt something settle in her chest, the feeling that she was finally grounded, that she was finally home.

EPILOGUE

THE AFTERNOON OF HAZEL'S EIGHTEENTH birthday was a warm one. The April skies were clear and impossibly blue, and now that they were in the middle of autumn, the air was no longer thick and heavy. Everything felt . . . peaceful.

Luca was there, and Red and Marc, and Maddie and Hunter—and, of course, Hazel's dad. Claire would be there too, as soon as she finished up at the restaurant. They were all sitting in the garden, Red and Luca manning the barbecue and making sure everything was cooked to slightly charred perfection while the rest of them sat around talking. When they had all eaten their fill, Hazel's dad produced one of the prettiest birthday cakes she'd ever seen, with eighteen candles alight on the top. "Make a wish," he said as she blew them out, but she didn't. She couldn't—there was nothing left for her to wish for.

She and her dad had spent the morning with her mum up in Tamoya Bay. The nurses had let them go down to the pier for a while. Her mum hardly spoke, but she was calm and comfortable, so it was more than enough.

It had taken almost two months and lots of paperwork to get it done, but they'd finally managed to get her transfer approved at the beginning of March. Hazel and her dad had traveled to England to sort everything out and had returned a week later with her mum. She lived a bus ride away in a lovely care facility on the coast, where she was well looked after and easy to reach. Hazel went to see her a few times each week without fail. Usually she went by herself, but sometimes she took Red or Luca with her. She liked going with her dad best, though. It wasn't often that her mum recognized her or her dad, but Hazel liked seeing the way her mum's face lit up when she did.

After she and Luca had sorted everything out back in January, the first thing Hazel had done was invite Maddie and Hunter over to tell them the truth. She'd been so worried that they'd be angry at her for lying—or at the very least disappointed—but they weren't. All Maddie did was ask if she was okay.

"I lied," Hazel had responded dumbly. "You do understand that, right? By not explaining the situation I let you guys think that my mum was *dead*."

"We know," Maddie had said. "But we also know that there are harder things in life than dying."

Hazel hadn't known what to do, how else to respond to their kindness, so she'd just cried while Maddie and Hunter hugged her tight. Since then, there hadn't been any more lies; honesty, as Red was so fond of saying, was the only way to move forward.

After the barbecue, when the adults had all gone inside to make tea and coffee, Hunter dragged the four of them through the hole in the hedge at the bottom of the garden and out onto the empty beach. "I have something to show you all," he announced, disappearing into the bushes. "Stay where you are!"

The four of them exchanged amused looks, and after a minute or two of rustling, Hunter reappeared from the bushes, dressed in a tight black wet suit with an orange surfboard tucked under his arm. "Prepare to have your minds blown." He grinned and then darted off into the waves before any of them had the chance to say anything.

"He's not actually going to . . ." Maddie trailed off, her eyes wide. ". . . Is he?"

"I think he is." Red snorted. "Shall we call an ambulance?"

Out in the sea, Hunter paused to wave at them, and they all waved back cautiously. Then, slowly, he crouched down on the board, looking back over his shoulder for the next approaching wave.

The second he was up on his feet, his whole demeanor changed. He suddenly looked in control, face set with concentration, well and truly in his element. He rode the wave in all the way toward shore, and by the time he made it to the sand, the rest of them were cheering and running over to meet him, because *this was it*, this was his sport, and he was so good at it.

"Why didn't you *say* anything, you tool?" Maddie said, throwing her arms around his neck and hugging him tight even though he was soaking wet. He just laughed and hugged her back, spinning her around and sending sand flying everywhere before setting her back down.

"Coach says he's thinking of creating a surf team just for me," he said. "How's *that* for a legacy?"

"I knew you could do it," she said. "I knew you'd find a way."

"Yeah, well. Now you can rub it in Callum's face."

Maddie rolled her eyes. "Hunter, I didn't help you because of that. I never cared about Callum."

"No? Then what did you care about?"

"*You*, you absolute oblivious idiot! I only ever cared about *you*."

"But I thought you told Hazel that would ruin our—"

"Oh would you *shut up*," Maddie growled, pressing her lips firmly against his before he could say another word. He kissed her right back, and when she went to pull away he stopped her, making a little noise of protest and looping his arms around her waist to pull her back against him. Luca and Hazel exchanged a look. *Finally.*

"All right, all right, that's enough," Red said eventually, clearing his throat, and the two of them broke apart. "Now I *really* need to find a boyfriend."

"Then we can all go on triple dates to the Anchor," Hunter joked, arm firmly around Maddie's waist, not missing a beat.

"Oh my *God*," Maddie said, cheeks flushing, and buried her face in his shoulder.

"You were great at the surfing anyway," Luca said, clapping him on the back. "Well done."

"I've only just mastered the basics, but I'm working on it."

"You're amazing," Maddie assured him as they began walking back up to the house, and Red made gagging noises as he pushed the two of them affectionately along the sand.

"Does this mean I have to cut him some slack now?" Luca asked Hazel.

"Imagine that." She smiled. "There's more than one athlete on the block."

Luca had sat his dad down over Christmas and told him that he was ready to start running competitively again. He'd found himself a couple of local track teams that had spaces, and together they'd figured out the best one for him. He'd only been training so far, but there was a scout coming down from the Charles Darwin University in a few weeks to watch him run in his first race, and they were all hopeful that the scout would show some interest. Hazel had complete faith in him either way, and Luca knew she would be there supporting him no matter what.

"Hey, at least you'll have someone to complain to about how much your muscles hurt now," she added with a grin.

"I do have someone! I have you!"

"Okay, let me rephrase," she teased. "Someone who actually cares."

He slung an arm around her shoulder, pulling her close against him and nuzzling into her hair. "You do care, really. Besides, I only say it because I'm angling for a massage. You just never get the hint."

"Oh, I get the hint. I just never take it."

Luca let out a groan. "You wound me. You know that, right?"

"Sorry," she murmured, leaning up on tiptoes to give him a soft kiss.

"Forgiven," he whispered back, and together they headed toward the house.

Later on in the evening, when the sun had just begun to set over the sea, Red dragged Hazel away from the others in the garden with promises of returning her very soon.

"Red! Where are we going?"

"Inside the house. I've got one last birthday present for you."

She pulled him to a stop outside her bedroom. "Wait, we can't go in here. Dad's still decorating."

"It's finished."

She turned to look at him, surprised. She'd spent the entire weekend at Maddie's house, having effectively been kicked out of her own room so her dad could repaint it, but he hadn't mentioned anything about it being done. "It *is*? How do you know?"

"I think that'll become pretty obvious." He grinned and pushed open the door. He stood back out of the way to let her pass, and when she stepped into the room her mouth dropped open. She stood gaping at the walls, at the ceiling above her bed. Gone was the bare, cold white—the room was an explosion of color. She turned on her heels, mouth still open, trying to take it all in. The wall opposite her bed depicted a sunset, with a black sky that faded down into an orange curve of sun. The wall to the left was the beach in daytime, and was the most colorful, all blues and greens and golden yellows. The third wall, behind Hazel's bed, was the beach at night. Red had captured the moonlight flawlessly, the navy blue of the sky, the silver of the sand. She raised her eyes to the ceiling. There, above her bed, Red had painted a sky full of brilliant stars, so that every single night could be a starry one.

"Red," she breathed. "It's perfect."

"I thought it was about time I truly showed you what I do at school all day." He shrugged. "Happy birthday, Hazel-from-England."

She threw her arms around his neck, hugging him tight. "Thank you! Thank you, thank you, thank you!"

He just laughed, hugging her back just as tight. "You are so welcome."

"So all this was happening when I was at Maddie's?"

"Yep." He grinned. "I spoke to Graham about it a while ago, though. We've had this planned for weeks. It's okay, then?"

"It's perfect," she said again, because it really was and she was a little lost for words.

In the last couple of months, Red's art had gone from strength to strength. Her dad had even commissioned a mural for the back wall of the restaurant. Hazel had already seen some of Red's mock-up sketches; it was going to be absolutely beautiful, and she was so, so proud of him.

He and Claire were leaving in a few days to visit a college out of state with one of the best art programs in the country. The college had already shown an interest in him just from seeing his portfolio—a fact that only really surprised Red himself. They all knew how talented he was. He'd gotten the best mark in his class for his assignment last year, and they'd gone to see his photographs when they were displayed in the gallery just down from the Anchor, after all. Hazel thought they were amazing, obviously, but her favorite was a shot that Red had taken of them all the morning after they camped out on the beach. His *honorary* family. Everyone looked sleepy and soft and happy, sitting around the remains of the fire. Red had captured the moment perfectly, captured the feeling of belonging.

Hazel crossed her bedroom to the balcony, sliding open the doors and stepping outside. Her dad and Luca and the rest of them looked up at the sound, and when they saw her they all broke into grins of their own.

"You like it?" her dad called up.

"I *love* it!" she said. Her eyes found Luca's. *I love you*, he was saying, without even having to open his mouth.

"Luc was here helping too," Red said quietly from behind her. "He painted most of the stars."

"He *did*?" she said. "But Luca hates art."

"Doesn't hate you though," he said. "Quite the opposite, in fact."

"He's such a sap."

"You two are so nauseatingly cute together," Red said with a shake of his head, pulling her backward until they were inside again and both lying flat on her bed, staring up at the starry sky. "It's gross."

"You don't mind," she murmured.

"I don't," he agreed.

Hazel settled back against the pillows and let her eyes wander across the ceiling, trying to pinpoint constellations. It reminded her of what Luca had said that first night they went to Bluehill, about the stars being spy holes for heaven. It was a thought that was both comforting and sad at the same time.

Luca still had his bad days, and Hazel still had hers; it wasn't as if they were *fixed*. But they were better. Now, if things got too much, if it hurt too bad, they talked about it. It had taken them a while, but they'd gotten there eventually. They'd gotten there together.

"We should go back down," Red said after a minute or two of warm, comfortable silence. "They're waiting for us."

And they were. Hunter had his arms full of wood, twigs and logs and branches, and Luca was holding the biggest bag of marshmallows Hazel had ever seen. Claire was there now too, fresh from her shift at the Anchor, and she beamed at Hazel as they approached. Everyone at the restaurant had been run off their feet lately, because after many late-night discussions with Graham, Claire had finally agreed to become co-owner. The two of them were in the middle of negotiations, and were hoping to open a new restaurant up in Tamoya Bay before the end of the year, and so everyone was extra busy. Busy, but excited too.

"Sorry I'm late, love," Claire said when they reached them, and Hazel just hugged her in response, happy they were all together now.

"So I was thinking," her dad said then. "We should go to the beach and make a campfire and watch the rest of the sunset while we roast marshmallows. How does that sound?"

"It sounds perfect," Hazel said.

They made their way down to the bottom of the garden and through the gap in the hedge at the end. Once they arranged themselves into a circle on the sand, Dad and Hunter made quick work of lighting the fire. They sat and talked and laughed and roasted marshmallows and watched as the sinking sun was engulfed by the sea and the sky above them turned black. The mood was relaxed, the company amazing, and the night air was sweet with the scent of autumn.

"This is nice," Dad said to no one in particular. Hazel met

his eyes across the circle, and he smiled at her, soft and bright and filled with fondness. She smiled right back at him, and then around at all the other familiar faces that were bathed in the warm, flickering light from the flames. She couldn't help but think to herself again just how lucky she was to be surrounded by so many people who loved her beyond reason.

A little way down the beach, dark waves crawled forward, breaking against the sand—it was a sound she'd become so used to that it was now merely a low hum in the background, like music. In and out, they went. In and out. She liked that, liked how comforting their consistency was, locked into a perpetual rhythm. It was reassuring to know that—if nothing else—those waves continued their journey to shore, day in, day out, all night long, as if nothing around them had changed. As if nothing ever changed. But the fact was things *had*, and *did*, and *would* go on changing in ways she couldn't even imagine, with every single breath she took from here until forever.

Hazel had to learn how to love and how to trust and how to forgive and how to open up and how to hold on and how to let go, and it was hard, but she also had to keep on going, she had to keep on trying. That was just life, that was how it went, that was how they—how she—had to live if they were going to survive.

Dear Mum,

I was eight years old when you bought me my first camera.

It was a pink plastic Polaroid one, where the photographs printed right away. You told me how important it was to take pictures of places and faces and things that were special to me, and keep hold of them in case one day I needed to look back on my life and remember all the moments that made it so great.

We took photos all the time after that. Birthdays, days out, holidays, even just of the two of us at home. We captured moment after moment on film, every smile, every laugh. We stored them all in a box, first one, then two or three, then five or six, until we had a whole shelf full.

But then you got sick, and suddenly there were things that were much more important than taking photos. The boxes grew dusty and forgotten, and the memories faded away until it got hard to remember a time when things had been happy. When things had been normal.

Slowly but surely I lost control of my childhood, and you lost control of your memory.

Recently, I sat down with some good friends of mine and sorted through each of the boxes. It took hours and hours, and I both laughed and cried at what we found. In the end, we managed to sort all of the best ones into two photo albums. One for you and one for me.

I hope that when you look at the photos, they'll mean something. That when you look at them, even if you don't remember the day they were taken, or what the weather was like, or even who was with you, you'll remember how they made you feel.

I remember, Mum. Not just the good bits, but everything. I sit each night and think of you, think of how things used to be, and I remember.

I remember how much you love the smell of rain on the dusty sidewalks in the summer.

I remember how you prefer black-and-white movies.

I remember how you were usually right, even when I wanted you to be wrong.

I remember how we used to bake when I was upset, and read stories together by the fire when it was cold outside.

I remember how we could just talk, about anything, anywhere, anytime.

I remember how you were always there for me.

I remember how you used to plait my hair each night and lie next to me on the bed when I had a nightmare because you knew that was the way I would fall asleep.

I remember how you believed that even something as

small as a snowflake was magical enough to change the world.

I remember how you kissed me good night, your lips soft on my forehead, and how your voice sounded when you told me that you loved me.

I remember.

I remember, I remember, I remember.
And Mum—I hope I never, ever forget.

Love then, now, and forever,
Hazel xxx

ACKNOWLEDGMENTS

Thank you to Silvia for taking a chance on my quiet little story, and to Margaret, Melissa, and everyone at FSG/Macmillan for helping me make this book the best it could be.

Most of the details about Australia come directly from my own memories of the country, and thus any discrepancies about its culture and/or education system are my fault; that being said, big thanks to Mitch for answering all my questions about life in Australia so patiently and thoroughly and for helping me give Hazel's story a real setting! Thanks to Arisha and Alicia for reading rubbish initial drafts and for being the first people to talk about these characters like they were real people, and to Samantha, Imani, and Kelcey for being my sounding boards and for taking my freak-out calls even when they're transatlantic. Thanks also to James and the rest of the creative writing staff at Roehampton—Leone, Ariel—for making me believe that I could really do this.

And last, but certainly not least, thank you to my mum, Clare—for absolutely everything else.